PATH TO THE PRIESTESS TEMPLE

DIANNE ADEL

$\mathscr{P}$ATH TO THE PRIESTESS TEMPLE

DIANNE ADEL

Lilith House Press

Lilith House Press
Estes Park, Colorado

ISBN 979-8-9858101-2-7 (softcover)

ISBN 979-8-9858101-3-4 (ebook)

Library of Congress Control Number 2023907120

Cover and interior design: Jane Dixon-Smith/www.jdsmith-design.com

Editor: Elisabeth Kauffman/www.elisabethkauffman.com

Copy Editor: Kara L. Stewart/www.blueimaginarium.com

Proofreader: Linda Shreve

Cover art: Melissa Stratton-Pandina/ www.deshria.com

Author Photograph: Candra Severson

In the depths of every woman rests a cave of thunder, so potent and pure it lives through all time. This sacred temple of the womb is the first story, alive with skin and silk, filled then pouring into the blood of our sisters of all shapes, all colors, all sizes, all ages, all nations. Together we step on the steep rock of the mountain. Together we hold a foot on the pulsing neck of the weak-minded man when he mumbles his arrogance into the dirt. Together we burn the lies of us, told through the centuries. The truth of our power needs no proof. The way of our strength, no cause to doubt. Our glory belongs to the hush of our veiled movement between worlds. See what I know through the body of the Goddess so you will forever remember this Holy Temple is you.

Anya of Mahet -
High Priestess of the Temple of the Arch. Malta, 2000 BC

THEN

I was once a child of the dark, born blind as the night. Now, at twenty-two summers as High Priestess of this temple, my inner vision is filled with the swell and shapes my sister Priestesses and brother Priests share with me. It was not always easy to pass image from mind to mind. It came to be that many depended on me for my inner vision.

My first practice at inner seeing began when I lived as a child of four summers with my Grandmother Oriana on the farthest side of this land surrounded by sea, four days' walk from this temple. Our loamy stone home rested in a forest cove near the lull of the shallow part of the waving waters. Life was simple with our goats, our garden and the carriage of the days in salt-scented peace.

When Grandmother handed me a soft pear from her favored tree, I thought she meant for me to only breathe in the pungent sweetness, yet she instructed me to roll it in my palm and feel the sense of it with my whole body. Then she waited in silence, for what I did not know. She was still for long breaths. She handed the fruit to me like this for many moons and nothing happened, until the time that something changed in the silence as she waited. I felt a tingle behind my eyes, deep in my forehead. When Grandmother embraced me, I felt her cheeks wet with tears. When she gave me warm goat's milk and lay down beside me in the grass, I knew I had pleased her.

The next time she gave me the pear, I felt the same tingle, then the sensation of warm water moving through my forehead. So rolling and pleasant it was to spill my mind open with no bounds. For many more moons we repeated this until I felt something different move behind my eyes. At first it was a wispy tickling, as if a family of spiders crawled there. Then a shape appeared that matched the contours of my questioning fingers. It was a round bottomed bulb with a nub of a top. A small but poking stub seemed rooted on the tip. I did not know to say so then, for until that moment my mind saw no shapes. That was when grandmother clapped her hands and pulled me into her breast and kissed my face again and again. The tingle passing between us connected our minds to see the same vision, like two shells of the same mollusk.

I recall my reward was to nibble the sweet fruit together under the olive tree, giving Eisha, our mother goat her share of the tender bites as she stood quietly by our side. Never had I felt so complete as in that moment. But even then, I sensed the need for my inner sight as urgent.

Now I lie on my mat of linens and cushions in my temple chamber that has been my home since Grandmother brought me here in my seventh summer. The age when all Initiate Priestesses and Priests are brought to live here and devote our lives to the way of Great Design of the Goddess.

On this night, when I hear footsteps and rustling fabric around me, I do not reach out for a mind-image as is my accustomed greeting. Instead, I quiet my inner eye to prepare for the taking of the tea, for what I see in my trance this night will decide if my Prophecy will come to pass. I feel the Prophetess Taniyeh probe my mind with a sudden thrust. I do not wish this. I lift a sharp hand toward her and I feel her bow her head and step back.

It is not as if I am unaware of the nature of what the Prophetess commands of me this night. I need no more urging from her. It is enough that I am shaking at the thought of this task and need my senses to be mine alone and not pulled into her drive to succeed.

I regret my sharp rebuff of her when I remember how much she has given of her life to prepare me for this moment. Her Telling has always been of the Prophecy that a blind Priestess of twenty-two summers who comes from within this Temple of the Arch will use her inner sight to travel beyond time to set our sacred work forward. This night may be the most important of her long life. To make amends I reach for her hand, still holding a curtain over my mind to shield my images so that she cannot intrude without consent. Her fingers are more brittle than usual.

As I roll my head back on the pillows, I feel my sister Priestess Lael next to my bed watching me with the eyes of the falcon. I forgive this scrutiny. All here fear I will die. I am not certain their worry has no reason.

Lael wipes the sweat off my forehead. It is hot in my room, with so many here, hovering. I take her hand and kiss her palm. She is as close to me as my own kin, since she raised me as her younger sister when we were Initiates together. I find solace in her lavender and rose scent, yet my pulse quickens when I hear Sondro's robes upon the stone floor as he moves to my bed. I restrain myself from reaching to his mind, as I know his images will distract me. He takes hold of my hand and brings it to his cheek. I inhale his smoky scent from the burning resin of the sacred fire in the Priest's chambers. His lips find mine and I shiver as I recall our morning together. He laughs softly for I know he sees my memory, even as I have not meant to show him. Unbidden I see his response is the vision of his hands moving across my breasts to between my thighs in the wet wake of the dawn this morning. I quickly close my mind to him so that I can bring my focus back to my immediate task. He vanishes his images for me, so that I need not strain toward my goal, although I much prefer to remember our coupling than the intensity rising in me. He presses my palm then lowers his body to the hard floor next to me, an easy feat for him as he and his Priest brothers are accustomed to many hours of prayer with their knees folded under. I allow our fingers to part. I feel his care not to show concern for me.

The Prophetess Taniyeh holds the clay cup of tea in one hand. Her bird claw fingers on my shoulder make my jaw tighten and my stomach knot. I do not wish to be reminded of our argument about this trance journey. In spite of her certainty, and her devotion to my destiny, I have found it too hard to believe that women and men in the future will not know what we hold sacred. She assures me that violence and the loss of reverence to all women is to come and will carry very far into the future. I think it impossible to lose the knowledge of women as the voice, body and soul of the Great Design of our sacred women's way, known to all here as the most honored of all truths.

I turn my attention to the sounds beyond the stone window next to my mat. I hear the sea that calls to me beyond the walls of the temple as it crashes below the cliff. I allow my body to relax into the rhythmic pull and sweep of the licking waves along the shore so close. Perhaps the ocean or her creatures can assure me that such horrors will not really come to pass. I feel Taniyeh again probe my mind to say otherwise.

I am saved from her insistence by a pulsing in my womb when my sister Priestesses begin their frame drums to start the Trance Ceremony. The twelve women play their fingers, palms, hands and even wrists to a purring pattern to awaken our bones. Soon they are moving their feet in spiral pattern around the fire, in steady beat. The shapes of the drums, in their circles of hide, bring connection to all things. I feel the sound awaken my body to the earth's heartbeat. I push myself up to sit higher with my back to the pillows leaning on the stone wall. I feel the vibration in the rock's thick body. The drums, the stones, the sea, my womb each take me back to my purpose.

I know when the Madre Paloma comes into my room from the hall that the Trance Ceremony has begun and I am close to taking the tea. The Madre leads such temple activities with calm. She enters with twelve Priests, each holding a crescent moon made of onyx. I hear them pass around the sacred fire, aflame in the fire pit at the room's heart center. As they settle to kneel around it, I hear their low toning chant begin. I thank them silently for holding my body in their sound. Sondro does not take his place among his Priest brothers. He stays with Lael beside me. He does not even ring the bell to sound with the Priest's deep humming note.

I have never taken this trance tea before. The Medicine of the Stinging Night is made from the sacred poisonous mushroom and must be handled with wisdom. We are taught as Initiates to commune with plants, herbs, bees and their honey, and all creatures of the earth, sea and sky. Yet Taniyeh and her cousin Na'akt knew best how to gather this deadly substance a day's walk from the West along the ocean's highest cliff within the depth of the great forest along the edge. Careful to leave an offering of drawn blood from their palms spilled into a bowl of honey, they secure honor to my Trance. The mushroom caps were then brought to the temple's herbal antechamber and laid on thatched grasses to dry close to their earth-host and the pounding sea. The temple's Priestess healers blessed the mushrooms for three sunrises with the living force in their hands and their chanting voices in preparation for my trance journey. Once dried, the caps were soaked in wine for six full moons.

Now, as I wait, I know to trust that Na'akt has mixed the mushroom and wine tincture with precision, using only a small drop into the fennel tea that I will drink. I will be given only a small clay finger-bowl full of the Medicine of the Stinging Night, for more means certain death. Yet its edge will be sharp, ready to sever me from this world.

For as long as I remember, Taniyeh has brought her Oracle Visions to us describing ways in which our world will change. Now her predictions are becoming real, as we hear of it through the traders from other temples across the sea when the ships come with fabrics, tools, knives, jewelry, animals and pottery to trade. There has been terrible talk of men from distant lands that dismiss our woman-governance and sacred seat in leadership. Such a refusal of our worth is not happening in temple life or by our townspeople who honor us with bounty from their farms and sea travels. Worse, these men regard our sex as theirs to take. Here, such an act would mean death by sword to those who commit such a crime, for it is the Goddess Herself that is defiled. Yet there have been accounts that have come to our Temple Council that times are shifting toward such violence. Taniyeh promises it will only worsen over time. For she has seen in her trances that wars will begin toward those who refuse to worship only one male God. She has seen that men will rule with force against women and will say such acts are this God's will.

As I think on all of this I begin to shake, still unable to fathom these things. The drums hold me steady. The Priest's toning returns me to courage. The Prophecy is that these changes will begin slowly. I pray they begin not at all. I force fire to my bones to burn my fear. I nod to the Prophetess Taniyeh that I am ready. She raises the bowl of tea to the moon and stars for blessings. Her voice is the scrape of stone.

"We pray for this tea to show Anya of Mahet the way. We pray she will travel through time safely. May the Great Design reveal Her path to us."

Taniyeh brings the cup to my lips. The grainy bitter taste is strong on my tongue, numb to the tip.

Suddenly I am spinning. Moving so fast I am pulled out of darkness behind my eyes into a swirl of flickering light. I am glad to feel the cushioned bed beneath my back, for I am too dizzy to move.

The tea makes my heart race. I am thrown like the twirling dolphin in my azure blue ocean. I expect to float forward through time and see what is to come. Instead, I am lifted to the past to where my life began.

I feel Mahet, my mother, birthing me as her body loses life, her heart stopping as I feel my newborn shape be lifted from her. The tea moves time so that it is happening now so much so that I smell the metal blood-soaked skin of my mother's thighs. I feel the hands pull me, and know they are Grandmother Oriana's hands. I feel the cutting of the long flesh connecting me to my mother's dying body. The hands swaddle me, then take me to a breast I do not know. I smell sour skin, and feel hunger and the oily drink of another's milk rather than the mother I never knew. I long to speak to my mother to ask why the tea has shown me this.

Instead the tea sends me to rise into the stars above. My inner sight tingles in awareness. I ask the tea to give me vision and I begin to see with my mind, as I am most accustomed. I look upon the Earth below. Sirius, so named as our guiding star, blinks to me. My inner gaze rests on the Earth below us. The tea shows me those I will protect should my Prophecy come to pass. I see them as a vast scattering of light-filled beings, covering the great Earth. The tea tells me these are all people, mine to guide. I shudder with this sudden burden.

I am pulled downward to a place I do not understand. I stand on earth rock, but so dense I feel no earth-pulse in my bones, as if the very ground has lost its beating heart. There is crushing noise of grinding bronze and scraping. My ears feel pain with the pressure of the shrill vibration. The Medicine of the Stinging Night shows me this is another world than mine, as I see three faces I do not know. They hover before me. They do not look at me. They do not know I am here.

I gather courage and ask the tea to help my inner sight see them more clearly. I am brought closer to their floating heads. Their eyes are blank. Their faces turn to and fro, like owls on the cypress branch. I think of Taniyeh and know I must try harder to see what they see. I must find reason for this image. Nausea arises as I prepare to move into their minds. I do not understand how these faces will secure my place in the Telling, yet I know I must try. I flutter a probe from within the deep flesh in the center of my head. I meet only a flat sound from them, like a crushing of acorns shells. I ask the tea to show me more.

When I view their faces clearly within my mind, I see they are women, all three. The first is a young face, with light-sand skin and hair the golden color of sun-kissed wheat. There are speckled flecks of brown in splatters on her face. Her mind is unfocused and drifting. She still does not see me. I slowly turn to the next.

The second is a woman with curling black hair, and touches of aging white that accent eyes the color of amber and night. Her skin is smooth brown like mine. I smell a bitter herb. It seems close to the scent of the yarrow we heat with water in the bronze pots over the fire we use to cut and clean our wounds. Yet this aroma is so potent it seems to make my mouth lose sensation. Like the first face, she does not see me. Her mind speeds in rapid circles and the pulses from her body are sharp needles finding home in my skin. I feel bile rising from the sharp taste and odor and turn to the last face.

I feel her mind accost mine and I am repelled backwards. Piercing green-fire eyes bore into my inner sight. Her gaze could cut through bone. Her black hair is like mine in color but not in shape, for it is too short. The tips are white with milk, it seems. I find I want to touch the pointy strands, for I have never felt such a thing. Her skin is a glaze of alabaster, her blood pumping in fierce ticks. I move closer to her, curious. The fire-eyed woman turns toward me.

I recoil in sharp pain. The look are such knives into my head, I feel I may faint. When I join her mind, it is a shock of high-pitched screeching that makes me cover my ears with my hands. The sound is even higher than the whale cry, making my head throb worse than the dagger cuts of her eyes into me. I am held as if made of stone and cannot move. I do not expect my voice to let loose a cry so loud my throat becomes raw. For what I see has shocked me to my soul.

Her emerald eyes are no longer hers. My black eyes, with my lifeless veil of blindness, look at me. Her face has become mine.

NOW

Scotty D. Jones uses her sweaty palms to hold firm as she bends over her dressing room table. Her bare ass tilts toward the pounding thrusts from the guy behind her. She manages to shove her beer can over without spilling and slides her makeup case to the other side. She leans facedown, her shoulder-length black hair fans out over her head, the bleached white tips drape on the Formica table top. Her leather pants slip below her knees, making it easier to brace for his pushing. Her pressed nose on the Formica makes a ringed puff of moist breath. She hears the opening band, *Arlo Tight and the Brigade,* begin their last song. The crowd's hooting peaks to a feverish pitch, "Scotty D! Scotty D!" When she hears it, she reaches behind her, grabbing the guy's butt flesh to move him faster and harder. The sound of the crowd makes her body shudder with electricity, which finally increases the sting of her rising pleasure.

The guy behind her is rutting hard now. She lifts her eyes through her mess of hair and sees his reflection in the mirror. His head is thrown back, eyes closed. His backstage pass dangles from his neck on a red string. Scotty watches the flapping plastic wrapper knock back and forth, the words a backwards fuzz in the mirror. The can of beer almost topples and she saves it from spilling on the guy's cell phone. She *always* takes their phones from them. That's the last fucking thing she needs—a viral video of this. As the pleasure intensifies, her body contracts through her tightened calves, her thighs, her jaw, deep inside and around his hardness. She closes her eyes, not wanting to look at the hamburger next to her face in its greasy wrapper that her manager Val left there for her to eat before the show.

"Scotty! Ten minutes 'til show time!" Val shouts through the locked dressing room door. "Do you hear me?"

"Fuck you, yes!" she gasps to Val. She hears Val's footsteps walk away on the other side of the door.

Scotty takes the guy's hand around the front of her and makes him rub her as he thrusts. She keeps her hand over his for the right rhythmic pressure. He's out of synch now, which is annoying. She focuses on the pleasure. Her breath is finally heated and her body goes full tilt with ache. She moans and contracts in intense release. She falls forward onto her make-up case.

"Hurry the fuck up," she pants to the guy, her face now too close to the hamburger. "I have to get on stage."

The guy tries to grab her hair but she dodges him and lowers her shoulders. He grips the flesh on her narrow hips, then goes into a convulsive moan. He shudders his body over her back. His chin grinds between her shoulder blades. She smells his sour breath behind her neck. She tips her shoulder to knock him off sideways.

Scotty reaches between her legs and grabs the edges of the damp condom to stop it from slipping off. When he's out of her, she slithers away from him then kicks the waste basket over to him so he can drop it in. She grabs a purple hand towel from the dressing room table and wipes her hands, her brow, between her legs, then pulls up her pants and zips and snaps them shut. She throws the towel at him and watches him wipe himself dry as she re-clips her thick belt with silver corners. The guy zips up, then stands there looking like he can't remember where he parked his car.

"Here." Scotty hands him his phone. "You can have this back now."

"Can I have a selfie?"

"You just got your selfie." She walks him to the door, unlocks it, and pats him on the shoulder.

"Can I see you again?"

"Sure. From the front row. But that's it, bud. It's been a good time." She gives him a gentle push out the door. "I gotta get ready. See you out there."

"Uh. Okay. Cool. Yeah. See ya."

She waves her fingers at him and closes the door. She drains her beer, reapplies her lipstick, runs her hands through her hair, checks her eye makeup and heads out her dressing room door to start her show.

***

After three hours on stage with the *Scotty D. Jones Band*, Scotty's body is a primal, speeding fever coming to a slow, edgy halt. Her throat is raw, her mouth dry. Her ears are ringing. Her drenched skin feels an icy shock from the air-conditioned hallway backstage. After setting the last guitar she used on its stand on stage for her roadies to pack, she sits on a black packing trunk smoking a cigarette. Her platform boots are heaped sideways on the floor. She rubs her feet, cigarette tipped between pinched lips. She squints one eye from the curl of smoke to peel off her sweat-soaked socks. She flicks the ash, then takes a deep drag, exhaling the smoke into a single stream.

Her body pulse is beginning to slow from the high of performing, enough to feel pain that was non-existent on stage. So much for youth—she's sore in places she never used to be. Especially her feet. She shoves her rolled up socks into her boots, which she grabs by the laces and pads barefoot backstage to her dressing room.

She drops her boots on the floor, pulls off her sweaty yellow tank top and throws it on the couch by the door. She flips the straps of her drenched black lace bra with her thumbs, lifts her boobs then flops onto the chair in front of the mirror. She drops her lit cigarette into the beer can. Her face is an exhausted smudge of sweat and makeup. Her eyes are dull and glossy as she comes down fast from the buzz of the high on stage. As she locks onto the image of her face, her hands move in mechanical digging to find the flask in her bag. Still gazing in the mirror, she throws back three gulps of tequila, then stops, her hand mid-air in a frozen clasp on the metal container.

Her reflection morphs like in the glass of a circus fun house. She slowly lowers the flask, staring intently at her image in the mirror. Her eyes aren't the cut of green with smudged black eyeliner. Instead, her pupils are black as night. They are covered with a blue film, cloudy and opaque. The life behind them isn't hers. The light brown skin in the mirror is not her pale, pink color. The hair is black like hers, but long and thick as a curtain. The small rose lips aren't hers and they're screwed into a silent scream. The face holds tight palms over its ears. The blue-black eyes are a dense stare from somewhere distant and untethered.

Scotty lifts the flask slowly to her own lips. She watches the figure in the mirror take no drink.

"What the fuck!" She shoots up off her chair, knocking it over and spinning away with her back to the mirror. "You better be fucking gone when I turn around." She drains the flask before her knees give out under her.

***

Dr. Abigail DiGiorno's 12-hour shift began at 8:00 p.m. Now, at 2:00 a.m., it's been a quiet night so far. Her hospital office is warm but not so much that she gets too drowsy. The computer screen throws a blue glow over her hands and face as she concentrates on typing. Her phone is live-streaming NPR news. She likes to hear words in the background since music could lull her to sleep. The newscaster's voice suddenly catches her attention.

"... in the recent overturning of Roe v Wade, the Supreme Court...." Abigail snatches her phone and clicks it off.

"Idiots," she mutters. "We're doomed. Fifty years of progress down the shitter!" She runs angry fingers through her thick black curls, twirling them into a taut knot that stays put like a lodged ball of yarn. Slivers of gray hair around her temple shake loose in wispy rebellion.

She forces her attention back to the article she's writing for the *New England Journal of Medicine*. She spent the last few months researching the *Tostana* herb discovered in Ghana, not yet approved of by the FDA. There have been some little-known cases in which the herb has proven to improve the symptoms of pre-eclampsia, a serious complication in some pregnant women that spikes blood pressure. Her data finally compiled, she figures she can pound out her first draft during this shift, but she can't find her sketch pad and needs it for the last quote she scribbled next to her charcoal rendition of the plant.

"There you are!" The pad's corner is just under a copy of *Us Weekly Magazine* that one of her patients gave her with some tired old rock 'n' roller woman on the cover. Abigail squints at the photo of the woman with the uneven black hair with bleached white tips, leaning against a brick wall with her guitar on her knee.

"I don't know who you are but you look like you haven't slept for a month." The green eyes are a glazed stare back at her. She flips the magazine over and pulls out the sketch pad to type her scribbled writing.

"Within 17 days, researchers have found that 4 out of 6 expectant mothers..."

Abigail pauses. She leans over to flip the magazine for another look at the woman on the cover. *Have I met you?* She looks more closely at the tattoos climbing up her arms. "Nope—I would remember you." She buries the magazine in her desk drawer.

"…who have been given up to 13 doses of the herb over a period of six months have successfully…"

She stops to open her desk drawer for another peek at the magazine but instead pushes her rolling chair back with an abrupt whoosh and heads into the kitchen to heat up her green tea. She sets her mug into the microwave and hits 2 minutes. She tries a sip, almost burning her tongue. She carries it back to her office and puts it on her desk next to her computer, then rolls the chair forward with her butt. Ellen, one of her favorite nurses, suddenly bangs on her door and enters at the same time. Abigail looks up, recognizes the look on Ellen's face, and hurries toward her in one step.

"A patient of Dr. Benson's," Ellen begins as they both turn to leave Abigail's office.

They start a quick walk down the hall as Ellen continues, "…just presented to triage at full term with extended fetal bradycardia. Her cervix is long and closed. We're wheeling her back to the OR emergently."

Abigail is on call. Dr. Benson is not. They hurry down the hall to the operating suite. As they rush forward, Abigail's brain is already laying out a rapid plan with clicking precision. The baby's abnormal heart rate requires immediate attention. Time is of the essence.

Within seven minutes, Abigail is scrubbed in. She enters the OR with the sleek grace of a seal underwater. Her gloved hands are up, her hair covered in a puff of the bouffant cap. Her mask sits snug on her face under the plastic face shield. She scans the room for proper equipment, room temperature and how many bodies are present. She notes the names of all nurses on hand within seconds. Ellen, of course, plus Cynthia and Tonya. *Good nurses. This should go well.* Her anesthesiologist, Dr. Lowell, rapidly performs the epidural. Abigail moves with calm and clear motion to her patient on the table, looking into the frightened face of the mother to be. Her wide eyes seem in a frozen stare over the oxygen mask placed over her nose and mouth.

Abigail knows she has only 30 minutes for the best outcome for the baby. She lowers her breath into her belly, which allows her voice to be reassuring, expertly masking the need for urgent speed.

"Hello, Fran. I'm Dr. DiGiorno. Your baby's heart rate is dangerously low, so we must deliver quickly with a caesarean section. We will take great care of you both and get started right away."

"Are vital signs stable?" she asks Ellen without taking her eyes off the anxious patient's face, noticing her clammy skin. Ellen and Cynthia are adjusting the surgical drape that covers Fran's whole body. They place her arms by her sides on elevated supports then gently strap them down. Dr. Lowell has placed the IV in her arm and the arm straps will ensure no accidental movements dislodge the needle. The nurses clip the extended top up at her chest to the two metal stands for a barrier between Fran's head and her torso. Her head seems separate from the rest of her covered body.

"Is your partner here with you?" The paper cap over Fran's hair vibrates with a turn of her head to see Abigail better. "Jim," her voice barely audible.

Abigail raises her eyes and nods to Cynthia to alert the man peering into the small square window on the OR door. An attendant on the other side opens the door. Jim's stiff body lunges into the room. His elbows are like two bent hangers, filled with rigid tension as he tries not to slip on the OR floor in the paper pads over his tennis shoes. He peers over his mask then adjusts his paper cap as it seems to be slipping off his hair.

"Hi, Jim. We may need to ask you to remain outside until the baby is out and stable. For now, please remain standing to Fran's left side so she can see you." Jim obeys by planting two feet on the ground and gripping his hands in a tight fist in front of him.

Cynthia reports: "Blood pressure 140/80, pulse 90, O2 sat 98%."

"Thank you, Cynthia." Abigail is swift to answer. "Dr. Lowell?"

"T4 level achieved," he reports.

"Okay." Abigail is a calm ocean. She says her secret, silent prayer. *Divine Mother. Bless this baby and this mother. Guide my hands with wisdom and care.*

She opens her palm to receive a scalpel. "Thank you, Ellen."

She has moved the scalpel to the mother's belly. She closes her eyes for three seconds and sees, in her mind's eye, into the body under her. It comes unbidden as if someone's holding a picture before her. She needs no effort to make it happen. The image of the pink tissue arises spontaneously, pulsing with red and yellow swirls. She suspects the baby is face down, which would be good. It will avoid cutting the baby with the scalpel when the uterus is opened rapidly. She suspects the cord is around the infant's neck. She'll know in a moment.

Her hands move as one long measured note. The skin on her palms and fingers feels as if it is made of electric fiber, able to translate to her brain the notion that the scalpel is no longer a separate instrument. Tool and flesh are now one. Her logical brain has no argument about this, as her fingers move as if instructed by another kind of mind. She makes the Pfannenstiel incision gracefully down through the skin, subcutaneous tissue, fascia and peritoneum. Within seconds, she is inside the uterus. As she suspected, the baby is face down with the umbilical cord wrapped tightly around its neck. She frees the cord from the fragile skin and bone of the cervical spine and delivers the head without issue. She bulb suctions the baby's mouth after its head is removed from the uterus and rapidly but gently delivers the baby. At first it's floppy and quiet, but with gentle stimulation she can feel the baby's life energy come up into her own, as the baby projects its first cry. This eases some of the urgency in Abigail's body knowing now that the baby is safe. Her own imperceptible and controlled tension softens. Ellen cuts the cord from the mother, then Abigail hands the tiny body to Tonya, who takes it to the warming table to examine, clean and wrap her for warmth.

"Fran and Jim, you have a baby girl." Abigail's voice is a melody.

Ellen hands the clamp to Abigail. She takes it with the same open feeling in her skin and fastens it on the cut cord.

Tonya walks the wrapped baby to Fran's side so she and Jim can see her. The new mother's cheeks are wet with tears. Jim's rigid elbows are now softly wrapping his shoulders as he shudders with silent relief. He wipes his own eyes with his sleeve. They gaze at the baby in wonder.

"You'll be able to nurse her in the recovery room." Abigail looks at Fran from her seated position on the opposite rise of the drape.

"90 over 40," Cynthia tells Abigail.

Fran's blood pressure is decreasing, which means Abigail needs to work quickly. She gently removes the placenta and hands it to Cynthia, who places it on a tray to examine it. Ellen hands Abigail the needle driver and vicryl suture, then swabs the incision area quickly as Abigail begins by stitching the uterus. This allows her fingers to do their job without forcing them to move with tense effort. Once the uterine incision is closed, the uterus contracts nicely to control the blood loss. She again feels her tension melt away. She proceeds to carefully close the fascia, subcutaneous tissue and skin incision with lithe and precise fingers. Abigail's thoughts seem to have dissolved and in their place is a blissful, no-think spacious vastness. The rhythmical and meditative act of *insert-pull-and-draw, insert-pull-and-draw* of her hands stitching into the life and skin of this woman seduces her into a zone. She feels it as a trance-like waltz.

Her eyes go heavy with the peaceful task. She's startled when she suddenly sees a face appear in her mind as if right there in the room. The eyes seem blind, with a bluish hue over deep black pupils. The unblinking gaze stares at Abigail with life behind them. The odd appearance of this face doesn't fit anything Abigail has ever experienced. Not a vision, or a memory. Abigail's skin turns to solid goosebumps.

"Doctor?" Ellen's voice gets her attention.

"Sorry." Abigail tries to steady her hands. "Vitals?"

"120 over 70." Cynthia reports.

"Thank you," Abigail says tersely, then forces a smile at Cynthia, who removes Fran's oxygen mask. Ellen unclips the drape for Dr. Lowell to pull out the IV drip, bandaging its port site. Abigail stands up and nudges her blood-smeared face shield with the tips of her gloved knuckles to lift it up. She tries to speak past the image of the face that has rooted into her brain. For a moment, she is without words.

"Congratulations!" she almost shouts, like she's just remembered how to talk. Then recovers with her normal bedside voice. "Fran, you can rest here for a few more minutes. The nurses will take your vitals for a bit longer. Then the three of you can go the recovery room and you'll be able to nurse your baby."

"Thank you so much, Dr. DiGiorno."

Abigail holds the practiced tone to respond. "You're very welcome, Jim. Have you picked a name?"

"Genevieve." Fran says softly.

"Beautiful name." Abigail forces another smile. "Welcome to the world Genevieve. We'll be doing tests and checking on you tonight, but the hard part is over."

Fran manages a chuckle. "I think it might have just begun!"

"You may be right about that! You can follow up with Dr. Benson tomorrow. I'll send a report." She waves to them, then hurries out.

Finally, alone, she stops in the doorway to the sterilizing sinks to lean against the wall, squeezing her eyes closed.

"You okay, Doc?" Ellen touches her elbow.

"I'll be fine. Just need more green tea." She steps forward to scrub out.

THEN

My return from the Medicine of the Stinging Night trance is harsh and sudden. I smell the sour rush of vomit as Lael holds the urn for me. The Madre pads a lavender-soaked cloth to my forehead. The sweet scent eases the bile's clinging odor. Until another lurch forces upward and empties.

"There is no more to let."

I lean back into the pillows on the wall, my body first ice then fire. Sondro moves into my bed, wraps his body around mine and pulls the woven linens over our shoulders. He has let loose his Priest knot from behind his head leaving his long silken black hair to warm us more. My trembling begins to slow.

"What did you see?" Taniyeh's voice is the barking wolf pup.

"Do not hurry her," the Madre chides.

The effort to recall what happened is like trying to remember a fading dream. It returns in small moments, then hides. The clinging smell returns. I remember now that this odor arose when I saw the woman with the dark curls. She had a cover upon her face that hid nothing and allowed her to gaze through. She was concentrating on something. Then I remember.

"She was stitching, yet it was no cloth under her fingers." I think I say this to myself, but my voice betrays me.

"Who?" Taniyeh demands.

I recall the woman's hands and her steady rhythm matching the Priest's even tone that still sounds in my room. As the vision arises, I slowly come to the knowing that she mends with a curative tool. Light emanates from her hands. This woman is a birthing healer, serving a mother in danger. The dizzying odor is indeed for cleansing, yet stronger than what I have ever known, making my skin and mouth tingle. Even with my curiosity of this healer's method, I am shocked with the bitter and repulsive taste of the scent once more and reach to Lael again for the urn.

I allow the Madre to wipe my lips and cheeks, then gently take her wrist to cease her movement so I may think more clearly.

"How is it I knew her task?" I regret to say this out loud, for Taniyeh moves to me, her voice an arrow.

"Who do you speak of?"

"The tea showed me faces of three women."

"Did they speak of the future?"

"They did not speak at all."

"Did they see you?"

"At first no. Yet even as they later did, they did not know me. Nor I them."

"But what of the future?"

I frown and send my mind to Taniyeh to instill patience into her.

"Prophetess. I cannot say."

"Show us what you saw!"

I sit up higher on the pillows. "One was a seamstress. The other with green fire-eyes...." *Her face became mine.*

"You say there were three."

"My nausea stopped my seeking."

"But you saw something that frightened you." Taniyeh probes my mind unbidden. "Show us more!" Taniyeh demands.

"Prophetess Taniyeh. This can wait. Anya must rest." The Madre's order is not to be denied.

I invoke blackness and secure my vision is gone.

"What has happened to you?" The Madre clucks, placing herself on my bedside and taking my hand in hers. The only mother I have ever known shares her face's image, intending to comfort me. I gaze on her fleshy cheeks, and frown at the little red specks like cherry stains that splatter across the smooth madrone bark of her skin when she is angered. Her aging white hair is pulled back with the Priestess crown wrap. I pat her cheeks with my palms, glad to feel her close. She pulls me into her heart.

"Madre, do not coddle her," Taniyeh says. "We need to understand the future and Anya's trance has brought nothing forth."

I turn to Taniyeh. I send a stern force into her mind to look toward me. From there, I join her mind and can see her with my inner sight.

There are lines of age upon the Prophetess's copper toned face. Her violet eyes are power and stillness. Past the fleeting emotion, she exudes pure life-force. Her head is encased in a gold cloth that runs down the back of her body in a long twine, the fabric twisted with beads of lapis and agate. I reach for her hand.

"Prophetess. I will tell you all I know." She bows her thanks to me, releasing her small fist from mine.

"Yet first I will bathe."

I hear impatience in her voice. "Summon me when you are done."

She calls to the Priestess Na'akt to follow her from my room. Na'akt comes to me and presses her forehead to my palms in my honor as High Priestess. Our minds merge and she offers her sight to me, to know of her tall frame, her gilded skin on long arms like the fig tree branch. I am thankful she will tend to the Prophetess and leave me in peace for now. I let her image go and my mind is again still and in darkness. Na'akt makes no sound on the stone floor as she follows the Prophetess out of my room.

I lean back again, this time letting my whole body surrender to my exhaustion. I could easily fall into deep slumber, but I have one more task I must complete.

Lael has begun to fill my copper bathing basin with water heated from the fire. I send a probe to her mind to call her to me. She sits next to Sondro making the cushions tip with her weight. I speak low to them, knowing the Madre needs no more worry than what already burdens her, should she hear me. The Madre has dismissed the Priests and the drummers of their duties. She sweeps with the broom in halting swats on the opposite side of my room, her mind not on me for now.

I share the face of the third woman with the sun kissed golden hair, the smattering of specks upon her skin. It is now I smell her. She is of the salt sea air. I feel Lael and Sondro merge with my mind.

"She is the one that did not see me. We must go back and find her."

NOW

Talia DiGiorno reaches to her nightstand to see what time the clock reads. The dream startled her awake. As she presses on the top of the little fold-up clock, 3:30 a.m. lights up in neon green. She tries to hold onto the fading images.

Show your face!

It's the recurring dream. Her thoughts have begun to distance her from it the more awake she becomes.

Look at me!

She rolls onto her back, smelling her Mom's organic laundry soap in the sheets. Rose petals and something like candle wax. It dawns on her that she's not in her college apartment in San Luis Obispo where she last had the dream. With her eyes still closed, her fingertips feel the bed's headboard. Then she remembers. It's the day before Thanksgiving, and she's in her childhood bedroom in her parent's house in Larkspur, California.

She's too awake now to return to the dream. She runs her hands through her short light blonde hair, then yanks it into a slippery twisted knot, as if that will hold the dream in place. Her silky hair won't hold, and it unravels onto the pillow. She presses her palms on her forehead, eyes squeezed shut to will the visual pictures to sharpen. Shapes, colors, sensations and sounds play back at her like a movie she's seen a hundred times.

She's on a mat on the ground. She hears the ocean nearby. There's a kitchen hearth with a fire going. She always hears the bleating of goats, maybe even inside this kitchen. The stone floor is always cold under her bare feet. She pads through the darkness holding the hand of a man she longs to see clearly, even though she seems to know him in silent trust.

His steady fingers are cupped around her child-like hand, like when Dad used to help her cross the street to the park.

The man leads her out of the stone kitchen, down a small hill to the ocean's shore. He lets go of her hand and she runs down the hill to the beach. The way he chases her playfully toward the water makes her think he's older than her, but still youthful. She feels the damp sand under her feet as he wraps her body with his to warm her. She folds into his comfort, her child body half his size. His presence feels wise, bringing her peace.

She turns her head to look up at him.

In all the years of having this dream, she's never seen his face.

Now her body braces, knowing she'll feel a sting with what always comes next. The man disappears into thin air. Then there's a triggering tug in the middle of Talia's head, and then the woman's face always appears.

Her face is as familiar to Talia as her own Mother's but couldn't be more different. That raven hair, those blue-black eyes that look at her but never seem to see her.

Then the woman's face fades, too.

A garbage truck grinds along the street outside Talia's window. It hisses to a stop then beeps like it's backing up. Talia is slow to roll to her side to tuck her long legs in a tight fold. She wraps her muscled arms around her knees, making a burrow of warmth in the nest of covers, that eases the hollow ache in her chest. Sleep will come, but she knows it won't be until after the sun begins to rise. The tremor in her body is a revving engine that won't quit.

***

Talia shuffles into the kitchen around 10:00 a.m., still hazy from the dream. It lingers around her like a heavy blanket, weighing her down, but at the same time bringing her closer to a sense of the earth. This is a good thing, since Mom's often telling her she's too spacey and not grounded, but this morning Talia feels like she's up to her knees in heavy sludge.

"Morning." Kate mumbles, not looking up from chopping onions.

"Morning, Mom. You making stuffing?"

"Yup." Kate's knife seems to speed up.

Talia sighs inwardly, moving to the coffee pot. She wishes her Mom would talk to her about how she's feeling. It's so obvious, anyway, so why not just come out and say it? Talia's not happy she's moved back home either.

"Dad around?" Talia blows the steam on her coffee, testing the hot liquid with a tentative tongue.

"Hot!" Kate says, looking up at Talia's coffee cup suddenly. She aims her eyes back on her onions.

"It'll cool down." Talia blows on it again.

"Don't burn your tongue."

"I won't."

"Dad's in the garage." Kate brushes her mousy brown hair out of her eyes with the back of her hand, the knife wavering. Talia sees her mother holding back onion-tears.

"I don't know how you do that and don't cry like a baby. Any time I cut even one onion, I'm bawling."

Kate points the knife at her daughter. "I have a lot of will power!" She half smiles. "We're going to Sebastopol to Barb's to pick apples." Kate's brown eyes are a mirror to Talia's. "Are you coming?"

"Is that an invitation?" Talia finally sips her coffee.

"It is if you want it to be."

"Thanks. I'll think about it. When's Aunt Abby coming?"

"She'll be here tomorrow. Poppa Roberto will be staying here, too. Dad's going to pick him up at the Redwoods when we get back from Barb's." Kate throws the onions in a heated pan, spiking in a sizzling burst.

"Good to know. I'll pass on picking apples, Mom. But thanks for the invite. I have some stuff I want to do here at home."

"Have you sent out more applications?"

Talia feels her shoulders brace. She wills them to soften with a forced outward breath.

"Sure. I emailed two this morning." Lying is easier than going into it with Mom right now.

Kate finally smiles. "That's good, honey. That's good."

"What's good?" Her Dad's robust voice sounds before he enters the kitchen.

"She sent out two applications already today."

"That's my girl." Almasto pulls Talia in for a hug. "You'll be hired right away. I'm psychic."

"More like psycho," Talia mutters, half laughing. Almasto shake-hugs her with one arm.

"That, too," he teases. "Coming with us to Barb's?"

"No, but thanks. I have…." She decides to stop talking. The more she says, the more they'll ask, the more she'll end up lying to them. She slips out from under her Dad's arm and pads back to her room, softly clicking the door behind her.

She lies across the bed on her stomach and scrolls through her texts. Then Instagram. Then Twitter. Then Facebook. She sits up and chucks the phone on the pillow. She jumps up and flings her closet's French doors open and stares at the rows of old clothes and shoes and crap she's outgrown. Her hands are fists on the glass doorknobs. Her mind is a mish-mash of the dream overlapping the overkill of photos she just saw of Aaron and Jasmine. There must have been at least 20 pics.

I mean, he's like, a day over me and then her, of all people? My best friend?

And they're both still in their college town, San Luis Obispo, where they were all living after graduation. For the last 6 months. No real jobs to speak of. And now this.

Shit. I should never have come home. If I stayed there, I could have stopped them.

But it's pointless. Aaron cheated on her before anyway, and even that was weird, because they weren't exactly together-together. She wasn't supposed to mind. So technically it wasn't cheating.

I mean we weren't a couple. Exactly.

Except they were exclusive for almost a year.

Staying in that town would have done nothing.

And, anyway, she had to come home. To break it to Mom and Dad that she is quitting her career path as a wanna-be architect. She only got that damn degree for her parents anyway.

Just because Mom's an architect, and Dad has his textile biz, doesn't mean that's her thing.

They're going to vomit when she breaks it to them that she's moving New York City with Rachel and her boyfriend.

And become an artist finally. And get tattoos and not care who my alleged boyfriend is sleeping with.

Talia's hands are still glued to the closet doorknobs.

Get a grip! We weren't a THING.

She has an urge to pull every single item out of the closet. She sees an image in her mind of throwing everything in a box without even going through it and driving it to Goodwill. At 70 miles an hour. Maybe 80.

She makes herself sit down on the bed, then slinks her butt to the floor.

Her head is leaning back on the soft mattress, the bed still not made. Her neck feels like it's getting a massage from the edge. She rolls her chin sideways back and forth, soothing the rock hard muscles in the back of her neck. Her mind drifts.

The dream. The man's hand holding hers. The woman's face. The blue-black eyes.

Her solar plexus lurches, pulling her up to standing, her legs tingling, her pelvis suddenly strong under her.

She listens past her door, to see if Mom and Dad have left for Barb's yet. She grabs her phone and pulls on one of dad's old button-down shirts from her closet. She likes to wear it over her T-shirt. It's a comfort how the cuffs go past her wrists. She shrugs at her bare feet. She won't need shoes in the garage. Even if they're still here, she can whisk past Mom and Dad and they won't even know she's gone.

***

Once inside the cool interior of the garage, Talia locks the door with an audible billow of breath. She lets her eyes take in the only space growing up where she felt free enough to be herself. Think her own thoughts. Have her own ideas.

When she was little, Dad made her a work table. It started out next to his own flat table overflowing with fabric, color plates and tools. When he began to travel more often to the warehouse in Rome, Talia's work table became the main feature. Soon hers was overflowing with her own art projects. Then she took over his work table.

Now, after four years in college, both tables have become just a place to store things. There's a twelve-pack of paper towels from Costco and four plastic bins that look like Christmas ornaments and envelopes, trinkets and photos that Mom likes to stash here.

Talia moves to the table and sets her coffee mug down. The cement is cool on her feet, making her body even more enlivened than it already is. The day is warm; November in California can go either way. Freezing rain and fog. Or relentless sun. September was soggy. But now it's bright outside. The Liquid Amber tree outside the garage window is bursting with rusts, oranges, yellowy-greens and earthy browns. Beyond that lies the stone wall Dad built. A spill of lavender, pink roses and dry grasses in magenta and green tones accent the dark gray rocks. The ground cover of redwood chips creates a scoop of brushing strokes along the green edges of the lush lawn. Talia's favorite granite rock sits next to the birdbath near the Wedgeleaf Goldenbush, which at this time of year sprouts in luscious woven folds, their filmy inner moments looking to the sun. Talia loves their wispy reaching out of the thin green stalks.

Her eyes rest on the swing her father built with her when she was six. Remembering herself as a little girl explodes the dream in her mind again, bringing back the sensation of the man's bigger hand holding hers.

She knows it's not her father whose hand she holds in the dream. Yet it feels like someone she's close to like that. A nameless man. But not someone in her life now. She's tried to figure out who he reminds her of. But she's never met anyone like him. And anyway, it's hard since she never sees his face. It's the same with the woman with the long black hair. When the memory of the dream woman's eyes appears in her mind, Talia kicks into sudden action.

She pulls the plastic bins off of her work table and sets them in a tower, leaning the paper towels next to it. She grabs Dad's step stool and moves it to the storage shelves. Standing on tiptoes, she reaches past a watering can and a cardboard box of empty mousetraps and pulls her oversized box to the edge. Carefully teetering down the stool, she slides the box onto her table.

She looks at her 10-year-old's misspelling on the cardboard top. *Talia's stuff. Not for Publick Consumpshon*, in black sharpie.

She shakes her head. *I'm still keeping secrets!* To tell anyone about these ships in bottles she's been making since she was a kid could mean losing the sense of where they came from. Since she was a little girl, she felt like these ships came from a special world that only she knew about.

Now, she's longing to touch that world inside these glass bottles. She starts to open the box but then stops. She packed these treasures before college. It's been four years since she's seen the bottles.

The unveiling needs music.

She connects her phone to Dad's Bluetooth speaker. She scrolls through her eclectic playlist, passing Florence and the Machine, Beyoncé, Bob Dylan, Nico, 4 Non Blondes, Eagle Eye Cherry, Led Zeppelin – she pauses. *Stairway to Heaven* might be the choice for this – but then she moves on to Hozier, Bon Iver, H.E.R. and more. Nothing satisfies. She finds her classical section, zips past the piano concertos she uses for creative inspiration, then lands on Samuel Barber's *Adagio for Strings, Op. 11*. Perfect.

When the music starts, Talia impulsively bows to her box, then slices it open with the x-acto knife that Dad keeps on the tool shelf. She removes the folded sweaters that she put inside on top to hide the lower contents. Before she digs her elbows past the Styrofoam peanuts, she remembers to check the locked the garage side door. Just in case Mom and Dad are still home.

One by one, she pulls out five objects encased in bubble wrap. Her heart is racing.

She slowly unravels the one on the top. It's the first one she ever made. It took her all through middle and high school to finish the five ships. The ship inside this glass bottle is still in perfect alignment. The tiny and precise sails and strings are set on the cherry wood boat bottom. She named this one *La Fenice,* or *The Phoenix* in English. She always gave her bottled ships Italian names. Maybe to honor her heritage, since Dad's side of the family is directly from Sicily. But also because she's always been drawn to the Mediterranean. Besides, Nanna and Poppa, Dad and Aunt Abby were always talking in Italian when she grew up. Italian names fit.

She remembers that *La Fenice* took a long time to make—more than 10 months. Especially since she did it in secret and had to pretend she was doing art projects for school. She made so many mistakes, she had to do the ship more times that she could count. When it was done, it was like it rose from the ashes like a Phoenix.

She hugs the bottle to her chest and lays it carefully aside.

Next, she half opens *La Farfalla,* in English *The Butterfly,* then puts it aside. That's not the one she's hoping to unpack. Then she finds *Il Tempio—The Temple* and *Il Vento Che Canta,* in English *The Singing Wind.* She loves these, but the only one left will be the one she wants.

La Signora Della Luna—The Moon Lady.

She closes her eyes as she lets the last bit of bubble wrap slip to the floor, holding the glass bottle in her warm palms, as snug a fit as if part of her hands. She opens her eyes. The ship is regal so upright in the bottle's bottom. She peers onto the bow of the ship.

"There you are," she says to the little clay statue she glued to the ship's deck inside the bottle. The tiny woman wears a blue robe. Her long black hair is made from the wisps she cut off of one of Dad's soft, unused paintbrushes. She remembers she used ink and paint for the blue-black eyes, but they can't be seen from this distance. As she sets her gaze on the figure of the dream woman, her body finally settles down.

She imagines the boat rocking under them. The sails taking the wind. The feeling of belonging with the dream woman, there in that little boat. Far away from here. Where she feels she never really belongs.

The violins stopped a long time ago. Talia holds the bottle to her chest and sways to music only she can hear.

***

Scotty steadies herself with a grip on the chair in her dressing room, saving her knees from buckling under. She makes sure her back is to the mirror.

"Val! Get in here."

Within seconds, Val's blue baseball cap appears around the dressing room door. Scotty watches her manager's face go blank.

"What happened Scotty? You look like you've seen a ghost."

Scotty holds the empty flask out to Val. "Do we have any more tequila anywhere?"

"I swear you need a 12-step program," Val says, as she takes the flask with a dainty pinch.

"Been there, done that."

"What the hell is wrong with you?"

"Nothing. Just get me more sauce." Scotty shoves her chin at Val. "Please."

"I'll find some."

Scotty looks over her shoulder and glances at the mirror. "It's gone."

"Is that the title of a new song?"

"I'd have to call it *I'm Fucking Hallucinating*." She pokes the hamburger sitting on the dressing room table and watches it wiggle.

"Don't eat that! It's like… a hundred years old."

Scotty takes the clothes Val hands her from the pile on the couch.

"Get dressed and I'll take you to a real dinner."

Scotty tugs on the T-shirt and throws the jeans over her chair.

"I'll come get you in five," Val says. "Don't forget you have a crowd outside the stage door. You are going to do autographs."

"That's the last fucking thing I want to do right now."

"No argument. You're doing it."

Val slips out the dressing room door.

Scotty aims her eyes away from the mirror. She yanks her sticky leather pants off, throws them on the couch then pulls on her jeans. She grabs her leather jacket from the clothes rack. She throws it on with clumsy punches through the sleeves, stands and wobbles on one foot at a time pulling her black UGGs over her still-sweaty bare feet. She stops, long enough to consider looking in the mirror. Instead, she hurries out the door and down the hallway to the stage door.

***

After dinner, Scotty showers at her hotel, then rubs her wet hair into a matted mess, throws on a baggy white T-shirt and dark green boy shorts, then grabs the half-empty bottle of tequila by the neck and shuffles into the living room of her suite, swigging as she steps to the floor-to-ceiling window. She leans her forehead against the glass. From the 17th floor, the city lights of Chicago lay out before her. It's like she's floating above the star-filled sky. She wonders if she's ever going to get a good night's sleep. It's already 2:00 a.m. She has to get up at 7:00 a.m. for the flight home to Los Angeles.

She reaches for a cigarette, then puts it away. She's already taken a couple of sleeping pills.

"Which are fucking not working."

She moves to the couch, deposits the tequila bottle on the glass coffee table and picks up her notebook. She clicks the pen. She scribbles as she sings.

You can have it but
It's over soon
Don't ever tell them
'Bout how you burn
She pauses.
Mirror, mirror on the wall…who the fuck are you

She growls and rips out the paper from the notebook, lights it on fire in the ashtray and watches it turn to ash. She swipes her phone open. No texts or messages. Her calendar alert beeps.

"Thanksgiving's in a week?" She punches the phone's power off. "Fucking bullshit holiday." She grabs the *Us Weekly Magazine* Val gave her on the plane to Chicago.

She sees her photo on the cover. She wants to look away but can't stop herself.

"I'm roadkill."

She sees herself leaning against a brick building, with her guitar resting on her bent knee. Her leg is folded against the wall with the flat of her black platform boot. She stares at the button-down shirt they made her wear.

"It's beige, for fuck's sake." Only a couple of inches of her arm tattoos show through. At least they let her keep her silver jewelry and black jeans on. Her eyes look bored.

Headline: "Scotty D. Jones—Can She Still Keep Us Guessing?"

She scans her article. Blah blah blah blah blah. The pages about her life go on and on. About her ex-husband Ryan, her two loser grown-up kids Zeff and Izzy and her wired, cagey but "very notable" music brilliance. The rehabs gone wrong. The oops-bad songs. The hits. She flips to the next page.

Her eyes begin to blur. She makes her way to the bedroom and falls flat on her back onto the bed. She holds her hands in front of her like she's framing a picture. The woman with the long black hair and empty eyes appears between her hands.

"Go away. I promise I'll stop drinking tomorrow."

She isn't able to stay awake long enough to know she finally passes out.

***

Scotty turns her SUV onto Montana Avenue in Santa Monica, just fifteen minutes from her house on the ocean cliffs. She went to bed early after she got home from Chicago and only drank a couple of glasses of wine at dinner last night.

"That's not really drinking," She tells Motley, who sits in the passenger seat. She scratches the pup's scruffy head. "Don't worry. I'm not taking you to the vet. Just the groomer." She pulls him into her lap where he balances on her knees to look out the window under her elbow.

"Almost there. Then Mama needs caffeine. Why didn't you make me any coffee this morning?" Motley licks Scotty's hand.

"I'll go to that café on the corner after I drop you off. Okay, Candy-Dog?"

Scotty always calls her pets candy-animals. They are always small bites of fur and flesh. Cats. Guinea Pigs when the kids were little. A Ferret for a while. It was a depressed Ferret so she gave it to her drummer Hans who gave it to his step-daughter. Now Hans' step-daughter has a depressed Ferret.

Scotty likes big animals enough. She grew up on a farm in Wisconsin and had a favorite cow named Rilke. But she doesn't like the maintenance of a large pet, even a good cow. A candy-dog is so small no one expects it to have manners, so she doesn't have to bother with training, like she even has time for that. Besides, candy-dogs make warm bedmates. Motley's little Chihuahua and Terrier mutt-body tucks perfectly on the pillow on the left side of her bed.

The Hot Cup is almost next door to the groomer, and lucky for Scotty the little café isn't too packed this morning. Even so, she pulls on her baseball cap lower and makes sure her black sunglasses are over her eyes. If she's going to be recognized at least let it be after coffee.

The waft of baked muffins and coffee beans fills her nostrils as she pushes the door and heads to the counter to order a double espresso, giving the name Mary Magdalene to a barista with an "Anne" nametag clipped to her shirt. Anne frowns. Scotty lifts her sunglasses just a hint and sees Anne's smile spread in recognition.

"Got it." Anne laughs and scribbles a name on a to-go cup. "You can pick it up over there, Mrs. Magdalene." She winks as Scotty moves aside.

Scotty spots her magazine photo cover in the news rack near the door. She hides it behind the LA Times. Her eyes wander to the woman at a table nearby. There's a paper cup of green tea next to her, untouched. She wears a denim jacket, over surgery scrubs, a hospital ID tag around her neck. Something about her curvy, full shape relaxes Scotty and for a moment she forgets she's there for a hit of caffeine. The woman's soft face is an amber oval. A mess of soft black curls fall around her shoulders. She seems lost in concentration as she swipes charcoal onto an oversized sketch pad.

"Mary Magdalene!" Scotty hears, interrupting her train of thought. She's not sure but she thinks she sees something on the drawing pad that startles her. Scotty beelines to the counter, bows a silent thanks for the espresso, then saunters casually back to the woman, slowly blowing on the steam in her cup, her heart pumping the closer she gets.

She lifts her glasses and pretends to look at a newspaper close by so she can angle her view of the pad more directly. When she sees the drawing, she freezes.

In one compulsive move, she balances her espresso cup in her hand and straddles the empty chair across the table from the woman, whose head is lowered in single minded focus. Scotty, taller and hovering, notices the speckles of gray dotting the dark strands in the lined part on top of the woman's hair, taming the two sides of spiraled chaos below. Scotty bumps her cup down making the woman look up, then yanks off her sunglasses and aims her eyes at the woman.

"Nice drawing," Scotty says, holding the woman's brown gaze steady.

"Thank you. Do I know you?" The woman flips the cover page over her sketch, hiding it, while keeping eye contact with Scotty's penetrating glare.

"No. But I know that face you're drawing." Scotty's voice is leveled.

The woman tilts her head.

"You don't know what to say to that, do you?" Scotty asks.

"You're right about that at least." The woman brushes a wispy curl away from her cheek. "May I ask why you think you know the face I'm drawing?"

"I don't *think* I know it. I just *know* it." Scotty punches her hand out to the woman. "Scotty D. Jones."

The woman hesitates, then smiles. "That's how I know you! The cover of *US Weekly Magazine*!" She takes Scotty's hand. "Abigail DiGiorno. Nice to meet you Scotty D. Jones."

"Next time you see that magazine cover, put it in the bottom of your parakeet's cage."

"I don't own a parakeet." Abigail sips her tea, makes a face, then puts it down.

"Cold?"

"I waited too long to drink it."

Scotty gets up and goes back to Anne. "Can she have another green tea? And can you bring it to us? We're having a very important meeting." Then an afterthought. "Please."

Scotty throws a leg over the opposite chair again.

"Thank you. You didn't have to do that," Abigail says.

"We're having a meeting. You need a beverage."

"What is it you want exactly?"

"That face. I've seen it."

"That's impossible. I drew it from memory."

"I saw it in a mirror."

"Let's slow down."

"Okay." Scotty sips her espresso as Anne brings the tea. "Thanks, darlin'. I'll pay after." Scotty waits for Anne to leave and then continues. "So Abigail DiGiorno. You want small talk?"

Abigail wraps her hands around her new hot tea. "It's a start."

"You're a doctor."

"An OB-GYN. I work down the street at Kaiser. But I also have a practice at The Women's Collective over on Judson St."

"So you're in the vagina business?" Scotty looks over the rim of her cup and sips.

Abigail blows on her tea. "Some might say that."

"And you like to draw faces of blind chicks?"

"How do you know she's blind?" Abigail puts her cup down. "And anyway, how do you even know this face is the same one you saw?" She air quotes the last word.

Scotty pulls the sketch pad toward her, twirls it on the table top to flip the cover and expose the drawing. "This is exactly what I saw. Same hair. Same look. Same weirdo eyes." She pushes it back to Abigail. "It's her."

"I'm not sure if I'm more shocked that you saw the face than I am that you just grabbed my sketch pad."

Scotty grins. "Both are fine with me."

"What exactly do you want from me?" Abigail pulls the pad off the table and leans it on the floor next to her chair.

"Look. I'm sorry I grabbed your pad. It's just that I saw that same fucking face. It was in the mirror." She shrugs. "I'd had a few drinks."

"So you want to see if you saw this face because you were shit faced. But now you think it's because she could be real."

Scotty leans in to her, her elbows on the wobbly table. "I am not shit faced now and that is the same fucking face, Doctor." She leans back again and crosses her arms over her chest, blocking the speeding thumps of her heart. She downs what is left of her espresso. "Where did you see that face?" Scotty zips up her leather jacket.

Abigail is still. Scotty watches her breath raise her chest in even swells a few times and wonders if that's helping anything.

"Listen, Doc. I'm sorry," she says. "This is just fucking weird. You said it was a vision. Did you see it in the mirror, too?" Scotty traces her finger over the top of her espresso cup, surprised that she hopes Abigail will say she did.

Instead, Abigail breathes deeply again, her hands quiet around her tea. Scotty notices her long fingers have no rings. Black and blue charcoal smudges dot her fingertips.

"I was in surgery," Abigail says. "The face came like a vision. I was wondering, before you came over, about the blindness."

"It's those eyes. You even sketched them all creepy the way I saw them with the blue you smudged over the black. It's like a Halloween mask. But a living one."

Abigail pulls her phone from her jacket pocket and checks the time. "Look, I have to go back to work. My break is over." She stands up and offers Scotty a grin. "Tell me, what do rock stars do in a case like this?"

Scotty surprises herself with a snort-laugh. "We drink, have sex and then write a song about it."

"That's a long way around a conversation, don't you think?"

Scotty opens her palm for Abigail's phone. "I never give my number to anyone, Doc." She types with expert fingers, then hands the phone back to Abigail. "But this is too weird."

"Mary Magdalene?"

"She had bad publicity," Scotty shrugs. "I can relate."

Abigail tucks her sketch pad under her arm, then holds out her hand to Scotty.

"Your phone please, Mary?" She ticks her thumbs over it. "Now you have mine. Just in case."

"One more thing, Doc. I need a photo."

Abigail's laugh is a calm hum. "I don't do selfies with strangers."

"Of your drawing."

"What does that accomplish?"

"Proof." Scotty's voice is the gritty, low scrape it always is, but there's a tremor under it. The more she seems to talk about this face, the more she shakes. Her knee starts jigging under the table. Abigail must feel pity, because she looks at Scotty like her dog just died.

"Here. Take your photo." Abigail opens the pad up to the drawing of the face.

The skin, eyes, hair, and even the neck have more detail than Scotty remembers. The look in the eyes is far away and detached. The woman's neck and shoulders are drawn wearing a sleeveless shroud of some sort. Abigail must have seen more of her upper body than Scotty did.

Scotty feels a shiver run through both of them, making the hair on the back of Scotty's neck stand up.

Scotty clicks the photo, her hand poised and unmoving after the image is captured. The room, which seemed to go silent when the drawing was uncovered, now heightens into high volume. The clank of dishes in a bus-tray. The barista calling a name in the background. Musty jazz piano chords over the sound of people talking in the room and the door opening and closing to traffic outside.

"I think we both need some time to digest all of this." Abigail folds the cover back over the drawing and shoves it under her arm.

"Okay, Doc. But if you don't call me, I'll come to the Women's Collective and make a scene."

"Something tells me you mean that." Abigail winks.

"True that." Scotty watches Abigail disappear down the sidewalk, her body like a billowing wave. Scotty is struck with a sudden feeling like she lost something tangible that she needs to get through the day—like her keys or her wallet or phone. She stands up to pay, pats her pocket knowing all those things are right where they are supposed to be. *You need a smoke, woman, is what you need.* And maybe something to take the shaking down a notch.

As she heads down the sidewalk to her car, she lights a cigarette and opens her phone. She looks at the photo and takes a long drag of her cigarette. She lets it out even and slow, finally taking one long breath.

THEN

Taniyeh and the Priestess Na'akt move past the drummers in the hallway outside of Anya's chamber. The Prophetess feels a creeping heat in her cheeks at Anya's dismissal moments ago. The tea trance must have yielded something important. Yet, Anya did not allow the Prophetess into her mind to view what must lurk there hidden. The older woman's tight throat closes even more against the threat of a coughing fit. She pauses to steady herself on the stone wall.

"Cousin, will you not let me help?" Na'akt offers her arm, but lowers it when she sees Taniyeh wave her away.

"I long for my own mat in our home," Taniyeh says, pushing herself off the wall to continue down the dim hallway.

"We will return there soon enough," Na'akt promises, her hand soft on Taniyeh's shoulder. "When you are ready, I will prepare for our journey back there. I pray you will be strong enough, although it is wise not to wait for the thunder and wet wind to challenge our day's walk."

"We are still needed here. We must wait until I know Anya is prepared. Yet, I long for our home. This temple is too cold."

Na'akt shakes her head, forcing her arm under her cousin's and taking her weight as they walk. "I think you find it colder here only because you are unwell, cousin."

Taniyeh holds her tongue. She does not wish to argue with her kin. The Oracle Tunnels, under the dusty road, is indeed damp no matter how the sun bakes above ground. Yet it is there that the Prophetess is most comfortable. The quiet of life underground is the only home Taniyeh has called her own. Her chamber, where she speaks through narrow echo tunnels dug into the walls made of earth, allow her voice to carry to all those within, calming them. Offering them what they desire and need through her visions. It is where she was born to a long lineage of women that were bestowed with the gifts of trance wisdom that tells of what lies beyond. She has never closed the city's door to any who knock. Those that seek her visions are tended to with care as they are prepared and cleansed to listen. They stay in the main hall while she rests fireside in her private chamber, seated on her pillows, her hands clasped around her calling horn. The hollow curved shape is placed in the hole in the dirt wall beside her. Those in need of her counsel, hear her voice as if it comes through the earth itself, as they never see her in these moments, so deep in trance is she in her separate quarters. Some come in dire need of healing. Some come in search of word from the world of the dead. Some leave feeling more complete. Some choose to stay and partake in the communal life that thrives within the walls built long ago in the depth of the earth's body. What is different from here is that those that come to the Oracle Tunnels wish for her help. Here she is rebuffed again and again by the High Priestess. Still, Taniyeh is sturdy in her decision to have come.

When Anya came of age for the Prophecy, Taniyeh and Na'akt came to stay at the Temple of the Arch, in promise of the Telling. It has been more than six moons since then and Taniyeh aches for her home's welcoming ways. Thinking on this, Taniyeh shivers.

Yet, not for the first time while here, Taniyeh knows the chill in her bones is not from the bite in the cold air here, but from the jagged frustration she has met with each passing moon at Anya's discourse and rejection of what she, a revered and respected Prophetess, knows to be true. This thought brings a sting to her eyes, as Taniyeh knows it must be through Anya that change must come.

"I must not fail," she mutters. In her distress she is taken by one of her gripping coughs.

Na'akt holds her steady as the coughing subsides. She attempts to console. "Anya will summon you and tell you what she has promised."

Taniyeh sways out of balance, holding her chest against a harsher cough that now overtakes her. She loses strength as it goes longer than the last, her throat burning with discomfort. When Na'akt touches her elbow in concern, Taniyeh is finally able to cease the spasms and right her body, pushing her cousin aside as they enter their room past the stone threshold. Na'akt's wolf, Ba-leh, rises from his slumber, moving to them. He greets them with a silent yet casual sniff, then lowers on his forefeet raising his haunch for a stretch. He yawns back into a curl on Na'akt's sleeping mat.

When she leans to murmur in his ear, he licks her face then lays his head on his paws, eyes sharp on her. If needed, he will be fully alert in less than a moment's notice, which Taniyeh finds unnerving. Yet the beast is a reminder of home and she is glad for his presence. She weaves in a weak shuffle to the straight-backed chair at a small stone-ledged table placed in the far corner. She grips the chair's back and forces herself to balance on shaking legs to sit with a heavy drop.

She looks about, her irritation still alight. The room does not help. With no windows and the smoke from the fire blazing in the pit in the center, she feels she cannot breathe. The four sconces along the stone walls are lit, flickering shadows in the darkened space.

"Your pain is worse." Na'akt kneels and removes her elder's slippers.

Taniyeh winces as Na'akt finds a sore spot on her foot but does not complain when she fetches her comfrey oil from her leather sack to rub the soreness on the bottoms of Taniyeh's feet and up along her ankles and lower legs.

"That helps. It is also in my back more than before."

Na'akt is quiet as she crumbles comfrey leaves and garlic buds into a pot of simmering water hanging over the fire. She uses a cloth to hold the hot handle and pours the liquid into a clay bowl to hand to Taniyeh.

The Prophetess sips the warm mixture, feeling a flood of peace soothe her. When Na'akt holds her hands over Taniyeh's sore back to bring healing to the surface under the silk robe, Taniyeh lets out a breath held there for too long.

"You must tell the others," Na'akt says softly.

"Not yet." She looks at her cousin, seeing the concern in Na'akt's dark oval eyes.

Na'akt stops her hands on the Prophetess's back and kneels again in front of her.

Surprised at her sudden grief, Taniyeh cups Na'akt's chin. "I will miss you most, you know."

Na'akt lays her head in Taniyeh's lap.

Taniyeh lets out a long breath. "I am running out of time." She strokes the Priestess's hair beneath the crown wrap. Na'akt raises her head, takes her cousin's hand and kisses the palm.

Taniyeh closes her eyes. "Help me to the mat."

Once settled under the warmth of linens, they sit in silence for some time, Taniyeh sipping her tea, their shoulders touching. Taniyeh's mind is finally slowing down from the gathering in Anya's room. She is not surprised when Na'akt speaks to what most troubles the Prophetess.

"Anya is more ready than you believe. Your need for her to be what you expect shadows your seeing what she is capable of. You forget that it was she who came into your life after so many moons of hoping for The Prophecy to begin. You must trust that she has been well prepared and that she knows her place in the Great Design."

Taniyeh frowns. "We need her to better understand how her blindness is the doorway."

"Do you think these faces she has seen are the way through?"

Taniyeh's shoulders are stones pulling her downward. "My visions do not show me. I do not trust these faces until I am told what Anya saw."

"You do not like to wait." Na'akt's words are a wasp prick.

Taniyeh's jaw tightens. She closes her eyes, braced for what her cousin will say next.

"This means you must tell them that you are dying."

Taniyeh lifts her hand to stop her cousin from saying more, but Na'akt continues.

"Your pride will be the end of you! Even before your body fails!"

Taniyeh regards her cousin with a steady stare. "I have reason to wait. None will want me to attend council here at the Temple of the Arch, and will fuss over me more than you do now!"

Her eyes are slits as she watches Na'akt's face attempt to remain without ripple at the Prophetess's outburst. She tries for a more neutral tone.

"When I call a council of all the temples to warn our people of the coming times, I will tell the others of my fate then." She lowers her empty tea bowl onto the floor, wincing at the sharp pain in her chest. "We will not speak of my illness again."

She rolls to her side, her breath rasping and weak. She hears the rustle as Na'akt slides away to join Ba-leh on her mat. Taniyeh is sure that she will not sleep until the moon is ready to turn to the sun.

***

"Anya, you have not touched your bread or milk." I hear the bronze plate and cup scrape toward me as Lael pushes them across the stone table next to the fire in my room.

"I have no hunger."

My mouth still tastes the bitter mushroom tea, reminding me of the sickness that came soon after. After my trance, only Lael remained in my room to sleep by my side, just as she did when we were young Initiates. I was glad to have her arms wrapping me when I slept, yet now my skin itches. I woke at sunrise feeling prickly and cross.

I lean away from the goat's milk, covering my nose. I feel the day will be hot, and I have pulled on my lightest robe, already soaked with sweat. I wonder how long I am to feel so ill-tempered.

"Do you wish to speak of your trance?" Lael hands me a cloth to wipe my heated skin.

"I do not."

Lael brings the boar brush to me.

"You try to ease my mood?" I lean into the stroking pulls of the boar bristle brush.

"I do not mean to, but am glad if I do."

"You do." I pat her hand.

When I reach for a piece of bread and nibble the edge I find I want more. I try a lick of milk on my tongue. My belly does not lurch. I tear off a corner of bread, suddenly ravenous.

"I am glad you eat." Lael's brushing still soothes. "What troubles you?"

"I know the third face is one I need to find."

"So you said."

"I plan to take the tea again. We must tell no one."

"I see the trouble in this. What needs such secrecy?"

"To invoke my Prophecy without Taniyeh."

"You believe these women are of the Prophecy. Yet you think now that Taniyeh has kept this from you?"

I drop my face in my palms to rub my forehead. "I hope it is not so. But she has never spoken of them."

"Perhaps the Prophetess has reason."

"You do not think of my reason! My blindness is the only reason I have been chosen."

Lael's hand has ceased its calming strokes. "And just how is it that you know how much to take to not die from the poison?"

I send her a mind image.

"Na'akt? You will entrust her but not the Prophetess? How is it you think Na'akt will agree?"

"She must."

The brush strokes so quick and harsh my head is tipped backwards. I find Lael's hand to stop it, bringing it to my heart.

"This burden is mine alone. Do you not know this, sister?"

"It is not that I do not know it. It is that I do not wish to."

"That you know it is what gives me courage." I stand up and take the brush from her. "Come now. Help me find my High Priest."

"What can Sondro say to this plan, except begrudge you for causing worry to us all?

"He will say that I must do this."

"What makes you so sure?"

"Because I will tell him he must take the tea with me."

***

The room Sondro shares with Eon, the young Initiate Priest in his charge, is set along the western side of the temple in the Priest's quarters. My mood lifts when the boy answers the door and leads us in.

"The High Priest has gone to his family's fishing boat, tied at the shore below."

My affection for Sondro's youngest student is hard to deny. Eon is only ten summers, yet his mind links easily with mine. When he bows his forehead to my palms he seems to know within his good heart to show me the image of his own kind face. With his dark eyes and dark brows, he could easily be Sondro's kin. Yet the mark at birth of the black crescent moon upon Eon's chin is his own. Sondro's soft beard would cover such a thing if he had been blessed with such a sign at his own birth. I greet Eon with a kiss on his cheek.

He steps back. I sense some strange import come over him, as if he stands on stiff legs like the egret in the marsh. He begins to speak in too grave a tone, as if the occasion is far more serious than our simple visit.

"High Priestess Anya of Mahet. I honor you with great…." He throws his arms around my waist. "I cannot remember the words!" His voice is the frog's croak, ready to lose its child's squawk.

"Little bird, such words are only for the Priests at High Ceremony." I take his braid around to the front of his chest and tease it with a tug.

He wraps his arms around my waist and leads me further into the room. My hand still grasps his long braid. "Do not fret. When you are older, you will have the Priest's knot."

"I will not deserve it! I am distracted with my practices. I try to sit still on my pillow but when my nose itches I think I must stop to scratch it, and then I can think of nothing else but my nose and forget why I sit on the pillow!"

"You will learn. Sondro is as fine a teacher as there is."

"I like it best when he plays pine cone paddle with me in the meadow."

"Is he to return soon?"

"He said only that I practice until he rings the bell." He coughs. "The bell is with him."

Lael joins my laughter. "Then we best go find him and bring him—and his bell—back to you!"

Eon begins a somber speech again, then stops as Lael and I squeeze him between us, trapping him with our kisses on his cheeks. His squeal is like the baby boar when our fingers find his ribs.

"We must take our leave now. To your practice now, young Eon!" I pretend to scold.

I hear his feet slap the stone floor then a thud as he throws himself downward to his pillow.

"You have yet to learn to move like the quiet fox," I tease.

"Do not tell!"

"It will be our secret." I seal my lips with mock seriousness. Lael takes my arm and leads me through the doorway.

As we move down the steps and leave the Priest's quarters, I hear their chanting tones coming from their ceremony room. The vibration echoes through me, reviving me further after our visit with Eon. We enter the open air main hall, where all walk, meet and tend to temple life. I smell the sea air, so close off the cliff. As a group of Priestesses pass I inhale the scent of mimosa clinging to their robes. I hear Priests moving by as well and smell the luscious peppery resin of their sacred ceremony herbs.

We come to the temple doors that lead to the outer circle, garden and meadow. I place my hands on the surface, feeling the life under my fingers. The twin panels of cherry wood need power to push them forward. As Lael leads me through the doorway, I remember Grandmother Oriana bringing me here to begin my life as an Initiate. Before we entered, she knelt to sing my mother Mahet's blessing chant, her hands upon my head. Thinking of my Grandmother, I realize how I long to see her. It has been too many moons. I hope she will take the long travel to celebrate our harvest season.

Out in the meadow, I hear the donkey's hooves on the dry dirt, knowing they pull carts with clucking fowl and bleating goats within. There are the calls and voices of those from towns and farms trading their pots, bowls, tools, etchings and carved statues. We pass the scents of animals, soiled hay, sweat, sweet mangos and strawberries, leather and the tang of heated metal being shaped with a rhythmic bang and the heat of fire.

Lael leads me through the tall grass and hefty flat rocks where we played as children. And then to where we had our classes in the Sacred Mudras inside the careful placing of the labyrinth's sacred spiral. The great oak still stands, with bark as rough as the oyster shell, that we sat under for our studies of healing plants, herbs, the star's mathematic design in the architecture of the rhythms of life.

We move past the caves, the cool rocks within making shelter set deep into the crevices of the earth. I smile to myself, remembering my first Sacred Union Ritual there, where we learned how the Goddess can choose her consorts to celebrate the fertility of life for all people. I can still almost feel the thick straw mats that softened the cool rock's ground. I recall when I first laid my lips on Sondro's sweet mouth within one of these caves. His were not the only lips I tasted, I remember now, my body heating from more than the sun. Until I chose him as my High Priest, leading him to my temple room on the Full Moon Ritual when the crops are gathered and shared in celebration of nourishment for all. Alone in my room, when we performed the Joining Ceremony, standing naked to bless each other's bodies with the sacred cinnamon and olive oil, the heat between us could not be contained. I shiver at the memory of how we forgot the words of our blessings in the haste of our slippery bodies drawn to each other like flint to stone. Now Sondro's lips are the only I taste. I wish for no other in my sacred bed. My hope to find him on the shore near his family's boat makes my heart skim faster with the current of these memories.

Lael untethers the leathers that hold the high gate on the wall that surrounds our meadow and the temple. The sun is above, casting heat upon the stone wall that circles us. It is only in the darkening time that we need shelter from the wolves and bears. And the hippos! So bold are they at times to charge through the temple if they have no restraint. Yet now, in full sunrise, we are safe with only the swallows and gulls near, and the scratching shrews digging in the earth to their nests. We make an easy pass down the path below the cliff to the sea.

"He is there, where Eon said he would be." Lael shares the image of Sondro with my mind.

His long black hair is in the Priest knot behind his head. His robe is tied to his knees, to keep dry as he steps in the sea. His deep red robe, made so from the linens soaked to bless the fabric with our menses flow, is a vibrant compliment against the cerulean blue of the ocean behind him.

I linger with Leal's shared vision. She is kind to move it within my mind with such textured detail. I squeeze her hand in thanks.

She holds the vision, showing me he bends barefoot and leans over the wooden rail, twisting a sail's end to tighten. I feel the wind casts only a slight breeze.

Lael stops the image to help me over the slippery seaweed and shale along the wet shore to move to him. When we reach Sondro our slippers grow wet as the waves move over our feet. I bend down and splash the sacred water, blessing my face in thanks for its pure life.

Sondro comes to us directly. "Is all well? I do not often find you here." He moves into my mind with worry, then eases there, seeing nothing to startle. He bows his forehead first to my palms, then to Lael's.

"Do you often come here to your family's ship?" Lael asks.

"I come as much as I am able to, for the memory of my mother and father."

"I see the painted drawing of the Moon Mother on the vessel's face." Lael turns her mind to mine to share the image of the figure on the wooden bow, her arms raised to reach above, palms open to the casting of the Moon, her Goddess robes black as onyx. She is the body of the darkened sky.

"Is this your mother's name for your boat?" Lael asks.

"My father's offering to the Goddess of the Moon, to keep us safe at sea."

A shadow seems to fall on Sondro. "The sea took them too soon." I touch his back, feeling the sorrow in him.

"I keep the vessel for their honor." Sondro's tone brings me ache. "When I am here, I feel them close. I was just fourteen summers when the sea took them."

"We are blessed you came to the temple." Lael says.

"It is my blessing the Madre raised me as her own. I would not know this path as mine to serve without her."

"Will you take the boat for fishing?" I ask, as Sondro leads me off shore to a dry place in the sand. I tuck my robes under to sit, with Lael beside me.

Sondro joins us on the ground. "I will take Eon to sea as a measure of his good practice." He takes my palm and kisses the center. "He enjoys the sway of the Moon Mother when we take her out under the stars. But this is not why you have come. It is about the last woman in the trance, is it not?"

"You see into my mind too easily." I turn my cheek to his palm, bringing a quickening to my skin. "We must take the tea and do the trance journey together. Will you do this for me, my Priest?"

"For what cause?"

I mean to only show him an image of the woman with the golden toned hair that will describe my reason. Yet, instead of a flicker of her face, she seems thrown at us through a dark tunnel. Behind her is a blazing light cast so thick it might run through our fingers. The woman with the golden hair reaches to me, then I am pulled into the tunnel, stunned by the need to follow her, like a mother to her child in danger. Sondro's voice calls from far away.

"Priestess, do not travel yet!" The image spills away. I feel Sondro's fingers tight on my shoulders. "So swiftly you moved to her without the tea!"

For a moment I do not know where I am.

"Do you now see why you must help?" Lael is quick to ask.

Sondro touches my arm. "You were pulled toward her with such power. Do you think she is of your Prophecy?"

"I feel I have to find her." I am shaking with the need. "It will be wise to find out more before we say so to Taniyeh."

"We do not tell Taniyeh of this plan?" Sondro does not hide his opinion.

"You sound just like Lael." Anger threatens to rise in my chest.

"Do you not worry what Taniyeh will do once she finds out?" Sondro's question helps me focus.

I am surprised that Lael speaks for me. "She must do this, brother. Taniyeh may not believe this woman is of the Prophecy until Anya can say why."

"What of the other faces?" Sondro's impatience is not well hidden.

"All three have come to her only," Lael assures him. "Not to the Prophetess."

Sondro is quiet. He holds a stone wall to me in his mind. When I reach to his inner sight, I see nothing. Now my face is cold.

When he speaks, it is with the slow, deep tone of his chants. "I will drink with you, Anya."

I do not know what has changed in him to say so. I let a breath out that I did not know I held so tight. "I thank you, my Priest." I nod to Lael. "Sister, make haste to speak with Na'akt. We must do this by the next full moon."

I stand and start to walk with swift steps to the temple, only to remember I need help over the shale and shells.

"Sondro, I believe it is time to ring your bell for Eon." I stop and hold my hand open to his. "He still waits for you on his pillow."

Taking my hand, Sondro joins my laughter. "It is my guess he long ago left his pillow and only plans a quick return when he hears us at the door."

Lael seems deep in thought as she follows behind. My smile fades. I am too soon reminded of the tasks before all of us.

***

Sondro stands at the rail of his family's ship watching the water glisten under the full moon, embraced in a dark sky with a scattering of stars above. The specks of light of the brine creatures on the sea's surface glow. For a moment, he thinks to fetch his net from the boat. If he caught them up, their slippery light bodies can be given to the Priestess healers to make a salve for aching bones. Yet he decides against it, having more important matters to face.

As he turns to Anya who sits on her pillow on the boat's deck, he keeps his thoughts protected. He does not wish her to know his concerns. His pillow rests across from where she sit upon hers, but he has been standing at the rail beside her. The wind picks up in a sweep around his body. His hair is in the Priest Knot, yet some strands come loose at the brushing breeze. If the wind grows stronger, he worries it might cause the ship to tip. Yet the sky is calm and the cypress and oak trees on the cliffs above do not sway with threat. He will spend the night here with Anya and Lael. Not only to allow all to rest after the trance, but to stay safe from the night animals that hunt along the shore.

He turns now, attempting to center and soothe his body. Since he rose with the sun, a shaky foreboding has been a veil over him. He watches as Lael sings the blessing over the mushroom tea, which she brews in a bronze pot over the small fire. Sondro managed to set some stones on the boat's floor to heat the tea in safety, for the shore would be too far from where they are to remain for the night.

Sondro pulls his wolf skin around his shoulders. He is glad Lael secured the tea from Na'akt with a trade in promise to tell Taniyeh what comes of their trance after it is done. He frowns to himself as the foreboding feeling increases. It is not good to keep this plan from the Prophetess.

Thinking on this his pulse increases. He knows the time to take the tea is near. He bends down to kneel onto his pillow, his legs under him in a comfortable fold. Seated now across from Anya, his heart surges at the sight of her. Long hair peeking out from under the wrap of her wolf skin, her legs folded, hands soft and resting. With the stone wall within his mind dropped, he sends a gentle image thread to her, only to see she has drawn her own barrier to him. He knows the black curtain he sees means her images belong only to her. He worries what she shields from him will bring her harm, yet he can do nothing. The hair on the back of his neck prickles, even so. He regards her to see if she notices his state.

She seems too deep in reflection. The smooth skin of her shoulder and wrist shows what is otherwise hidden by the wolf's fur around her. His body ignites at the sight of her, his want of her the same strong pull of the tide to the shore. Such a fit are their bodies, as moon to ocean. He wraps his fur into a tighter hold around his shoulders, if only to contain his desire to touch her. With her mind curtain drawn, he knows she cannot see him as he looks at her open eyes, so black with that rare blue over them, like a living precious stone at the bottom of the sea. The kind he pulled from the deep when he fished with his father as a boy.

Not for the first time, he wonders if he will ever be able to say to her what it means to him that, of all the others she could have chosen, it was him that she made High Priest. He came to the temple at already fourteen summers when the other Priests came at seven. Now at his twenty-three summers, his devotion to his path has never faltered, yet he never expected Anya to choose him that full moon night, when all the Priestesses choose their consorts for the Sacred Union Ceremony. Some, even Anya, had already had their time with him in their sacred exercises in the meadow to learn the early steps in how Priests are taught to unite with the essence of the Goddess in the Great Design. When Anya, already High Priestess, chose him by guiding his hand between her legs and leading him to her temple room to the Sacred Union bed, he went with his heart ready to burst. Yet, instead of the warmth that always comes with this memory, tonight it causes him to shift uneasily on his pillow as the foreboding sensation surfaces again.

This talk of the threat to all he has known has been a tsunami in his soul. He wonders how he will be able to serve as High Priest, when the Prophecy tells of such horrors to come. He knows this Temple of the Arch, named so after the balance and harmony of the bridge between Goddess and God, must not fall prey to a future of such instability. Yet it is said that it will be so.

He sets his back straight. With sudden clarity he lets his elbows rest soft to his sides. His fingers, wrists and all his bones awaken to his task. He must hold his vows and move past this ominous feeling and set his mind to the promise of this night. As High Priest, he is there to anchor the High Priestess in ceremony.

He sets his tone, even and low.

Through the sound of his deep chant, he reaches his mind to Anya. He is ready.

NOW

Abigail parks her sky-blue Prius in the driveway next to her brother Almasto's black BMW. She often finds herself musing on how the twins can be so different yet so the same; their choice in cars only one small example pointing to that fact. She knows his car's interior will be as tidy as her own, yet the vehicles couldn't be more different in cost, appearance and display. She glances at the shiny surface of her brother's car, the obsidian black tone overwhelming. The hubcaps sparkles in a silver mockery of her mud covered wheels. His tires even seem as if they haven't touched a road. She brushes a layer of dust off her car's roof and shrugs.

She lets Rufus, her labradoodle, out to pee then clips on his leash. She checks to make sure her sketchpad isn't bent when she stuffs it over her folded clothes inside her suitcase. She closes, re-zips and pulls the suitcase out of the trunk. She grabs her backpack and throws it over her shoulder. Seven hours in the car from Los Angeles to this sleepy little town of Larkspur, just outside of San Francisco, has made her walk like she's been on a horse for two days. The feeling comes back to her butt and feet as she makes her way up the path.

When Almasto opens the door, Abigail has just enough time to drop her backpack before Rufus charges to the end of his leash the second he sees the family cat—named, of all things, Cat—dart away. Her niece Talia appears from her bedroom and throws open the French doors to provide Cat the needed escape. Rufus is whimpering on what is now a tangle of the front hallway carpet.

Almasto rolls his eyes at his sister and takes the suitcase from her. Abigail has Rufus by the collar and smiles weakly at her brother.

"Sorry about that, bro."

Almasto bends over and carefully replaces each corner of the carpet that Rufus turned askew, then kisses his sister's two cheeks. "You are a terrible dog mother."

He rubs Rufus' head. "Scruffy beast. If you don't want your eyes gouged out, then leave Cat to her feline ways and stay clear." Rufus wags his tail and whimpers, his eyes keen on the French doors. Only he seems to hear Cat lurking, likely in sullen insult.

When Talia kneels to greet him, Rufus licks her face with mad abandon, his tail pulling his hind end in an uneven see-saw. He seems to have forgotten Cat and looks at Abigail with his ears in lowered flaps of regret.

"Are you going to be good now?" Abigail asks. Rufus cocks his head. Thumps his tail once more. "No more Cat terror." She unclips the leash and he remains quiet, looking at her for instruction. Abigail points her index finger toward the floor and he slowly lies down with clear disagreement at this idea. He places nose on paw, eyes showing decisive conviction that this plan is unwise.

"Come here, precious," Abigail opens her arms to Talia. "I've missed you!"

Talia moves into her Aunt Abby's waiting hug and squeezes her. "I've missed you, too."

They turn as one body still embraced to stare at Rufus, who remains in his obedient pose, tail thumping.

"Thank you, dog." Abigail flicks her wrist to release Rufus and stands back to take a better look at her niece. "You look amazing! So like your mama—and look at your silky hair! I'm jealous. It's so straight. Not like mine. Or your Dad's, of course!" They hug again. "I haven't seen you in what? Six months?"

"Yup, since my graduation in May." Abigail sees tension in the edges of Talia's eyes.

"We'll have to catch up." Abigail moves past her niece to embrace Kate, who has appeared from the kitchen with a towel still in her hands.

"Kate! Come here for a hug."

Almasto rubs Abigail's and Kate's shoulders. "My girls! You are le mie ragazze! My girls, yes? Let's go sit with Poppa."

"You guys go ahead. I just have to do a few more things in the kitchen. Talia, can you help?" Kate raises one sharp eyebrow at her daughter.

Rufus slinks to Talia's bedroom door, lies down with his nose in the crack of the doorframe, and stares ahead.

Almasto leads Abigail to the sun room. Abigail can barely hold back a sudden suck of air as soon as she sees Poppa's back. It's not just his forward-curling body. He looks enfolded in a sunken shroud. The sunroom's pure light only makes the dimming sense of him more acute. He faces the large floor-to-ceiling window. Abigail knows by the lean of the *San Francisco Chronicle* newspaper in his hands that his eyes are elsewhere. She follows his gaze to a black squirrel hopping off the low hanging branch of a Douglas fir. The tree's looping branch rattles in a spill toward the rose bush off the deck.

"Scoiattolo fastidioso!" He shouts at the window. "Pesky squirrel!"

He claps his hands together, seeming to forget his fingers holds the newspaper. He rolls it into a tube.

"Bang! Bang!" He waves the rolled-up paper wildly.

Almasto looks over Poppa's head at his sister. His eyes warn her not to speak. His voice is steady. "Poppa, we will have no murder in the house on Thanksgiving, unless you want Kate to boil that rodent and give it to you for dinner."

Poppa throws the paper aside and stands up. He grabs his son's arm and points frantically at the squirrel. "Prendi la mia fionda!"

Almasto speaks to the old man, but his eyes bore holes into his twin's shocked eyes.

"No Poppa," he says. "No slingshots either."

Abigail watches her brother gently guide their father to sit back down.

"Poppa, tell me about that article on page fifteen. You said it was about the new PG&E plant in Milpitas?" Almasto hands Poppa the discarded newspaper.

Abigail is thankful her brother is giving her a moment to collect herself. She moves to her father.

"Poppa, it's me. Abigail." She presents herself as if just arriving at a dinner party.

Her father stares up at her for a moment from his chair. "There's a squirrel." His voice sounds tired.

"It's me. Abby." *Your daughter!*

She kneels in front of him taking his hand. She hopes she can at least connect with him through touch. Poppa looks past her at the window. He pulls away a twisted pointed finger. It's bone and thinning life force.

She stands erect and mouths the words at her brother. *Why the hell didn't you tell me!*

Almasto squeezes his eyes shut. "I don't know. Too hard."

Abigail's doctor voice takes over in a sharp bark, as if demanding a scalpel from a surgery nurse. "I'm here for Thanksgiving, Poppa."

"Gina's at the store." Poppa looks down at the newspaper.

"Yes, Poppa." More doctor voice. "I will go find her at the store." She kisses the top of his head and turns to her brother. Almasto puts his arm around her shoulder. She lets herself be led out of earshot into the living room.

"Dovrei prenderti a pugni!" She hisses to her brother through clenched teeth. "I should. Right now. *Punch* you." Instead, she lets him lower her body down on the couch. "How long has he been like this?!"

Almasto's voice is flat. "Not long. A few weeks really. But you know, it's been building since Nona died last year. He goes in and out now." He lowers himself next to her.

Abigail's sitting with her back arched. Her toes turned in. Her knees are tight little steel doors to close off all sensation in her body. Her fingers are fists.

"He thinks Mom is alive!!" She makes Almasto look at her. Her eyes are ping-pongs, flicking at his, iris to iris.

"Why didn't you tell me!? Merda!" Her nails rub her scalp in furious strokes. She brings her cutting gaze back at him. "You knew seeing him like this would shock me! What the hell is wrong with you?"

Almasto stares down at the rug. "I don't know." He suddenly looks a hundred years old.

"I'm sorry, sis. I probably felt like if I told you about it, then it would be real. And maybe I didn't want to make you feel worse since you were already upset about breaking up with Nicole."

"But I feel worse now that I'm finding out like this!"

She grabs his cheeks and squishes them into pads of skin on both sides of mushed lips. She puts her hand over his whole face the way she used to when they were little when she wanted to literally rub him out of existence when he made her this mad. He always makes it worse by not fighting her but by turning into a puddle of goop under her hands. She feels like a bully roughhousing a sad kitten.

She runs her fingers into his curls, pretending to yank them out of his head. Kate appears from the kitchen. She crosses her arms, then leans against the doorway of the living room.

"You just found out about Poppa, I'm guessing?"

"I'm punishing your husband! And you will send him to his room without any dinner." Abigail points an angry finger at Kate.

"Okay." Kate smirks at her husband. "I told him to call you. I see that he didn't."

Kate moves behind them on the couch. She places her hands on her sister-in-law's shoulders. "And I'm so sorry about Nicole, too." She bends to kiss the top of Abigail's head.

Abigail leans back into the cushions. "Well. At least Poppa is too far gone to remember that he hates lesbians."

Kate grins. "Maybe now you can walk around naked with a woman on each arm and Poppa won't even care."

Abigail groans. "I hate this." She aims her head sideways, landing in Almasto's lap. "And I hate my own twin brother's heinous acts of negligent narcissism. His utter stupidity...."

"Please don't stop. Surely you have more fine words for me?" He strokes her hair.

"Arrogance, selfishness, did I say stupidity?"

"You did." Almasto ties her curly locks into a loose twist then watches it bounce open.

Talia enters the living room. "Family feud?"

They turn toward her and bob their heads in unison.

Abigail's heart feels raw as Talia leaves the room. It looks like her niece is about to burst into tears. Abigail feels torn. She wants to follow Talia to her bedroom and sit with her away from all this tension. She knows she should stay put.

Her brother's voice decides for her. "I'm sorry, sister."

Abigail thaws just a little. She'll find a moment to chat with her niece later. Her head thumps onto the couch cushion when Almasto gets up.

"I will join our nutty father in the sunroom and tell him it will be his fate to meet a parade of lesbians at the pearly gates. But I'll tell him at least they will all be Italian. *And* Catholic."

Kate takes Abigail's wrists and pulls her off the couch. They straighten their clothes and adjust their shoulders and elbows and head to the kitchen.

They hear Almasto's soft question.

"How 'bout those Giants, Poppa?"

"There's a squirrel."

Abigail lets Kate lead her away by her shoulders before she can think about any of this another second.

THEN

The tea throws Sondro into a raging sea. His voice breaks from his toning chant as he is churned into a senseless chaos. He feels his body like a stone drifting downward toward the silt at the ocean's bottom. A part of him knows this is not possible. His calm body sits across from his Priestess, yet the trance has him in its swallowing grip and the ocean's pull seems real.

The tea speaks. *This is what it is to drown.*

Panicked, he flails his arms, splashing in useless motion, until he understands that his limbs belong not to him, but to his father.

This allows him to yield into the hum of his own voice, which begins to carry him to the surface of the angry waves. He no longer feels water soaking his robe, weighing him down, or the terror as the salt water seems to fill his lungs.

Now he watches from above the ocean's thrashing surface. His father drifts to the deep of the sea's bottom. Sondro can see his father's tunic catch on the rugged spike of black coral, as it must have happened when the sea took him, his body never found. He sees his mother pulled away by the ripping tide. His memory of her body washing ashore chills him to the bone, lifeless and drenched, hair like seaweed, eyes open to the sky. From his vantage point, Sondro sees the family's empty fishing boat turning over and over in the storm, the shredded sails diving and surfacing in violent stabs.

The only thing left of his father. His mother.

The tea brings a message to Sondro, stopping his chanting once more. *Your own test is near.* This sets Sondro to shake with fierce intensity.

He knows Anya tracks his mind as he feels her fingers press his arms. He brings his attention to her, glad to move from the terror of such an unwelcome omen and back to the work ahead to stay in the trance and seek the face of the woman with the golden hair.

Path to the Priestess Temple

Call her, he hears Anya command to his mind.

Sondro is slow to understand.

My High Priest and consort. Take your place beside me for what is to come. Call her to us with your chanting tone.

Sondro's smooth voice hums low into the Priest's tone, yet he feels outside of his body, still altered and dispatched to the tea's consuming state. Yet he calls out the low vowel to awaken the name of the Goddess embodied in the woman with the golden hair.

Sondro feels his voice connect in body and mind to her as she emerges from the tunnel of light. It's a clicking sensation, like a tool finding home in a work of metal. In spite of the confusion she emits, she moves to them in haste, almost running. Sondro is taken aback by the sense of need to open his arms to her, as if to allow her to fly into them. The tea speaks.

She is a memory yet to come.

When she reaches them, the Golden Hair Woman places an offering at Anya's feet. Sondro's mind sharpens in harmony with Anya's as he shares the sight of the small object laid out for them.

My family's fishing boat? Sondro's chanting halts. *It is a small toy!*

He withdraws his hands back, palms stretched out to ward off this omen. But the Golden Hair Woman lifts it to his face to implore him to look. The ship rests inside a jar that Sondro is confused to see through what can only be clay. Even more complex is the statue as small as Sondro's thumb that stands on the miniature bow. He sees the long black hair, the blue robe. Then the eyes.

She has made an offering to you, my Priestess.

To us, my Priest.

The Golden Hair Woman lowers it to the earth again, then stands back to regard them. Sondro looks into her ticking, brown eyes that flash like a trapped wildcat, causing Sondro to feel the need to protect her. The light skin on her face is accented with specks of brown, like the splattering of squid ink. Her hair is short, cut evenly across at her shoulders. Her look is one of begging, turning Sondro's heart in a twist, as if something in her yearns too deeply to be known. The woman sets her beseeching look to Anya, who takes her hands strongly in hers.

You are to be Priestess.

The Golden Hair Woman seems to shrink backwards. Anya folds her fingers in tight constraint.

It is my promise to you.

55

The woman's arms are rigid in tense caution.

My Priest, prepare for the Priestess Initiation. Anya commands, her hands still steady.

Sondro readies to take the mudra pose to unify Earth and Sky as fitting for any Initiate Priestess, then stops. Anya's questioning sense moves through him. He fills her mind with his concern.

Priestess, surely this desire must come from her own heart?

She does not yet know her heart.

Sondro is taken by a stab within his mind—not a gentle probe as he is accustomed to sharing images with Anya, but a clunky knock inside his skull. Then his mind is a whirling motion, untethered, as if she cannot contain the mass of her own world and unburdens the images into his mind too fast and without skill. The Golden Hair Woman withdraws the contact. She drops to her knees before Anya, her forehead pressing the ground, her hands laying in fervent need on the High Priestess' feet.

I am between worlds! The Golden Hair Woman's distress is a haunted cry.

Then we will make you stronger for our world. Anya gently raises the woman by her shoulders to stand. *Do not fret, little bird. We will show you the Way.*

Sondro moves behind Anya, his body a strong anchor now.

As Anya slowly releases the Golden Hair Woman's hands, he watches her slowly recede backwards into the tunnel, her gaze locked on them, her face breaking in grief.

Sondro is pulled to float upward, losing sense of Anya, of the Golden Hair Woman, of his memory of ship, sea, his father, his mother, his body and all time.

***

I wake to my lover calling to me as he sleeps, *Anya, my own.* I do not wish to disturb him. As I shift my body to move, I feel the sharp pain in my head from the tea. My mind seems a coil of spider webs.

I feel the boat move underneath, rocking me. I have only slept for a short while after the trance and it is still the deep of the night. Yet I am not in need of sleep. I burrow my back further into Sondro's chest, glad for his arm around me. His hand gently cups my breast, his palm soft on my skin. My legs are folded with his knees. His breath a whisper on my neck. Our furs are cast over us, warming us in a nest of heat. I do not wish to wake Lael, who I know is asleep under her fur not far from us. I think the fire must be out, as I do not feel heat or hear it cracking. I ready to untangle from Sondro's body to stand up in quiet care.

I am still spinning from the tea. The bitter taste is repulsive, yet I am relieved to feel no nausea. I bring the memory of the Golden Hair Woman back from the haze of the tea. I remember her hand in mine. I remember my call to make her Priestess, how she seemed to desire it yet how she faltered. I remember the need in her to be near me, so great it was a knife in my heart.

I raise my head to the sky, only to realize I see the stars spread in a world above without Lael or Sondro showing me the image. I wonder how this sight has come to me without them. I have learned to feel the tingle within my mind only when given sight by another. I grip the rail of the boat. *Do I still travel in my trance?* Yet that cannot be.

I hold the ship's rail tightly. I am overwhelmed with looking out at the night like this, for it is the energy of life that my mind sees that is so new. The moon and stars fill my mind with their vital power. What looks out are not my eyes, but a knowing wisdom far beyond my inner seeing.

I walk along the boat's floor to the front, at first grasping the rail to balance and guide me along, until I realize I do not need to hold this way. This wisdom that sees from within me, in its own knowing, can see the rail, the wooden floor, the turn along the edge to the other end of the boat where I find certainty in my step and can stand alone. I am not the one who is seeing anymore. The energy within all things is what is seeing itself through me, and for this I need no eyes.

The moon's light is an orb floating on the water and also in the sky. This is enough of a sight to bring me to my knees, for I see two moons! One moon in the sky and her sister upon the dark water below.

Two faces of the same moon. The Golden Hair Woman shared her face with mine. Ours were two faces as these moons.

I hear Sondro stepping toward me and I turn.

I look at him in wonder. He has let loose his Priest Knot. Every crevice, every line, every silken hair I have only seen through his sight comes into my mind on its own as waving particles of light. It seems impossible to behold. I trace his face with hungry fingers as the light dances off his skin. The bones along his cheeks, the contours of his nose, the soft hair on his chin, his supple lips, all sparkling with light. I bring my mouth to his, linger there, to taste, feel, see into him, then lean back. I unwrap his fur, let it drop to the boat's floor and untie his robe.

I send my hands over his shoulders, his skin's surface glowing in the cool air. His hands stroke my hair, his fingers drifting through the strands. I bring my own hands between his thighs around his ready answer to my touch. We need no words as he kneels before me and opens my robe. He leans into me, his hands wrapping the flesh of my hips, pulling me forward to his mouth, his tongue flicking, my bliss ever building, my eyes now raised to the stars joining the spill of glimmering light.

I look down to the cascading display of colors and shine off his kneeling body and lift his beautiful face to me, beckoning him to rise off his knees.

"I see you as never before." My words are elation.

"I see you as always. Now and then," he answers.

"I feel the tea's wisdom still alight. When it is gone, so will be this way to see."

"Then see me now, Priestess."

I place my hands on his head. "This One sees you with the eyes of the Goddess."

He reaches his mouth to mine. Our salty teardrops are easy licks on our mingled tongues.

My hands guide his shoulders downward until he is under me on his back. I kneel low to stride him, sliding him into me. The light radiates with every move. His hands are warm on my hips, his palms first moving with my rhythm, slow as the sun rises. Then gripping in the quickening of the rushing river in spring. Our breath becomes the cresting waterfall. Now all the world erupts with us as my inner flesh contracts around him. As he fills me. We lie together, our breathing still catching hold, my face turned on the rise and fall of his chest, his arms around my back.

I know from the stir within my temple womb that my body received his seed. I say a silent welcome to our daughter, promising to keep her safe.

NOW

Talia feels like she's been holding her breath all day. The dream she had last night left her unable to settle. Nothing took the edge off. When she woke up, she was so agitated and had so much pent-up energy that she thought she might need to go on a run before breakfast to take the edge off. Even better, though, was when her old high school rowing partner, Lynn, called and invited her to scull in a double out on the Corte Madera creek. Talia borrowed Dad's car and met Lynn right away.

As they set out, Talia felt her mood shift. The fog was rising off the bay in wafting mystery. Bundled up in her winter hat, down vest and running gloves, she felt no chill, but only a burst of liberation from her mind as they cast off in one sleek motion. The gulls were awake and hunting, the sounds of Highway 101 slowly receding, opening her ears to only the sound of the oar's movement of the tap down to the rigger and the back splash of the oar sinking into the water. As Lynn's body moved with hers, their rhythmic slide and the synchronized pull of the oars through the water began to settle Talia. As her muscles engaged and released, compressed and lengthened, her breath started to flow again in steady relief.

But when she got back home her thoughts started to go in circles again. She knew that the dream wasn't complete. She knew she was supposed to remember more of it but only had bits and pieces. And she had no way to get it all back in one place. There was a sense of urgency to remember it, making her body clench. Like when she's supposed to do a homework assignment and she can't remember what it is.

She did her best all day to hide from the noisy Thanksgiving preparations. The last thing she needed was to be teased about being too spacy when she felt so thin-skinned. Thank God Mom put her in therapy those years ago even though it was because Mom thought the dreams were some kind of wacked-out mental issue. Luckily the therapist ended up helping Talia understand that her dreams and her spacy attitudes weren't a bad thing. In fact, the therapist told her that her dreams were real and had value and belonged just to her. The whole thing backfired for Mom, since Talia's trust in her dream world got even stronger after that. Remembering how much Mom's ideas about her stung when she was young, Talia ended up staying in her room most of the day, drowning out the chaos behind her door with her ear buds plugged into her playlist.

By late afternoon, Talia was like a coiled wire again. Thanksgiving dinner went on forever. Talia tried to keep up with the conversation, but it was like she was sitting at the table with a group of strangers. Mom was up and down from the table so much, making everyone nervous. Dad was telling stories Talia's heard a million times. Aunt Abby kept looking at her with concern. And it was hard to see Poppa talk about Nona Gina like she was still alive. All of that shifted her jagged alertness to a dull, heavy weight. She went from being like a raw nerve to a lead balloon, hardly able to move after dinner. When Aunt Abby, Mom and Dad sat with Poppa and started scrolling for a show to watch, Talia finally slipped away to the only place she could relax.

Now finally in the garage, she locks the door behind her. She turns and leans back on it, her flat hands like pancakes on its firm surface. She looks around, letting herself finally let the tension out of her body. The sights of the oversized metal shelves, the rock-hard walls and cold cement under her feet, bring her the sense of being encased in stone. She pulls out the step stool and sits, turning the power off her phone. The dark blue night is easy on her eyes as she peers out the garage window. She leans back against the shelves, rocking her butt back and forth to get comfortable on the step-stool.

She closes her eyes. Now that she's finally letting her brain slow down, the dream is right there behind her lids. She starts to remember details, filling in the lost gaps. There's a rush of it all coming back so fast, she can't believe she spent the whole day with no access to the memory. It's like she's right there again.

There was a low tone that she distinctly felt vibrating in her bones. As she recalls it, she starts to feel more solid in herself. Oddly, she realizes now, it was like the voice was singing to her, as if the tone was meant just for her. As she remembers the long low note, an electric pulse of energy makes her body thrust in an upward spiral then release. That makes her legs and feet feel more here than they have all day, which accents her contact with the hard surface of the step-stool. That connects her to her pubic bone, her seat bones, her pelvis, hips, and sacrum. Then it's like the tone she still hears fills inside her womb, like warm liquid captured in a bowl. The note seems to go on for an eternity. Repeating and repeating and repeating. Soothing every inch of her.

As her body relaxes with these sensations, she remembers how she felt pulled forward in the dream by the resounding tone. She has no other way to describe it than being carried through a hollow opening. Maybe a tunnel? The image is fuzzy because there was also a massive surge of light. Almost blinding.

The most remarkable memory, however, is that when she emerged through this passageway, the woman and man seemed to be waiting for her. She shivers, elated.

Then the unexpected. She saw the face of the man in her dreams.

Talia has to slow the visual picture down to savor the details of the face she's wanted to see for so long. Dark hair, in a knot behind his head. Beard, mustache, dark eyebrows. Lips, nose and cheeks delicate but strong. Light brown skin. She remembers how he looked at her.

She tries to find the word for how it felt. It was thoughtful, like he was a wise teacher of some sort. She remembers wanting to run to both of them, the need to be in their arms so great it almost consumed her. Protective! That's the word. He wanted to protect her. Like a father would.

In fact, they both reached to her, arms open, their robes swaying. She realizes they were both in robes! His was a deep reddish brown. The familiar long haired, dream woman standing with him was wearing a blue tunic-like robe. Even though she wanted to run into their arms, Talia is curious why, instead, she laid the Moon Lady ship in a bottle at their feet.

Is this the part that was so urgent?

Talia closes her eyes harder and bites her lip.

Do not fret, little bird, we will show you the Way.

Talia startles to hear the timbre of the woman's voice so clearly. Like she's in the garage now. A lullaby of vowels and syllables, deep tones. Like an oboe. Or cello. A song she feels like she's forgotten with an ache that is almost too much to bear.

An image shoots into Talia's mind of throwing herself at the woman's feet.

Why would I do that?

Talia's never done such a thing in her life.

You are to be Priestess.

Talia's eyes fly open. She swivels on the stool, hopping on it and climbs to pull her box off the shelf. Her hands are moving like quicksilver. Digging through the Styrofoam peanuts, she pulls out the Moon Lady and unwraps it quickly.

She holds the bottle up, peering inside. *You were going to make me a Priestess? Does that mean you're a Priestess? And he's a Priest?*

She sits down on the stool in a daze, suddenly filled with regret.

I didn't let you.

She startles when she hears Rufus scratch at the door. She unlocks and opens it.

"Hey pup. C'mon in."

She pulls the quilted packing blanket off Dad's shelf and lays it on the floor. She sits down on it still holding the bottle to her chest. Rufus lies down next to her, curling his paws into little nubs, with his nose on her thigh. She rests her back on the shelves behind them, holding the bottle in one hand with her other on Rufus' curly, furred back.

Rufus's cozy body is making Talia too sleepy to think anymore. After a whole day of total tension and how it's finally letting go she realizes she's exhausted. She surrenders to the drowsy release. Her eyes close in a peace she's been trying to capture since she woke up this morning. She's almost dozing off when Rufus pops ups and wags his tail at the door before Talia realizes Aunt Abby is standing inside the garage.

Talia grips the bottle, but doesn't move.

"Hi," Abigail says. "I don't want to intrude. I came to get Rufus for a walk." She holds up his leash.

Talia can't speak.

"Should I leave you alone?"

For a moment, Talia wants to burst into tears feeling flooded by the sudden need to tell Aunt Abby her secrets. A calmness then comes over her.

"Aunt Abby. Can I show you something?"

"Of course." Aunt Abby starts to sit but Talia points to the door.

"Can you lock it, please?"

Aunt Abby clicks it locked, then sits down. "Now I'm really intrigued."

"I have a secret, as you probably figured out with the locked door thing." Talia holds the bottle up. "This is part of it." She watches her aunt

62

carefully. "I'd like you to meet La Signora Della Luna." The worst thing to happen is that Aunt Abby will laugh. The best thing to happen is that she won't. Talia's sure her relief must show when Aunt Abby folds her hands in her lap.

"Tell me more about this secret. I like the name. La Signora Della Luna. The Moon Lady."

"I made ships in bottles since I was about ten years old. I never told anyone." She looks into her Aunt's kind brown eyes, the rims so dark and inviting. The long lashes resting at ease. "Until now."

"It's beautiful." Aunt Abby seems in no hurry to push Talia, which makes her want to say more.

"I've had recurring dreams for a long time about two people that I sense are important to who I am. That somehow hold me up. In ways I can't fully explain. The ships in bottles keep me connected to a feeling of another world. Their world, I'm realizing now. I sometimes feel like I don't belong in this world."

"I get it."

"I'm glad you do, Aunt Abby. Mom never got it. She even put me in therapy." Talia feels too shaky to look at Aunt Abby directly now. "I've made a few more like this ship in a bottle. But I keep them in a box I hide from your nosy brother and his overprotective wife." She snorts, then manages a sideways look at her Aunt. "Sorry."

"Not at all. I agree with your assessment. Please, continue." Aunt Abby smiles broadly. "I find this amazing."

"It's like I know these two people. And now I've had more dreams." She stops herself from saying more. Even though Aunt Abby seems like she'd understand, Talia decides to shift gears.

"Would you like to take a look inside?"

"I'd be honored."

Talia hands the bottle to her Aunt. Talia sees how her careful fingers curl to take it. In her mind's eye, Talia sees what her Aunt looks like in scrubs and a medical mask, gloved hands feeling the heartbeat and slide of a newborn baby. For the first time, Talia's glad to see someone else handle her cherished creation.

"Wow, honey." Aunt Abby whispers. A hush falls over them. "I've really never seen anything like this." She gazes into the bottle to see the ship more closely. "Is that a person?"

Talia's body tenses.

"It's a woman, right? In there?" Aunt Abby is still squinting to make out the tiny figure.

"You'll keep this secret, right?"

"Of course."

"Then yes, it's a woman in there."

Aunt Abby quickly hands the bottle back to her niece.

"Aunt Abby, you're shaking!"

"Yes, I'm definitely shaking."

"Did I say something wrong?" Talia's up on her feet, putting the bottle back into the box.

"This is the same woman you dream of?" Aunt Abby asks.

Talia feels frozen.

"Does this little lady in the bottle have long black hair? Did I see that correctly?"

"Yes. You're scaring me! Do you feel okay? Should I get Dad?"

"No! Watch Rufus. I'll be right back."

"You look like you've seen a ghost."

Her Aunt's face is ashen. "I think I have."

"In my bottle?" Talia lets out a nervous laugh. "I don't understand."

Talia unlocks the door, holding Rufus's collar and then waits for what seems like hours. Aunt Abby comes back, out of breath, with a sketch pad under her arm. She locks the door and flips through the oversized pages until she finds what she's looking for.

"It's this lady, isn't it?"

Talia turns it to see better. "I don't know how that's possible."

"But it's her. Isn't it?"

Talia feels her stomach lurch. "So you must dream of her, too? And of the man?"

"No, I don't dream of her like you do. I didn't see the man. But I saw the woman. I was awake. Her face appeared when I was doing surgery."

"Like a trance vision?"

"I guess it was like a trance vision."

Talia takes her Aunt's hand in hers. "Can we take a walk? I'm all jittery."

Aunt Abby clips Rufus to his leash. "That's the best plan I've heard all night."

She hands her niece the sketch pad, nodding to the box. Talia places it carefully next to her ships and shoves the box out of sight.

They hurry out of the garage and down the sidewalk to the gate.

***

Scotty's Malibu house is on a cliff overlooking the Pacific Ocean. It spreads over only two acres surrounded by cliff and rock, without the disturbance of close neighbors. What hints there are of nearby homes are far enough away along the coastal hills for privacy, yet close enough to lend an illusion of community. Because of the heft of the 7,000 square foot, two-story home, it feels as if it's on more land than it actually is. The grounds include a pool, pool house and a stand-alone sound studio. There's a three-car garage next to a manicured garden with plants she never handles. The four oversized bedrooms on the second floor are emptied of family, except for her bedroom directly above the kitchen, where Scotty stands, eating a piece of toast.

Even though it's already 78 degrees out, there's a chilly morning breeze blowing through this side of the home. Scotty likes the windows thrown open so she can hear the sounds of the surf, the birds and boat horns. She has her loose white T-shirt and her dark green boy shorts on, her black UGGs and a Shapka on her head. The Russian winter hat is made of rabbit fur, with side flaps that fit over her ears. It has two strings meant to tie the flaps down for the vicious tundra climate. The untied strings dangle under her chin. Because the flaps aren't tied, they scoop like upward curled puppy ears. She's also wearing one red mitten. Its pair lays on the counter next to her. Motley sits at her feet staring up at her. Scotty is reading texts on her phone while nibbling the toast. Motley's attention to potential crumbs keeps him in an unintended drill. Sit. Stay.

Scotty is biting down on the toast when her phone chirps. A crumb falls down her shirt. She holds the toast between teeth and touches the phone flat on the counter to speaker-mode with her free hand, and tries to locate the toast crumb with her mitten-hand. She hears a voice.

"Mom?"

She spits the toast into her mitten. "Who the fuck is this?"

"Not funny, Mom."

"It is to me. I haven't heard from you in a century or so." She flips the spit piece on the floor for Motley.

"I'm at Starbucks."

"I'll have a Frappuccino."

"Mom! Please be serious. I need a ride. Will you come get me?"

"Yes, I'll come get you. I'll be there in fifteen."

She ends the call, still looking for the other toast crumb. She shakes her T-shirt. Motley finds the crumb on the floor, snapping his teeth.

Scotty hasn't seen Zeff since he got out of his thirty days in rehab. It's been at least two weeks since then. Ryan told her that their son was doing okay. Also, that he was coming home. She didn't know which house he'd end up at. Now she's thinking it's her turn.

She sighs. "We have to hide all the liquor, Motley. My addict son is coming home."

She scoops Motley up in a cradle hold and showers him with kisses on his furry head. "We'll have to drink in the bathroom now. Okay?" She holds him to her face and he licks her nose then wiggles to get down. Scotty bends at her waist to lower him gently to the marble floor.

"Candy-Dog, where'd you put my keys?"

***

Since today is a "Hide Your Rehab Son in Your Car" day, Scotty takes her Ford F-150 truck with the tinted windows, so nobody can see inside. She's thrown jeans over her boy shorts, pulled her UGGs back on and donned an oversized cotton turtleneck that goes to her knees. As she pulls the seatbelt on, she makes sure she has her sunglasses handy. The mittens are staying home, but the hat is still on. Motley is eyes-forward in the passenger seat, ready for adventure. Scotty texts Zeff to meet her in the alley outside Starbucks. There's a place to pull over there where she won't have to get out. Before she eases out of the garage, she checks to see if there are any photographers outside the gate off the driveway. She's been in the habit of doing this for so long, she doesn't think about it. It has, actually, been a few years since the hungry press has appeared outside her house.

"Motley, we need a scandal. We're irrelevant." Motley wags his nub-tail.

Still, Scotty hesitates, just in case. She sees a woman walking a dog on the sidewalk on the other side of her gate. The woman carries a plastic Target bag. Other than that, there's nobody near her house.

The phone startles her. Scotty buzzes the gate to open while she fumbles with the Bluetooth, then drives forward onto Sweetwater Canyon Road as she answers.

"Hi Doc. Why are you calling? I haven't made a scene yet."

"I figured it was better to call before you do." Abigail sounds breathless.

"It's not on my list today."

"That's a relief."

"More visions of our blind-lady?"

"Not by me. By my niece."

"What's that supposed to mean?"

"I called to tell you my niece has been dreaming about the face we… allegedly… both saw."

Scotty swings the truck to the left, hits the gas, then brakes with a jolt. Motley tumbles to the floor, then hops back onto the passenger seat, panting. Scotty resumes driving, but slower now.

"Scotty? You there?"

"Yeah. I'm here. But you better fucking explain." She hears Abigail take one of those long breaths.

"My niece Talia. I was with her last week at Thanksgiving. She's been dreaming of this woman. And a man, too."

"Man?"

"Are you listening?"

"What the fuck are you talking about?"

"Can we meet in person?"

"I'm picking up my addict son. I'll call you back when I get home."

The silence on the other end of the phone is like a slap. Scotty realizes she's gone too far. "Sorry. I just have shit to do and this isn't the best time."

"Your addict son?"

"It's a long story."

"Okay. I'll leave it at that. But you'll call me back, right? We need to meet."

"I'll call you back." Scotty pulls into the alley. Zeff opens the back seat door and throws in a duffle bag. "I gotta go, Doc."

She ends the call as Zeff opens the front passenger door. He scoops Motley onto his lap then pulls down his seatbelt.

"Nice hat, Mom."

"It was Grandpa's." She looks at Zeff's mirror image of her face.

She sees the sleek black hair. The piercing green eyes, yet his have an amber cat-tone. Skin the color of peach yogurt. His naturally blushed lips are in a tight line. He looks like he's lost a hundred pounds. His cheeks are sunken in. She wonders if she can feel bone under the shoulders of his knee-length black camel coat. His hands, on Motley's back, are ring-less for once. She sees the creeping dragon tattoo under his coat sleeve. She leans over and hugs him, rubbing his hair.

"You look good for a month in prison."

"Just drive. Please?" He hugs Motley closer.

"Okay. You hungry?"

"Can we just go home?"

Scotty backs out onto Main Street. She pulls off her rabbit-hat. Flips her sunglasses over her eyes. The day just got really long.

***

Scotty's in her study on her couch. Zeff's been home only two hours and he hasn't come out of his room. The one Scotty left unchanged for him, even though he's been away from home for more than three years. Izzy's bedroom, too. Not changed. It's been so long since anyone else has been in her house besides Motley that she startles when she hears a thud upstairs. She wonders if Zeff is hungry. Or if they'll watch a movie tonight. She pulls her mind back to herself.

Scotty blinks at the photo on her phone of the weird face. A blank yellow legal pad and black pen are on the couch next to her. She swigs the bottle of Eclipse Stout she's holding, then turns the phone over so she doesn't see the photo. The beer bottle clanks on the glass table making a wet ring.

She hums a melody, adding words to chords.

"Just another... hmmm hmm." The chords are coming fine. The words are not. 'Just another… hmm mm."

She stops to set her guitar on the couch. She slides the red velvet curtains over and throws open the deck doors that open to the ocean view. The sounds of the day rush in. She moves to the piano bench and picks up her cigarettes and lighter next to the ashtray on top of the piano. She lights one and inhales.

"Da da… hmmm hmm… da da Queen…." The smoke makes a stream and then she quickly rubs out the cigarette. She tries a different melody, attempting another chord.

"Da, da da, then from the fall…." Another chord.

"Da, da, da what came before…." Another chord.

"The Queen she's falling…." Her hands go limp on the keys. *That sounds like shit.*

She stands and lights another cigarette, takes a drag. Rubs it out and moves to her guitar.

Zeff knocks.

"Come in," she tries a different riff.

Zeff hovers in the doorway. "Don't just stand there."

Zeff comes in and sits on the floor with his back leaning on the couch, stretching his feet under the glass coffee table.

"You writing a new song?"

"Trying."

"Is it about me?"

"I'm saving that song for when I'm famous."

"Ha ha."

"You don't want me to write a song about you. Trust me son. This one's about a queen."

"The royal kind of queen?"

"Not from England. But some kind of ancient one, I think."

"Different type of song for you, Mom."

"You settled in?" Scotty strums the guitar again.

"Yeah. Don't know how long I'll stay." He peeks at her from under his black bangs.

"You can stay as long as you need to. Just don't drink my liquor."

"Lock it up if you don't trust me."

"I don't. You're an addict like me."

"I know you think rehab is for babies."

Scotty stops playing and lays her hands over the top of the guitar. "It didn't work for me. As you know."

"But it's going to for me, Mom." He looks sideways at her again.

"Okay. But how are we going to do this? You're here. So is my liquor. So am I."

"I don't have to fucking stay here!" Motley startles at Zeff's shout. "I can go to back to Dad's," he says more softly.

"That's worse. Your Dad doesn't really know what it's like."

"And you do?!"

"More than your Dad, yes." Scotty resumes strumming.

Zeff snorts.

"Okay Mr. Smart-ass. Weren't you there for the two weeks you didn't call me?" She play-shoves her son's head sideways. "How much pot and cocaine did you see him consume? And whatever other drugs were around to tempt you? You know how he is. Do you really think you can stay clean and sober there? At least here you only have to ignore my liquor."

"Sorry I didn't call, Mom. I was mad at you. Rehab therapy made me see what a shitty mother you are."

"Fair enough." Scotty starts to strum again. "But stay here. We'll make it work. I'll lock my liquor up. If that helps."

"Maybe. I don't know. I have to go to 12-step meetings a lot, you know."

"And mommy has to drive you since you lost your license." She rests her hands again.

"Forget it! I'll go to Izzy's!" He jumps up.

"Izzy's is boring. Sit, son. I Promise I Will Be a Good Mommy."

Zeff stares at her. She pats the couch. He sits on the edge.

Scotty puts her guitar on the coffee table, making a lap for his head. "Come here, son. Come here."

Zeff leans back on the couch. He drops his head first on her shoulder, then slides down with his head on her lap. She strokes his hair. Zeff reaches over to the coffee table and turns her phone over, flicking on the photo. "Is that the Queen?"

Scotty is silent, feeling the whisper of her son's soft hair between her fingers.

***

It's 1:00 a.m. and as discussed with Motley, Scotty has taken two cases of wine and a case of tequila out of the garage and brought them up to the bathroom. She also carried two open bottles of vodka and a six pack upstairs from the fridge. She cleaned out her bar off the living room as well. The bathroom looks like a 7-11 minus the junk food and twirling hotdogs. The good news is that this plan has made it easy to drink while she bathes.

Motley's curled up on the bathmat. Scotty didn't bring any glasses up, but the half-full bottle of vodka rests on a windowsill over the bathtub. The bath water is lukewarm, the bubbles dissolved.

She slips her head under water then comes up for air. "Time to get out, Candy-Dog."

She steps over Motely, the vodka bottle neck wobbly in her hand. He jumps up and darts out of the way, but not fast enough to avoid the drips of bath water on his back. His collar rattles with his body shake. He stops moving to see what Scotty does next. She finds a corner of the bedspread and pulls it so hard that she almost falls backwards, then half wraps it around her, rubbing her wet hair with the corner. She weaves out the bedroom door, down the hallway past Zeff's room and stumbles to the stairs, slugging as she goes. She leans against the wall, teetering on the top stair. Her feet find the steps and don't stop until she's downstairs in her study. Motley pads behind her. She thuds onto the couch and drains the bottle then lets it drop to the floor. Her phone is still on the glass table.

"Looky! Here'z my phone!" Scotty brings the phone an inch from her nose and squints. She pokes a single finger, muttering to herself, and watches the text zip away as she pushes send. She scrolls her photos then brings the phone with the picture of Abigail's sketch to Motley's nose. "Candy-Doggie, here'z that ghost-bitch." He sniffs and puts his head on his paws. The fuzz over his eyes wiggles as he watches her.

Scotty lets the phone drop to the carpet. She slips lower on the couch. Her head rolls to the side into the quiet hush of unconscious oblivion.

***

"Mom?" Zeff's feet are soft on the stair carpet then slap the kitchen porcelain tile.

"Mom?" He peers around the edge of his hoody.

He thought he heard her stumble past his bedroom to go downstairs at 1:30 a.m. He couldn't fall back to sleep. She must be in her study since Motley appears from that direction. His dog-toes click on the kitchen tile. Zeff picks him up but Motley wiggles out and trots to the side door that leads to the pool and garden and wags his tail. Zeff opens the door and watches the dog hurry down the path then lift a leg on one of the low bushes in the garden. The little dog turns, shakes, does quick back-feet brush-digs, and runs back into the house.

Zeff picks him up. "Mom?"

His hands are iron tight around Motley who escapes the gripping hold to trot past the dining room into the partly open study door. Zeff follows. He sees a picture in his mind of what he knows is coming. He pushes the door open with stiff fingertips.

Scotty is rolled up in her bedspread. She's passed out on her back on the couch. Her bare leg and part of her hip are hanging off along with her arm and one breast. Her head is turned into the couch back. Oddly this is the thing that comforts him. That he can't see her face. An empty vodka bottle is turned on its side next to her phone on the floor under the glass coffee table. Zeff can hear the rapid thump of his speeding heart in his ears.

Motley hops onto the couch between Scotty's covered and uncovered legs. He sits alert, his eyes wide.

Zeff stands still in the doorway for a long time. He takes one step backwards toward the kitchen, hesitates, then rocks forward on both feet into the study. He lifts Scotty's limp arm and checks her pulse. He leans down, kisses the top of her head. She stirs, then moans. She rolls her face deeper into the couch back.

Zeff pivots quickly, crosses his arms over his chest. His fingers squeeze his elbows. His knuckles are blanched white. He walks past the kitchen and slowly makes his way back up the carpeted stairs.

***

At 1:00 a.m., Abigail interrupts her stare into the drone of her computer's screen so she can look at her phone. For the fiftieth time. Still no call from Scotty. *How did I get myself into this?* She slams her computer shut and steps out of her office to go down the hall to the kitchen. The Birthing Center at Kaiser is usually pretty quiet this time of night. She has to start rounds in a few minutes, but she only has two patients on the floor tonight. They each had smooth births, but she needs to check them before they are released with their babies in the morning.

This whole waiting-for-someone-to-call thing is triggering the last two years with Nicole. Especially right before they broke up. Her chest tightens at the thought. She clicks the power button on the teapot and pulls a green tea bag open with a rough rip and tosses it into one of the kitchen's clean cups. She looks at her phone again. Still no call.

Another doctor shuffles into the kitchen and Abigail gives her a tired smile. "Mornin' Jeanne. Hot water?" She lifts the teapot to offer.

"No thanks." Jeanne reaches for the coffee pot. "My eyelids are shutting on their own. I need rocket juice."

"Coffee makes my hands shake. I don't know how you don't nick an artery."

"Yeah, I know," Jeanne says. "But I'd rather not fall asleep with my head on the patient. You finish your notes yet?" She leans her butt into the counter behind them.

"No. Going now." Abigail raises her cup as a wave goodbye and goes back to her office.

But instead of sitting at her computer she sits in the small standard couch next to the door. The seat is like a bouncy trampoline, with no cushy squish, like her favorite chair back at home.

She lets her eyes travel to the window and into the unique darkness of this hour. She sees the street lights below and only a smattering of house lights. Three floors below, the highway is a moving flow of dotted lights traveling like shooting stars, calming her until she startles abruptly.

This time she's not surprised to see the face. It reflects in the darkened window glass. She sees the eyes. The blank stare. This time Abigail's not in surgery, or in a trance. Behind the face now is a tunnel, its bright light contrasting the sheen of night in the window. The woman is dressed in a blue robe. She floats backwards into the tunnel. Abigail feels as if a fish-hook finds her solar plexus, making her ribcage jut forward. Her hips feel pulled into the vortex, like an undertow has taken her hostage, the gravity of it like nothing she's felt before.

She throws a pillow at the window. "If you're going to come when I'm awake, at least make some damn sense!"

She closes her eyes, shutting out the images, then forces her eyes open again. The strange scene is burned behind her eyes, even when closed. Like she's looked right into the sun. She rubs her eyes. *I'm losing my marbles.*

She grabs her tea and heads to her desk, then hears a text blip on her phone.

It's an address. Then "Breakfast 8:00. Bring coffee."

She looks at the time. Only six and a half more hours. *Then what?* She's already wondering if Scotty takes her coffee black.

She sits back down on the couch and looks out the window again. No face, no body, no woman and no tunnel now. But the night sky seems alive.

***

Scotty stirs on the couch in the study. Her hand automatically cups the razor pressure in her forehead. The throbbing pulse is a sudden engine telling her of her whereabouts. She squeezes her eyes against the rush of understanding. She has no memory of coming downstairs. She has no memory of how the bedspread became her night clothes. Her movements have caused her stomach to lurch.

She throws off the bedspread, racing her heaving guts to the powder room off the study before the puke hurtles up and out. Sharp pain shoots through her head. She makes it to the toilet just in time. She flushes then sits on the rim. More comes up into the sink. She rinses the sink bowl, scoops water on her face. Grabs a hand towel and rubs hard. The movement is sickening. Motley's in the bathroom doorway standing on four stiff little legs. His eyes are intent on her.

"I bet you want breakfast." She croaks at him.

She heads back to the study to wrap herself back into her bedspread. She lights a cigarette from her pack on the piano. Takes a drag then stubs it out. The flutter of the early morning light is playing on the ocean, the deck, the wicker porch chairs. The world. She pulls the bedspread closer around her shoulders.

"Okay. It's morning enough. You can have breakfast." She shuffles into the kitchen.

Her feet halt in a freeze. She sees an empty vodka bottle on the counter. A folded note leans against the bottle's belly, her phone laid next to it. The note is written on her yellow legal pad paper. The black pen lies neatly next to it. She wonders, just for a single moment, if she wrote herself a note. Then realizes this is a ridiculous idea.

She bolts to it, her head stinging with the movement.

Mom. I love you but I can't stay here. Don't call me. Please get help.

Her low melodic voice wretches in an intolerable moan, rising from her gut into the echo of her empty house. She tips one hip on the stool next to the countertop then splays her head onto her folded arms. Her nose is pressed on the marble surface. She smells her own sour breath. In her mind, she sees those blue-black blind eyes. They could be her own eyes steeling into her, racing, probing and diminishing her until she disappears. She holds her palms over her face wishing she were the blind one so that she didn't have to see what she knows is true.

***

Scotty sits at the kitchen counter in one of Zeff's old sweatshirts, her hair shoved under the hood. She clutches her mittens around a cup of strong coffee. The day seems like it's going to be a hot one even though it's not quite 8:00 a.m. The sun is already poised to begin its baking ascent over the ocean. She left the windows closed this morning. She doesn't have the energy to open them.

Her phone is off. The last thing she wants is to be reminded of the photo of the creepy drawing. And there's no way Zeff will contact her. No one else is worth talking to right now. She takes off one mitten to run a finger over the side of the empty vodka bottle she left on the counter. The glass is smooth. The note on the yellow legal paper is folded under it in a small square. Motley is somewhere in the house.

"I don't blame you, Candy-Dog. I don't want to be near me either right now."

There's a knock on the door. Motley barks from wherever he was and scampers to it. Scotty turns in shock. Nobody ever knocks on her door. Unless it's Zeff? She pulls off her other mitten, jumps off the kitchen stool and runs to the door. She throws it open to see Abigail standing there. Scotty hauls Motley up into her arms, twisting her fingers over the mutt's barking mouth, her head a slice of sharp pain from bending over.

"What the fuck are you doing here?"

Abigail stares at her.

"How'd you even get my address?"

"You are by far the most annoying person I have ever met in my entire life." Abigail pushes past Scotty. "I just came off a twelve-hour shift. I'm hungry and tired."

Scotty drops Motley and watches him slink away. "So?"

Abigail turns and glares at her. "You invited me here."

"I did not." Scotty pushes the door closed and buries her fists in the hoody pockets.

Abigail has red specks in her cheeks. "I called you yesterday morning! You said you'd call me back. Then it's… what… an entire day later and you just text me your address saying 'Breakfast?'"

"I did not."

"You did." Abigail pulls her phone from her jean's back pocket. "At 1:42 a.m. Look!"

Scotty studies it, their heads together.

She saunters past Abigail into the kitchen. "Well, I missed you. Coffee?"

"I brought you a cup." Abigail holds it up. "Your instructions. Or didn't you read that part of your text just now?"

"I take it black." She lifts one side of the to-go lid and inspects.

"You're welcome." Abigail smirks. "You don't remember texting me, do you? Judging by the smell coming off you and the glazed look in your eye, you were too drunk." She picks up the vodka bottle and holds it up.

"I'll thank you to leave my bottle alone." Scotty snatches it back and replaces it on the yellow square of paper. "So? Beverage?"

"Tea. Green."

Scotty rustles through an open drawer for a box of tea for Abigail. "I suppose I'll have to cook you something."

"I think you should. As penance."

"Are we Catholic?" Scotty fills the electric kettle from the filtered waterspout.

"Recovered." Abigail takes a seat on the counter stool across from Scotty.

"Omelet?"

"Yes, please."

"You're very polite." Scotty pulls a pan off the hanging rack above the stove. "Nobody ever comes here, you know. I don't allow people here."

"You are very Not Polite." Abigail looks down. "Sorry. I'm really, really tired. And upset and… I'm…."

"Shhhh. I have a bad hangover. If you start to cry, I'll punch you."

Abigail laughs. "I'm not that tired. Let's eat. Then talk. And thank you for letting This Person in your home. Which is gorgeous by the way. I know your privacy must mean a lot to you, but you invited me. Just remember that!"

"I don't remember."

"Obviously. But I'm here. So let's eat." Scotty doesn't move.

"Go sit. I'll do it. You look like crap." Abigail takes her denim jacket off and washes her hands.

Scotty shrugs. "I feel like crap."

Abigail moves Scotty out of the way by her shoulders, steering her to the stool. She sets about the kitchen as if it were her own. "I'm Italian. I cook. Now put on your mittens and go sit."

***

Scotty's glazed eyes glance over at Motley in his hopeful sit/stay below the kitchen counter. His front legs tremble with anticipation for dropped crumbs. His eyes are bullets, Scotty the target. She sits next to Abigail on the high stools.

"Try? While it's still hot?" Abigail waves a fork loaded with egg and tomato.

Scotty picks up her fork and pokes at the omelet. She nibbles it slowly. Swallows. "Not bad, Doc. I bet you do a good ravioli."

"I'm not gonna lie. I can cook. My mother was a pasta genius. At least she taught me that."

"Bad mother?" Scotty takes a bigger bite.

"Good enough. Except for the homophobic part. And obsessed with that guy with the white beard in heaven."

"That can make a long life." Scotty stabs more egg. "Do you guys talk?"

"She died last year. We didn't talk much before then. She never accepted my ex, Nicole."

"That sucks. What about Dad?"

Abigail takes a breath in and out. "He followed Mom's lead in most things. He has dementia now. My own brother didn't tell me."

"That sucks, too. Is that your niece's Dad?"

"Almasto. My twin." Abigail pushes her clean plate forward and sips her tea. "What about you?"

Scotty pulls the hood off her head. Puts her fork down. She leans back in pointed assessment at Abigail.

"What?" Abigail says, clearly confused.

"Are you recording this?"

"Are you nuts? Why would I do that?"

"I have a history of making stupid mistakes telling people shit that shows up on Twitter a minute after they leave my sight."

"You've got to be kidding. I'd never do that!" Abigail reaches over and wraps her hand around Scotty's arm.

A current of energy clicks in Scotty's skin through the thick cotton sleeve. Abigail appears to notice the buzzing sensation and drops her gaze. She draws her hand away slowly.

"Scotty. You don't have to say anything more."

Scotty shakes her head. Her mouth is dry. Her stomach clenches. She crosses her arms. "My son's an addict. He hates me. My ex-husband's an addict. He hates me. My daughter's not an addict. But she won't talk to me. My dog loves me." She throws Motley the last little bit of her omelet. She shrugs at Abigail. "He likes Italian food."

"I'm sorry to hear that." Abigail breathes and sips her tea. "About the humans, anyway." She gives Scotty such a beaming smile, Scotty's surprised she suddenly wants to say more. The words pour out.

"Mom died when I was seven. Car accident. Dad died ten years later.

Lung cancer. I grew up on a farm in Wisconsin. It was just me and Dad after Mom died. They were both in Poland during World War II. Came to America as teens but met when they were in their 20s. A lot of Polish German immigrants fled to America during the war from that area that's now Poland. My parents were lucky to get out. We're Jewish."

"So Scotty D. Jones is not your birth name?"

"No comment."

"Siblings?"

"Rilke the cow. Named after my maternal grandmother."

"Your music?"

"Started early. I could play the piano when I was three. So later, piano lessons. Then guitar lessons. Singing lessons. But I was an oddball kid. Rilke was my best friend. I hung out more with trees and farm animals than humans. School was suicide. I'm a lefty." She waves her hand at Abigail. "Back then that wasn't okay. I flunked every class. Music saved me. Especially when I discovered Sister Rosetta Tharpe. Back then, music was a man's world. Still is pretty much, even though it seems like it's starting to change."

"Same as medicine," Abigail adds.

"Yeah. Right. Don't know if there's anyone like Sister Rosetta in medicine, but that woman was a fucking force of nature. She paved the way. A woman shredding like that? That woman could rock. And a black woman? In those days? She was unstoppable."

"We still need more women role models." That seems to remind Abigail of something. She slides off the stool and goes to her back pack. She pulls out the sketch pad Scotty saw at the café and slides it across the counter.

"Let's get to this now, Scotty."

Scotty braces for the viewing of what she knows will be the drawing. But when Abigail flips the cover, it's a different sketch. There's a long hallway like a tunnel sketched in gold and pinkish white tones. The woman is drawn in full body in a blue robe with the long black hair. The beginning of the tunnel is in the bright tones, the end of the tunnel is a black hole, disappearing into nothing.

"What's this?" Scotty's skin prickles at the sight.

"It came to me when I was just sitting in my office."

"That tunnel is intense."

"It felt like I was being pulled into it."

"That explains my body chills." Scotty rubs her arms.

"But my niece, Talia, acts like this is all normal. She likes all of this! She even builds ships in glass bottles for a hobby and made one with the figure of this woman standing on the deck of the ship."

"Ships in bottles?"

"Shoot! I'm supposed to keep it a secret."

Scotty zips her lips. "Are the bottles some weird-ass clue?"

"I wish I knew what they mean. Have you seen the face again since that time in the mirror?"

Scotty looks at the empty vodka bottle, still on the counter. "I see her every time I close my damn eyes."

"That's why I keep sketching." Abigail brushes the drawing with her fingertips. "I feel like these are all clues." Her eyes search Scotty's. "We need Talia."

"Then get her here." Scotty steps into the study to grab her cigarettes on the piano. She lights up then flings open the velvet curtains to the deck. She turns away from the bright sun beaming in and rubs her temples. Her head is still pounding and the light makes it worse, but she wants to see the ocean now. Abigail has followed her but stops in the doorway, sketchpad under her arm.

"So you're gonna just stand in the doorway?"

"Maybe." Abigail crosses her foot over her ankle and leans on the door jam.

"You must have picked up that I don't let anyone in here. Usually. Except my kids. And Motley," who jumps on the couch as if on cue.

Scotty drags on her cigarette, then paces the carpet. She stops in the middle of the room in an abrupt halt.

"Holy shit. I need to show you something." She twirls around to stub out her cigarette and crawls on the carpet behind the piano. She comes to a shelf of books and pulls them off to get to the safe. She ticks Izzy's birthday to open it: 12-17-92. When the safe opens, she digs under birth certificates, divorce settlement papers, a manila envelope with $50,000 in cash and her will. Her hands encircle a large wooden box.

I haven't looked in here so long I forgot it was here. Her heart is thudding in her ears. She crawls back with the box under her arm. She sits on the couch holding it in her lap.

"You better come in and sit down, Doc."

Abigail moves in slow motion to the couch. "Our blind friend has something to do with that box?"

"You'll see. My father gave this to me a few months before he died."

Scotty opens the lid and pulls out a pair of red child mittens. She smooths out the wool, then lays them next to her knee on the couch. Next are two pieces of white paper, stapled and folded. Before she opens them up, she pulls a cassette player out of the box and puts it on the glass coffee table.

"You sure you want me here for this?" Abigail leans forward. "This stuff looks very personal."

"You need to be here."

Scotty unfolds the two pages of white paper. The crayon-colored figure on the first page is shaped as any seven-year-old kid would draw. She touches the long black ponytail she drew on the top of her mother's round head. It bounces in a scooping curve, like a cartoon. She remembers drawing the oversized eyes into the big round circles in bright green crayon. Filling them in the same color as her own.

A yellow sun is drawn in the corner, with sparks of light in uneven shards poking around its circular shape. Seeing her rendition of her mother's stick arms and legs reminds her of how young Scotty really was when she drew this picture. She remembers how hard it was to draw hands and how she gave up and made five little sticks poking out. She sees the pink snow boots she drew, easier than toes for sure. Scotty's fingers brush the perfect triangle for the red dress she drew for her mother's body. She punches her eyes, then rubs the dampness on her knee in a harsh wipe.

She catches a sideways glance at Abigail, who is intent on the drawing, no expression on her face. A doctor's face, Scotty thinks. Yet she can feel a tidal wave of sympathy underneath. Abigail's face flickers, showing it a little. *Go on,* she seems to say to Scotty, without words. Scotty sees the little hand that she drew holding Mom's stick fingers. She brushes the joined hands as if she could feel her mother's fingers woven with hers now. Her young self wears an identical red triangle dress and pink snow boots. The difference is that she's half her mother's size. And her black hair is in two stumpy braids that stick out in odd angles, much less elegant than her mother's long sweeping pony tail.

She knows Abigail has seen the words on the bottom of the page.

The lettering is precise. "Welcome Home Mommy."

Scotty lets the paper crease to a half open pause. "She never came home."

"What happened?"

Scotty begins to explain but her throat wells up. She shakes her head like Motley after a bath. "Listen to this and maybe you'll get it."

Scotty pulls the cassette recorder closer and hits play.

Scotty's mother's voice crackles. The German twist accents over broken English.

"You do a concert for me pretty girl? *Bitte?* Is concert when you play!"

A sound of feet on the floor. A slam in the background. "Jonah! We have concert. You come now?"

Scotty's father's muffled voice rises in the same lilting English. "Not now, Darla! I shovel sidewalk. Where's my Shapka? There's foot of snow last night."

Footsteps. Slam.

"Mommy. My hands are cold. I can't play with cold hands."

A chair pulling out on a wood floor. "Let's warm those pretty fingers. Here! Your red mittens… put them…"

The tape clicks off. Then starts again. A muffled sound as if the recorder is being moved.

"Your hands warm now?"

"Yes, Mommy. I wanna play *My Girl.*"

More footsteps. "The Temptations! I love that one. I will be audience!"

The piano intro starts. Then stops. "Mama, you sing the My Girl part!"

The piano intro starts again.

Scotty's voice is smooth butter.

I've got sun-shi-ee-ine on a cloudy day….

She sings through the first verse until the piano stops suddenly. "Mommy now!" The piano starts again. They sing together.

"My girl, my girl, my girl
Talkin' 'bout my girl.

More laughter. Muffled movement. "We stop now. To go to market. What you want for dinner, my girl?"

"Banana splits!" Scotty's laugh.

"Silly, silly. That's dessert. You come with me to market?"

"I wanna stay here with poppa and play my piano and draw. Will you sing with me when you come home, Mama?"

"What do you say?"

"Please."

"Of course Schatzi, you play and I…" then the sound of muffled movement and a click as the recorder is turned off.

Scotty is relieved when Abigail speaks first. "I'm so sorry, Scotty. Was that the last time you saw her?"

"Yes."

"You made the drawing for her when she was at the market?"

"Yes."

"And she never came home?" Abigail asks softly. "She died that same day?"

"Same day."

Scotty watches Abigail's doctor-face melt. She's sure she sees pity in Abigail's brown eyes.

Scotty flings her body off the couch to grab her cigarettes on the piano. "Like any of this fucking matters." She spits the words, digging into the pack and pulls one out.

"Scotty! I didn't ask you to show this to me!"

"I know." Scotty's teeth are set on the cigarette. Which won't light.

"I'm so sorry that you went through all that."

"It was a long time ago." She clicks and re-clicks the lighter harder.

"What does all this have to do with the face we saw?"

Scotty cups her hand around the lighter, finally flickering a flame. She takes two full drags before she answers. "Turn to the next fucking page."

Abigail does. "Oh my God. When did you draw this?"

"The day after Mom died."

"But why?"

"Because it came in a dream the same night she died. I thought it was mom. I thought if I drew what I saw in the dream, my mother would come back."

Scotty stubs out the cigarette and sits, her knee jigging. "So now you know. It wasn't mom."

The black crayon portrait is of a woman with jet black hair, long and spilling over her shoulders. She wears a sleeveless blue dress. Her eyes are shaped to stare forward. The sky-blue crayon has filled in around pupils black as night. The woman has stick figure arms raised to the skies with palms upwards as if holding up the stars. She is floating askew in the middle of the page, unattached and falling.

Scotty's knee stops jigging. "It's time to call your niece, Doc."

THEN

The moon has gone from full to quarter since Sondro and I took the poison tea. Now I sit with my head resting back on the rim of the straight-backed chair in my room, as Lael prepares my bath. We ready me to lead the council meeting, yet my mind is on other matters, my heart heavy.

The Medicine of the Stinging Night continued to soar with the light behind my eyes for many sunrises and sunsets. In that time, all that I looked toward came to me with the same crystal glimmer that I saw on the boat with Sondro. Sometimes the light shaped faces and objects. Sometimes it was pure movement of bright lines, cones of energy and flowing specks. My steps needed no help. My images no probing measure from another's mind. My elation grew with each passing moment. Then it was no more.

After the sun rose and set again and again, the light dissolved, leaving me in darkness once more. It has not returned. I mourn the loss as I would the death of a loved one. I am no longer able to claim eyes that see the un-seeable. I sit now behind a curtain of black, with no desire to share images with others. For if I do, they will see what great sorrow rests in my heart.

With that worry comes the sense of another reason to lament, for when the Golden Hair Woman was drawn backwards through the tunnel of light, it seemed she was pulled by some force greater than her desire to stay with us. The image of her grieving face stays with me after she vanished through the tunnel of that brilliant light. I recall now how she laid her offering before us, I remember how it seemed she yearned for what we have, for what we know. Perhaps for what a Priestess and Priest can be. The ache of her words persists even now.

I am between two worlds.

My vow to help bring her to become stronger for our world was not just for her ears, but for mine as well to unlock my Prophecy. My covenant to Initiate her to become a Priestess seems a grave key.

Lael's light touch on my shoulder motions me to stand and I remove my robe to hand to her. The scent of the anointing mimosa and pine oils is easy to notice in the jar on the table next to us. She leads me to the heated water in the bronze bowl by the fire, her hand firm in mine. She steadies me as I step onto its slick base. My shoulders sink into the welcoming warmth.

"Are you unwell, Priestess? We have not met within our minds for some time now." Lael begins the thick tangerine-salt and honey soap's journey over my skin.

"I am once again dependent on images sent to me from others. The light needed no such thing." My fingers play at the water, reminding me of a child. "The Golden Hair Woman may never return, either."

"There is still time for both to return." Lael balances me to rise me to my feet, my legs still deep in the water. She once again takes my hand firmly so I may climb out without slipping. I rock off balance as she rubs me dry with the clean linens in chaffing haste. I hear her sleeves rustle as she raises the jar of anointing oil above her head to ask for Blessings.

Great Mother, Bless this High Priestess to be embodied by your wisdom to lead the council.

She brings the dabs of pungent oil to my feet, knees, vulva, womb, chest, palms and forehead. I inhale the familiar scent, knowing this means we are close to my leading council with my High Priest by my side for the invocation.

Lael holds up my robe for me, helping me to secure the tie. She takes my cheeks between her hands. "I believe you will again see with the light-filled eyes, sister. As I too believe you will see the Golden Hair Woman again. And her sisters."

"Are you now the Prophetess?" I tease.

She makes a grunting sound.

"Was Taniyeh angry when you told her of Sondro and I and our tea trance?" I ask.

"I only told Na'akt. Taniyeh may still not know," Lael confesses. "Do not fret about this now. We will come to a way to talk of this with the Prophetess after council. I hear the drummers preparing for ceremony. Turn to me?" Lael lifts the headdress above my head.

"Is this the lapis?" I spread my fingers on it to know it by touch.

"You must let me into your mind, if you are to know." Now Lael teases.

"Very well," I laugh. I let her probe enter. Lael shares the image to my mind of the horns of onyx holding the full moon's orb of bursting lapis lazuli, the sharp blue hue a radiant spread of texture. My heart soars to feel her within my mind once more.

"I have been foolish to keep you out." I bring my cheek to hers in remorse, then take hold of the headdress.

"I will place it. You pull it too hard!" She taps my fingers away, laughing. She guides the headdress more gently onto my head, its weight causing me to wince.

"The heaviest of my headdresses," I complain.

"It fits your task well, sister." I hear Lael's robe swishing on the stone floor as she moves to gather the jar and linens.

The headdress makes my neck strain. I let the gold inlay flaps cover my ears. The discomfort is great.

"You speak the truth, sister. This task is of great import."

There are thirteen temple leaders who have traveled to hear the Prophetess' oracle vision of what is to come, of my trance and of the movement of my Prophecy. The plans to prepare for the coming times are to be decided. The leaders have traveled long and far to join us. By cart, steady walk for many sunsets and ships upon the sea from temples known to us through trade. In copper, leathers, glass and fire baked clay, sacred stones like the lapis upon my head and the sacred tablets that have been inscribed for this Telling.

I hold the headdress steady as I try to stand without it toppling sideways. I hear a shuffle at my door, realizing Lael has gone to open it for Sondro. I strain to hear what they whisper together, but cannot make it out. Sondro comes to me and lays his hand on my shoulder, his own headdress of the sun in topaz stone preventing him from leaning down for the more formal offering of his forehead to my palms.

"Shall I walk you to the ceremonial room, Priestess?" His voice fills me. I offer my neck to him, holding the side of the headdress away.

"First find your lips here, for I have missed them!"

"Ah!" He holds his own headdress so not to tip it, his mouth a soft reminder on my neck. The hair upon his chin tickles my collar bone, sending quivers to my spine.

"Must I stop?" He does not, making me laugh.

"I wish not!" I take his hand. "Promise me you will continue later." His laugh joins mine.

Lael stands patiently holding the dried olive branch that will burn to purify and bless the meeting upon my arrival. I take her hand in mine, still clasping Sondro's in the other.

"After council is over, let us all walk along the shore and breathe the sea air as we used to when we were young. When trouble did not grip us so."

"To pick chamomile from the meadow," Lael's sweet voice comes easy.

"Play chase in the grass," Sondro's voice adds.

I embrace each. "I will be along. Will you both leave me here to pray?"

When I am sure they are beyond my door, I remove the weighted headdress and lay it on the table.

I rub my sore neck and stand for a moment and listen to the Priests chanting in the council room, down the long hallway outside my room. This means they have already built the Sacred Fire and begun the ceremonial preparations. I feel the Priests' singular tone resound in my body as the homage to the Great Goddess reminding me of my vows.

Vows that I must uphold whether I see with eyes of light or not. Whether I am sure of my Prophecy or not. Whether I know that I will again be with the Golden Hair Woman and her future sisters or not.

I move to my chamber's fire pit and kneel before its stone circle. I lay my hands over the rocks, feeling the vibrations. Stones have always given me their song. Their humming fills my body, joining the Priests' sounding. I lift my palms over the fire. There is no flame, yet the coals are still warm.

I feel to my side on the ground, glad to find the oak branch there. The one we use to read the coals. The shells captured in leathers on the end make a rattling sound as I take the pointing end to stroke the coals, separating them. Although I cannot see without the help of others, and my trance sight is gone, I can still pray to the coals. I drop the branch and cup my palms onto the rocks warm surface, my head bowed low.

Empty me of all but my vows to the Great Design. I pray to the coals.
Great Mother, may my life be bound to your Wisdom and Truth.
Guide me to carry the burden for my people.
Give me a sign from the Golden Hair Woman. The Fire Eye Woman. She of the Wise Hands.

The stones suddenly scream under my palms, all hair on my body stands on end. "No!" I shout to the stones and turn to run. "No!"

The movement under my feet is a terrifying shake. I lose balance but find the door and thrust it open. The ground is tipping and rocking. I lean my palms on the walls, willing the stones to hear my plea. *Do not fall!*

The three women of the future are quick to my side. I do not have time to think how they come to be here. They surround my body, coursing it forward as fast as a shooting star. With them, my feet know where to run. My sight comes sudden, with blazing light of the eyes that see the unseen. I have no time to feel elation at the light's return. I recognize the doorway to the council room, which I see as steady crossing lines of energy and light. I run to it. The women shout to me as they pull me to a stop under the door's heavy wooden frame. They push me to the ground. I feel the Fire Eye Woman throw herself over me, protecting me. She of the Wise Hands covers my legs with her body, heavy on my bones. I lift my chin only to look up and see the eyes of the Golden Hair Woman, who lies down facing me so close I feel her breath on me.

She holds her hands to my cheeks, forcing her steady eyes into mine.

"I will not leave you again!" She shouts. "We give you our sight!"

I hear the rocks crumble all around from the floor, the walls, from the ceiling, from all sides above, around and below in a raging fit, breaking into pieces with a deafening and pounding crash. The cracking of the shards of stones spill and spew in endless splitting. They shatter in a thundering cascade on all who are gathered in the council room. The ground is a sea of scattered, broken stone. The world goes black.

NOW

Abigail sets the brightly colored, reusable Trader Joe's grocery tote bags on her dining room table, ready to bring them when they go to Scotty's tomorrow morning. She picked Talia up at the airport late this afternoon, and so she only has to do a few more things to get ready. Homemade ravioli is easy enough to make, but she assumes Scotty doesn't have a pasta maker. She wraps hers in a hand towel and tucks it into one of the bags. She moves around her kitchen reaching into drawers and cabinets for the other items she'll need. Rolling pin, a cutting board, a tin of flour, her cheese grater and garlic press. She grabs garlic, French bread and a tube of tomato paste that she bought from her favorite gourmet Italian market. All she really needs from Scotty is a pot to boil water, although she considered taking her favorite sage-colored Gibson, then realized that just seems over the top. Of course Scotty will have a pot. *Right?* She hopes she's right. She checks the fridge for the perishables she'll take, mentally going over her check-list one last time.

Ricotta. Fresh parmesan, cream, heirloom tomatoes and homemade chicken stock for the homemade sauce. She'll even bring her own butter. *Will Scotty have spices?* Probably not. She grabs some fresh oregano, basil and thyme from her garden that she has in the crisper and lines them up on the fridge shelf in obvious sight so she won't forget.

She brushes her hands together, satisfied.

"Rufus, you'll stay home tomorrow. I don't think Motley will want you there."

She turns off the kitchen light and heads down the hall. She stops at the guest bedroom door on the way and leans her ear against it. She hears Talia watching a video on her phone. Some kind of sit-com, since she hears tin laughter. She pads down the hall past the photos on the wall of

Nicole and Rufus at Yosemite two summers ago, after a hike to the Vernal Falls. Both are soaking wet from the section of the Mist Trail where the water pours onto the hikers like a wide rimmed shower on the walking path. She makes herself move on. She knows she should take the photo down. It's been almost a year since they broke up.

She flicks the hallway light off, making sure the night light works for Talia to find the bathroom if she needs it in the middle of the night.

Once in bed, she turns the bedside light off and pats Nicole's side for Rufus. "C'mere Bud. I need a doggie snuggle."

He hops up and curls with his spine to her belly. She wraps herself around him cupping her fingers around his popcorn-scented paws. The last thing she remembers is wondering if she should bring flowers to Scotty's when her eyes become too heavy to hold open.

She doesn't know how long she's been in deep slumber. It feels like she hasn't even been asleep.

The dream comes like a movie that she's watching but she knows she's also in it, seeming to be both awake and asleep.

She's standing inside that tunnel she sketched. Only this time, it's a hallway with high ceilings and long arched windows and a fire pit with a blaze of orange at the far end. There's a terrible thundering sound. She knows within the dream that it's an earthquake. She's been in some small ones. This one is massive. She feels no terror, but rather responds with the objective neutrality that happens when she's in surgery, where she can act and not react. She isn't even surprised to see Scotty and Talia there.

They flow forward together like a pod of dolphins. They carry something? No—they are pushing it along…but like a conveyor belt. It's the woman from her vision. *Their* vision. They move the woman along, as if under water, yet they make her run forward, racing fast to get to the end of the hallway. They all seem to know they have to get her to the safety of the doorway. They seem to be showing her through their sight where to go.

When they reach the doorway, with one telepathic thought, she and Scotty throw their bodies over the blind woman's small frame. Abigail feels the woman slip to the ground, face down. Abigail's aware of her weight across the woman's legs and lower limbs. She feels the bony protrusions of ankle joints. Knee joints. The woman's body is fragile. Yet her power is a live wire under Abigail.

Scotty acts as quickly, lying sideways across the small woman's back and arms, joining Abigail in shielding, protecting without hesitation.

Abigail knows the rocks will not fall on them. It doesn't occur to her that she or Scotty are in any danger from the avalanche of stones.

Talia lies on her stomach in front of the woman. They are a sight, the two of them face to face, like two animals finding each other in the chaos of danger. Talia's hands grip the woman's cheeks, forcing her to keep her head from turning sideways, her blue-black eyes hollow and full of fear.

Talia shouts at the blind woman.

Abigail wakes up with a start. She's slathered in sweat, her heart racing. None of this makes any sense! She sits up and throws her legs over the bed, not sure where she's going to go or what she's supposed to do now. She jumps off the bed and begins to pace in a frustrated circle. She can't help but wish she could have stayed in the dream longer to figure out what this was all supposed to mean.

What she hears next from the guest room makes her bones set to a cold and deadly grip. Her feet stop her dead center in her bedroom, her skin on fire with fear. Talia yells something in her sleep. It takes only a split second for Abigail to realize she's hearing the same words she heard just moments ago.

"I will not leave you again! We give you our sight!"

***

Scotty leans back in her patio chair watching a hiss of cigarette smoke poof upwards. A boat horn sounds in the distance. The morning looks good on the blue of the ocean below. Motley's tucked into her lap, his cold nose on her wrist. As she pets him, her mind is not on the little wiry hairs around his neck but on the weird-ass dream she had last night.

It seems true that Doc's niece Talia has a handle on understanding this blind woman. Even though Scotty still hasn't even met this Talia kid, it was clearly her in the dream, holding the blind woman's face. Like they were long lost friends. Then she said, "I won't leave you again."

Why say that?

Of course there was an earthquake.

Then that fucking thing with her own eyes.

When she was lying across that woman's back, Scotty's own eyes went blind. Then—like a bomb—a display of light exploded in her head. She saw energy. Light. Like the whole fucking world blew up with burning, brilliant light.

90

Not like a cartoon, but real-ass light. So thick and alive, she could have touched it and it would have had texture. Density. Movement even.

She needs tequila.

She gets up, spilling Motley off her lap. He scrambles on the patio tiles, but then the doorbell rings and he takes off barking.

Scotty stubs out her cigarette in the ashtray on the piano and follows Motley to the front foyer. She flings open the door.

"You're early." Scotty grabs Motley up.

Abigail gives Scotty a Trader Joe's bag. "Here. I need more hands." She leans down and grabs two more bags.

"You staying for a week?" Scotty peers into one of the bags past a bouquet of flowers. "You brought your own pot? Man, you're a serious cooking machine."

Her arms full, Abigail tips her chin sideways. "Scotty, meet Talia. Talia, meet Scotty."

Scotty looks into the same brown eyes. Same short golden blonde hair she saw in the weird-ass dream.

"Scotty?" Abigail looks worried. "What's wrong?"

"Nothing's wrong." Scotty gazes at Talia. "Feels like we met already."

Talia looks like she's going to say something, then follows Abigail into the front hall.

"So you make ships in bottles, I hear." Scotty winks at her, lowering Motley to the ground.

Abigail's shoulders slump. "Sorry Talia! It just slipped out. I didn't mean to tell her."

"I think we might be past that now, Aunt Abby. Given our circumstance." Talia takes a seat on one of Scotty's kitchen stools.

"You have a point, kid." Scotty says.

As Abigail starts to unpack, she waves a tin of flour and a stick of butter at them. "It turns out that Talia and I had the same dream last night." She twirls around to organize the groceries on the counter, making little piles in a neat line. Her voice drones in the background as Scotty only half listens. "… and then I heard a sound and…"

"Hold on." Scotty stops her. "You dreamt the same fucking thing?"

Abigail finally stops fidgeting. "Why?"

Scotty feels Talia's eyes on her. Little poking pebbles. "You know what I'm going to say, don't you, kid?"

Talia doesn't answer.

"Oh no." Abigail seems like a deflated balloon. She puts one butt cheek on the tall kitchen stool, arms limp.

Scotty looks at both of them. "I saw Talia in my dream last night. She saw me, too. And you know you were there, too, Doc."

"What is this? The Wizard of Oz?" Abigail puts her face in her hands. "How can this be?"

Talia's voice is even. "It just is. That's how. What did you dream, Scotty?"

"Hold on. I need food. Let's do this after I cook." Abigail gives them a pleading look. "I'll make us some tea first."

"How about some tequila to go with it?"

Abigail takes Scotty's wrist pointing to an imaginary watch. "It's what? 11:00 a.m.? But it's your house, so you get to drink whenever you want."

"Thank you, Judge Judy. I'll be right back." Scotty heads to the upstairs bathroom. "You can start cooking, Doc. I think this is going to be a long yackity-yack."

***

Scotty can't remember the last time she sat around her dining room table. The ravioli's steaming in an orange ceramic bowl Scotty doesn't even know she had. She drains her second shot of tequila as Talia passes the loaded plates onto three linen place mats. Abigail must have dug them out of one of the kitchen cabinets. The flowers Scotty saw in the Trader Joe's bag are in a vase she thinks Ryan gave her a million years ago. The flowers look perky in the center of the table.

Abigail's eyebrows are a jagged pinch. "I promise to talk after we eat."

"She has low blood sugar," Talia explains.

Scotty rolls her eyes, but she already has her fork raised. She didn't realize how hungry she is, too. The ravioli is melt-in-your-mouth soft. The sauce a perfect blend of savory and spice. There's even garlic bread, which Abigail passes to her with a block fresh grated parmesan and a snappy looking cheese grater with a red handle.

"You weren't lying, Doc. You can cook." She chases a little square of ravioli around the plate then slides it into her mouth, licking her fingers.

When she's finished her second helping, Scotty pushes her chair back, tipping onto the back two legs.

"Now's the time, Doc."

Abigail takes her plate into the kitchen and sits back down. "Okay. I'm better now. You start, Scotty."

Scotty's chair legs thump back down to the ground. "The dream went fast, but it was real. I knew I was dreaming but I felt like I was awake. We were all behind the blind chick, pushing her along, like we were all on a treadmill. She needed us to see for her. Everything was stone. The hallway. The building." She pauses. "Does this sound familiar?" Her skin spreads in goosebumps.

Abigail's holding her shoulders. "Go on."

"Then an earthquake happened, and we threw our bodies over her. You and I, Doc. So the stones wouldn't fall on her. Like Florence fucking Nightingale. Then you," Scotty points at Talia, "laid down in front of her and grabbed her face. I swore it was so you could keep her from turning to see the rocks falling on the people nearby, in some kind of room with a fire going in a stone fire pit of some kind. Not that she *could* see, with those eyes."

"But she could," Talia interrupts. "Through our eyes."

Scotty pauses, the blinding light a palpable memory. "Yeah. I guess you're right." She looks carefully at Talia. "You yelled at her. *I will not leave you again. We give you our sight.*"

Talia inclines her head. "I did. Yes."

"So that's supposed to mean we see for her?" Scotty sounds more like she's in a courtroom than her own house. "Sorry."

"I know it's a lot." Talia folds her hands.

"And the part about never leaving her again? Why say that?" Scotty asks, aiming for less of an accusing tone.

Talia goes quiet, looking like she's deciding something. "I don't want to leave her again. It's just a strong feeling I've had since the last dream."

Abigail seems to pale. "This is nuts."

Scotty watches a ripple pass through the two of them. "I need more liquor. I'm keeping it in the bathroom." She shrugs at their confused looks, then trots upstairs.

When Scotty comes back with a bottle of red wine under her arm, the table is cleared and the teapot's whistling. She flicks it off with a twist. As the whistle whines down she grabs three wine glasses from a cabinet.

"Fuck the tea. We need this." She presents the bottle formally. "It's an Italian Sangiovese. Good for wacko occasions like this one."

She rustles through a drawer in the kitchen for a corkscrew, wedges the bottle between her thighs and pops the cork off. She chugs her first glass, refills, then sits back down. "Talia?"

Talia holds up her glass as Scotty pours.

"Doc? Better than tea." She wiggles the bottle at her.

Abigail holds up her glass, keeping it there until Scotty fills hers, then says. "*Del basso verso l'alto!*"

"Nana used to say that. Bottoms up." Talia drinks.

"Yes. Bottoms fucking up." Scotty drinks and pours another.

"So, Talia." Scotty rolls the wine glass stem in her fingers, watching the red liquid swirl. She points her eyes sternly at the young woman. "You need to tell us about the last dream."

"It's a long story."

"We have time."

"It's not the first time I dreamt of them."

"Them?"

"I already told Aunt Abby. I dream of two people. Not just the woman. But also a man."

"And?"

"And it's like I know them."

Scotty stands up suddenly. "Talia, you were younger when you made those ship bottles, right?"

"Right."

"And you made one with the woman from our dream inside one of the bottles?"

Talia nods, looking at her Aunt, who has no expression.

Scotty moves with swift motion into her study. When she hurries back to the dining table, they drag their chairs together and sit at the end of the table.

Scotty unfolds the two white pieces of paper stapled together and flips to the second page, pushing it across the table to Talia.

"That's her." Talia looks at Scotty. "You drew this?"

"I was seven years old."

"The day her mother died." Abigail adds.

"You knew about this?" Talia's tone is accusing.

"I had no reason to tell you."

"No more holding back shit." Scotty says.

"I agree." Abigail smooths the papers out carefully.

Scotty feels a creeping sensation in the back of her neck.

"You're holding something back right now," she says to Talia.

"It has to stay between us," Talia whispers.

"Who the fuck would we tell?" Scotty snorts.

"I don't know—you're famous. You might have an interview with Fox News and slip."

Scotty's laugh sets them all going.

"First of all," Scotty grins, pointing a wagging finger at Talia, "I draw the line with Fox News. And second—what do I get from that? Just casually say 'Oh yeah, my two friends and I had a dream about a blind woman that we saved from an imaginary earthquake! And this chick is from another time and she's fucking haunting us.' That would go over great for my career."

"It's true, you know." Talia's stopped laughing. "You're not making that up, Scotty. She *is* from another time." She looks about to cry. "We're supposed to help her. Why else would we all be having this dream?"

"But what is it that we're supposed to do?" Abigail asks.

Talia's eyes are intense arrows into Scotty. "I've been keeping this secret for so long."

Scotty surprises herself when she reaches for Talia's hand. "It's okay, Nugget. We all have your secret now."

A ticking energy surges through the three of them.

"It's like she's part of me." Talia's face flushes. "She's been in my life through dreams so long, I feel almost like I'll die if I don't see her and the man again. My Mom put me in therapy when I was younger. She thought having these dreams meant I was sick or something. Like it was wrong. To believe them so much."

She looks up at them, tears welling up. "I wish I could say I feel like I belong here. But I feel like I belong with them."

Talia squeezes her eyes shut and says it fast. "And now you guys are in this world with me and I don't know how to deal with it." She jumps up from her chair and starts to head out of the room.

Scotty's body freezes. She makes herself stand up. "Sit down, Nugget. We're not going to send you to the funny farm. We have your back. Right, Doc?"

Abigail's hands are folded on the table. She gets up slowly and walks to her niece.

"That's right. We do. Come sit." She leads Talia back to the table, her arms in a bear hug around her. Talia's tears brim over and let go in a flood. Like she's held them back for two hundred centuries or more. She turns into her Aunt's arms.

Hearing Talia's muffled sobs, Scotty goes rigid. But the last thing she expects to hear is Talia's confession.

"They wanted to make me a Priestess." She steps back from Abigail, rubbing her eyes. "I didn't let them."

Scotty slowly moves to the study, knowing they will follow. She points to the couch. Motley climbs into Talia's lap. Abigail sits down next to them.

Scotty picks up her acoustic guitar off the stand. She sits on the piano bench facing them. She puts her hands on the strings. She starts to strum.

It's a melancholy melody, eerie and slow. Her voice blends with the ache in the chords. Scotty's mind quiets as the notes seem to find themselves.

"I was pretty sure this song was about a Queen." She looks at Talia. "But now I know, it's about her. And she's sending it to me. To us. It's not just a Queen. It's a Priestess."

Her fingers are part of the strings, the wood of the guitar, her body. The shape of the notes fills the room. Reaching. Stretching. Landing.

Scotty feels the low tone echo deep in the cavernous cervical hollow of the guitar.

"And we are her instruments." She looks over at the couch.

Abigail's holding Talia's hand. They breathe in and out. In and Out.

***

That night, in Aunt Abby's guest room, Talia sleeps in a half-awake state. She hovers in the tunnel mid-air, floating but not moving forward or backward. She twists around, seeing only particles of light dotted within a hazy mist. Even now, in this odd place, her surroundings bring her a calm the way she knows home is supposed to. She looks around, hoping to see the Priestess. Instead, the man appears in front of her, alone. This time, his dark hair is under a headdress with a yellow-greenish stone, shining like the radiant sun. His brown eyes penetrate into her. He lays a small odd-shaped offering at her feet. The round headed stone statue has a block body with no arms or legs and hollow eyes.

For the first time, the man's speech is audible and not within Talia's mind. His tone is the embers of a low lullaby, vibrating through her bones.

Cross the seas to the High Priestess Anya of Mahet. Take this offering to her and bury it at the site of the dead near the Temple of the Arch. He bows to Talia, laying his forehead deep into her palms. *My child, I will not come to you again.*

THEN

Na'akt crouches under a corner of the fallen council table, her ears still ringing from the overwhelming sound of the rocks falling. Ba-leh's wolf nose is cold as he licks her face and whimpers, shaking. She takes his head to her forehead, cupping his face, feeling along his body for anything broken. Other than a bloody paw, there is no damage. The ground below them is still, yet she fears it will set to shaking again. Her arms ache from the tension it took to cover her head. She feels her skin stinging on the outer edge of one arm, her legs, her face. Her robe is torn across the middle and she has lost one of her goat skin slippers. She slowly inspects her body. The stinging is only from deep cuts, no broken bones. She breathes a prayer of thanks. Her teeth begin to chatter, so she knows she must be coming out of shock. Her ears, ringing less, hear moaning. Her mind snaps to clarity. She must find out if people are trapped. Every inch of her body aches, yet she makes herself crawl forward on her knees, which she now sees are cut and bloody. She feels nothing but the need to find Taniyeh. Before the ground shook and the rocks fell, they stood beside each other ready to sit at the council table as they waited for Anya's arrival. *Anya? Does she live?* Na'akt's thoughts whirl.

She sees Taniyeh's hand lying limp on the ground. She rushes to her, with Ba-leh close behind. She is relieved to find the Prophetess still breathing, if only a rasping rattle.

"Cousin! I am here." Na'akt feels along Taniyeh's wrist to find her arm is wedged under rock. "You are hurt!" She tries to remove the stone, but stops when she hears Taniyeh gasp.

"Come closer." Her cough is harsh, her face wincing at the pain.

Na'akt slows her breath, trying to become calm.

"I did not know this fall was to come...." Taniyeh's cough is weakened now. "...There was no vision."

Na'akt feels her heart grip at the burden her cousin feels. "You could not know."

Taniyeh's eyes become hardened. "You must see this as a good omen."

"How is this good?"

Taniyeh's voice is now so quiet Na'akt must lean in to hear her. "This crack from the earth opened the portal. Tell Anya she can now move between the worlds. Give me your word you will tell her." This time blood spills with her cough.

"I give you my word," Na'akt whispers. "Let me make you more comfortable." She gently removes Taniyeh's head wrap to lay it under her head and is startled to see Taniyeh's eyes soften then close. Even though she expected this, it still stuns. Na'akt watches her cousin let go as the death rattle sounds through her lungs. There is not enough time to mourn properly, so Na'akt pushes down her grief, laying her head on her cousin's heart, praying for strength to handle this. As she whispers the blessing death chant, she holds her hands over Taniyeh's head to release her spirit through the crown of her head. Na'akt knows she must move on to see if others live. As her ears orient to the room once more, and the moaning she heard before increases, Na'akt tears herself away.

"We will give you a proper burial, cousin." She kisses Taniyeh's forehead and makes herself move on, not bothering to dry her tears. "Ba-leh. Help me."

The wolf wiggles forward, squeezing his body around a rock and leads her to their left, turning to make sure she follows. Na'akt crawls on her hands and knees following Ba-leh to the sound of the moaning. It is coming from the doorway. She cannot see who it is over a pile of rocks blocking her view, so she shifts her body around the fire pit, where flames still rage contained within. Ba-leh has sped forward and turns to yip at Na'akt to come close. When she reaches the door frame, Na'akt sees Anya's body splayed downward under it, her face turned away. She lies in a clearing where no rocks fell, inside an unseen circle of protection. Na'akt rushes to Anya's side.

"Priestess, are you hurt? Turn your face to me."

When Anya does, Na'akt feels Anya's mind image as if lightning enters her mind. The explosion of brilliant shine comes with such force she almost falls backwards with the power of it. Three women's faces flood her mind that she sees as clearly as if they stand before her, in spite of the brightness of light. She cannot look away from the lure of it, knowing these faces are from the trance.

"They were here," Anya murmurs. "They saved me. Can you help me up? We must find Sondro and Lael."

Na'akt helps Anya to stand, her own skin in unbearable sting from the movement.

"You are hurt!" Anya does not conceal her angst.

"Just cut. Nothing broken. You must stay here. I will find the others."

Na'akt makes her way over the rocks and looks around in haste for the Madre. She stood nearby before the falling rocks. She hears a small scraping and peers under the table. Ba-leh has begun to dig at the wooden shards of the table and broken stones.

"Madre!"

"My arm. I cannot move."

Na'akt finds a sturdy splint of cherry wood from the council table leg, which she inserts next to the rock that is closest to the Madre. She pushes with all her might and dislodges it, then reaches under the table top to help the Madre crawl out, offering her own arm where the Madre's cannot take weight. "Breathe with me Mother, this may hurt."

She manages to slowly pull the Madre out, helping her rise. The Madre locks her arm across Na'akt's shoulder. She is tall with the strength of an ox, but Na'akt cannot carry the Madre's ample body. Na'akt unties her robe's silk rope and makes a loose sling for the Madre.

"This will do for now. Keep the limb close to your body," Na'akt instructs, guiding her away from the rubble.

"Stay here with Anya. I will search for Sondro and Lael. Ba-leh, guard her." The wolf drops to a sit, his golden narrow eyes on her.

Na'akt leaves them as Anya leans into Ba-leh, her body swaying in feverish prayer. Na'akt has no time to think of anything else but the bodies she finds. She has counted five Priests and six of the temple leaders so far that begin their journey among the dead. She hastily blesses each, then stops. She sees his topaz stone sun headdress lying on a rock before she sees him. Her heart sinks.

When she reaches Sondro's body, she finds Lael lying over him. Na'akt carefully touches Lael's back and is relieved to feel the breath under her hand. Lael turns to her, her face covered in blood.

"I could not save him." She falls back onto Sondro's chest.

Na'akt softly reaches to roll Lael toward her, soothing her. "Anya lives. Come sister."

Na'akt's tall frame lifts Lael in a cradle and carries her to the High Priestess.

Na'akt lowers Lael to Anya. All it seemed to take was Lael to embrace her Priestess sister for Anya to know, without words, what has come to pass for her beloved High Priest. Na'akt watches helplessly, as Anya slithers past Lael's embrace, sinking to the ground, her fists clenching her long hair, her keening wail so full of sorrow, the hollow sound cuts through Na'akt to the bone. Na'akt kneels and wraps her like a mother, reaching for Lael and pulling her into the fold, rocking them.

"I will bring his body to you," she whispers. But she cannot move and instead holds them tightly. For long minutes they rock, the grief too harsh to bear. Ba-leh curls under them, licking whomever he finds near, his low howl blending with their moans.

Na'akt turns slowly when she hears running footsteps along what is left of the hallway, whatever strength remains drains from her limbs. Priests, Priestesses, healers and survivors from the town spill into the ruins of the council room. Na'akt lets her body sink to a flat rock. Soon she is surrounded as hands find her and hold her head. She points weakly to those she has found in the rubble. Her mouth is dry yet she manages to tell them where the High Priest lies. Her tears flood as Ba-leh licks her face, her hands, and again her face, until he begins to shake enough for both of them. Na'akt lays her hand across his withers, a numbness overcoming her.

Young Eon has come with the others and rushes to Anya, falling into her arms. Anya's head dodges side to side, reminding Na'akt of a trapped wild creature.

"I did not tell him I carry his daughter." Anya's words shatter Na'akt, yet she is sure she feels Sondro move across them and cover Anya's body in the wash of brilliant light that again holds her captive and shaking.

NOW

Abigail glances at the clock on the wall next to her china cabinet. It's already 8:15 a.m. Scotty will be here in a couple of hours. She wonders if she should wake Talia, but her butt is glued to the chair in spite of the strong urge to get up and get moving. She curls her fingers around the empty tea mug in front of her.

Her eyes wander to the glass doors of the cabinet. Her mother Gina's dishes, cups, serving plates and tea set are neatly stored there. Abigail hardly ever uses any of them, not only because it's been ages since she had enough people over for dinner, but also because they are antiques from her grandmother's set from Sicily. She'd hate to break them. Mostly the top of the cabinet is a shelf for her vases and favorite tchotchkes. Her hands tingle suddenly on the tea mug, making her skin rush with goosebumps. She's not cold. *Maybe just wired?*

Rufus had done his business in the back yard soon after Abigail got up at 7:00, but she wants to move her body and take him for a walk to help these jitters she can't seem to shake. Her mind is a magnet and won't let go of the events of yesterday's conversation at brunch. She slept like the dead, but woke up with a twitchy brain. Still, she doesn't move from her chair.

Her phone chirps in her back pocket. A text from Scotty. *I'm almost there.*

She's too early. Abigail texts back *See you soon.*

"Hello sleepyhead," Talia shuffles into the dining room. "Coffee or tea?"

"Coffee, please." Talia adds cream from a pitcher on the table then sits to pat Rufus's back. "Going for a walk?"

"I was, but Scotty's on her way over." Abigail finally gets up. She feels like her head is on backwards. There's so much going on that she doesn't understand. Scotty and Talia seem to take all this unusual mystery in stride, like they're somehow prepared. She wonders if it's because they both had experiences with this… Priestess… when they were both younger and she hasn't. Or is it just because Abigail is more suspicious and they're more trusting? Maybe all of this is just about fear. *Which makes sense!* Whatever it is, she feels the least like herself than she has in a long time. Her musings are interrupted by Rufus's bark as he scoots to the front door, tail wagging. Abigail moves to the door to open it, but Scotty's already in the house and squatting to greet Rufus.

"Hi boy. You're a lot of doggie." Rufus licks Scotty's face with enthusiasm.

"Rufus, down." Abigail shoots her finger to the floor and Rufus lowers to lie down. "Good boy. I thought you were coming at ten o'clock, Scotty?"

"I assume you make better coffee than I do. So. I'm here."

Abigail feels heat in her cheeks. "You're in luck. Coffee's already brewed for Talia." She heads to the kitchen to pour Scotty a cup. "Does that mean you've already had breakfast?"

"Not yet. You make better breakfast too, I bet." Scotty warms her hands around the hot cup. She flops down next to Talia at the table. "Hey Nugget. Good sleep?"

"She slept for ten hours," Abigail says over her shoulder from the kitchen.

"You look like you need ten more," Scotty says.

Abigail brings out a plate of chocolate croissants, butter, three containers of yogurt and a bowl of fruit. She pours herself a second cup of green tea from the loose tea press, then brings silverware and the pot of coffee to the table. She looks sideways at her niece.

"Scotty's right." Abigail is suddenly concerned. Talia looks like she's about to cry. "What's wrong, honey?" She puts her hand over Talia's forehead. *No temp.* "Are you okay?"

"I have to tell you guys about what happened." She hops up, only to return seconds later. "This is my dream journal." Talia holds up a red leather notebook as if it explains everything.

"The dream I had last night was different."

Abigail feels chills and sits down slowly. Something is off.

"It was with the guy. The man. I dream of…" When Talia pauses Abigail's stomach grips. Her niece looks like she's gone somewhere else. Exited her body. Her eyes are glazed. She seems to shake it off then resumes talking.

"This time he was wearing a ritual headdress of some kind. It was with white and yellow stones… that glimmered. He…."

Abigail moves her chair closer.

"He spoke." Talia's voice seems to break. "In all the other dreams, I've always known what he says but I never actually hear him speak."

"Go on." Abigail sets her hands still in her lap. She's starting to buzz like she's had too much caffeine. Which doesn't happen with her green tea. Ever.

Talia continues. "I know this sounds really crazy, but I know he's gone. I think he spoke that way because he meant to give me a message. I remembered every word and wrote down what he said."

Talia smooths the journal pages softly. She looks up, seems to gather courage, then begins to read.

"*Cross the seas to the High Priestess Anya of Mahet. Take this offering to her and bury it at the site of the dead near the Temple of the Arch.*"

Talia's eyes stay glued to the page, her mouth still reading. But only to herself.

"Then he gave me a statue."

For long minutes, they all seem under a spell.

"Who the fuck is Anya of Mahet?" Scotty bursts out.

"I think that's the Priestess' name." Talia looks at the journal.

Energy clips through Abigail's body. She rushes to her bedroom and comes back with her laptop and sets it on the table.

"Let's see what Google says." But after several searches, there's nothing about Anya of Mahet.

"Is Mahet a place?" Abigail types it in. "No. It's a name. Could be a sur-name, too? Interesting. So this dream lady is 'of Mahet.' Does 'of' indicate a family name?"

"Maybe. But I remember a class on History of Women in college. I read about Matriarchal cultures that take the women's surname as the family name." Talia says. "And also, why is it even called a 'sir' name, anyway? That's so lame."

"Good point. All that male influenced jargon is in our subconscious, right? But, given we believe she's a Priestess, it *would* make more sense if it were her mother's name." As she says it, Abigail feels that crackle of energy again. This time with goosebumps.

"Talia, you said there was a statue? Like an offering? What did it look like?"

"Do you have a pen?" Talia asks.

Abigail grabs her sketch pad and charcoals from her bedroom. She joins Scotty in watching Talia draw a little statue with a knobby head, long nose, hollow eyes and no arms or legs.

"About how big was this?" Abigail asks.

"About the size of my palm." Talia holds her hand up. "It was limestone, I'm sure of it, from the color and texture." She shrugs at Scotty's look of confusion. "I studied temples in college for my architecture classes. This was limestone. Trust me."

Abigail Googles "Limestone statue. No arms." Scotty and Talia lean over her shoulder. "Do any of these look like it?" Abigail scrolls down dozens of photos of statues of various size and shape.

"No. None of them." Talia squints as Abigail scrolls more. "Try adding 'Long nose' in the search."

Abigail types it in. Nothing. She closes her laptop. The others sit back down at the table. Scotty's leg is jigging. The motion of it brings Abigail back to Scotty's living room when they looked at her child drawings. Instead of goosebumps, this memory sets an odd heaviness over Abigail. The energy rush is gone, replaced with a wash of sadness.

"Now you're about to bawl?" Scotty looks at her. "Does this habit run in the family?"

"Apparently." Abigail pats Scotty's knee.

"But why are you sad all of a sudden?"

Abigail puts her hand on her chest, trying to locate the reason. "I think it's because you and Talia both saw this Anya woman as kids. I'm sad that I don't have that connection with her." She leans back and gasps. "Wow! I haven't thought of this in years, but I just remembered something random."

"That's spooky timing," Scotty says. "What is it?"

"It was like the visions I've had, when I'm awake and seeing things. I remember I was walking to school alone. Almasto was sick with the flu or something. I was crossing the bridge that goes over the highway and I saw a dead cat next to the freeway, lying deep in the dirt below. It was partially decomposed. I remember I was riveted by the look of the remains of the body lying there so peacefully. Maybe something about the natural state of seeing something in a regulated cycle of life took hold of me. Whatever the reason, all of a sudden I had this vision. It came out of nowhere, it went really fast through me, then it was over. I forgot about it until now. How many decades later?"

Abigail tracks the memory silently then describes it. "In the vision, I was frantically searching for something I lost in church. My mother shoved me into the confessional. Instead of the Priest, there was a woman on the other side nursing a baby. She tried to touch me through the divider and then I felt her standing by my side. When I looked up at her, she had the black hair and blue-black eyes we've all seen. So it must have been this Anya of Mahet. She put her hand on my head and said something. What was it? It had the word Goddess in it... something like 'Divine Goddess. You will never forsake me.' Or something like that. Seems rather dramatic, which must be why I remember. And probably why I also forgot!" Abigail chuckles. "It was like she was ordaining me or giving me a secret task or something like that. It felt like a blessing the way the Catholic Priests offer communion, but this felt more like ... a part of me." The energy is surging through Abigail's body again. "I wonder now about the baby she was nursing. Because about a week later, I decided to become an obstetrician. Even though I was only about twelve years old at the time."

Scotty's knee has stopped jigging, her voice an altered lull. "That was not a coincidence."

"It was her, Aunt Abby." Talia reaches over to squeeze her aunt's arm.

"I have to agree. I think I even say a little blessing to her whenever I do surgery. I never made the connection."

Talia seems to track her Aunt's thoughts. "I'm getting we're all somehow connected to this woman. If we can figure out where the statue is from, we might be able to figure out what century Anya's from."

"And why the fuck this is even happening to the three of us," Scotty adds.

"Doesn't that temple from your dream have a name?" Abigail starts another search.

"Try typing in Temple of the Arch," Talia offers.

"Nothing."

"Try adding Greece? Or Egypt? Or try Malta."

"Why Malta?" Scotty asks.

"It's the location of the oldest temples in existence," Talia explains. "We might as well go through the temples chronologically. I know they were built with limestone. So maybe there's a connection."

Abigail types. "Statue. No arms. Limestone. Temple. M-a-l-t-a."

She pushes the computer back with a quick shove. "Bingo."

"No way!" Talia's up on her feet. "That's it. That's the statue."

The long-nosed, no-armed, no-legged, hollow-eyed, round headed little statue is the first photo to pop up.

"Holy shit." Scotty points to the screen. "They are a set of," she counts "Nine. From a *burial site* in Malta."

Abigail's trembling. "Is anyone getting goosebumps like I am?"

"Affirmative." Scotty says, hugging her arms. "So who wants to go to Malta with me?"

"Are you serious? That's nuts." Abigail closes her laptop.

Without warning, a vase tips off the top of the china cabinet and crashes to the dining room wood floor. They all turn in shock.

Scotty whistles.

"What made that fall?" Abigail gets up to pick up the pieces. "Shoot. Nicole gave me this vase." She starts piling the shards in her palm. Her hands freeze. She stares an upturned broken chunk of the pottery.

"What is it Aunt Abby?" Talia kneels beside her.

"What?" Scotty squats next to them.

"Look," Abigail whispers. She points to the words printed on the curve of the vase's broken bottom.

"Made in Malta."

Abigail feels like she just jumped off an airplane. The surging energy pumps like she's already falling through the air.

***

The next morning, Scotty sits on the edge of her bed with her mittens on. One hand is wrapped around her cell phone, the other on her jiggy knee. She pulls the mitten off one hand with her teeth and punches the phone keys. She clears her throat as she waits for Zeff's recorded greeting to end.

"It's Mom. I'll be gone a while. I promise I'll only contact you if I stop drinking this time." She pauses, trying on the words in her mouth before she utters them. "I love you, son." She stabs the end-call button.

She stares at the phone as if it could talk. She taps the screen for Val's cell number. "Hi."

"What's wrong? You never say 'hi.' Are you okay?" Val's voice is a high-pitched squeal.

"Calm down. I'm fine." Scotty puts Val on speaker and puts her phone on her lap. She puts her mitten back on. "I'm going away. I need you to cancel my next two tours."

Silence.

"Val? Cancel the next tours. Now through the end of spring."

Silence.

"Fucking answer me!" Scotty croaks.

"Sorry. You caught me off guard. You sound different."

"Well, I'm the same bitch I've always been." She pulls the mittens off. Puts them back on.

"Going away, huh?"

"Yes, nosey. Cancel the tours. Got it?" She takes the mittens off again. Throws them on the bed. Lights a cigarette.

"What the hell am I supposed to tell the band, Scotty? The fans? The venues!"

"Tell them the fucking truth. That I'm a drunk. And I have some shit I have to fix. And pay the band for the tours. Please."

"No warning here?"

"I'm a compulsive addict."

"Okay. Okay. I'll make it work."

Scotty draws deep on her cigarette. She slow-streams smoke into the air.

Val's voice is lower now. "So where are you going?"

Scotty pulls another long drag on her cigarette. Blows. "Malta."

"As in the Island of Malta in the Mediterranean?"

"As in I leave two weeks from today. And I need three one-way tickets. Can you call our travel agent? Please." She blows more smoke, then walks to the bathroom to spray the cigarette butt with sink water.

"That's it? That's all you have to say? What the hell, Scotty?"

"I'll call you later."

"Jesus Scotty. I need the names of the other two travelers. And why one way? What the hell?"

"I'll text you whatever you need to know. And Val?"

"What now?"

"You've been a good friend." Before Val can respond, Scotty ends the call.

She's still standing in the bathroom so swings around in a circle, taking the view of her bootleg stash, still there since she moved her whole liquor supply upstairs.

"Hello motherfuckers," she says to the bottles. "Today is the last day of the rest of your life." She twists the cap off a bottle of tequila, drinks deep.

Euphoria washes through her, throbbing ecstasy at the heat rolling over her tongue. The sting in her nose. The gripping in her throat, slippery and clinging to the taste. She draws another huge gulp. Then again. Her body loosens. Warms with the perilous bliss starting to cook in her belly. She wipes her mouth with the back of her hand.

The mirror is above the toilet. Full size. She sees her body in blurred reflection. She watches herself bring the bottle to her lips, the last lover's kiss, tongue finding the little droplets around the rim. She turns the bottle upside down and watches the perfect golden liquid drain in a single stream into the toilet. She throws the empty bottle in the garbage, then leans in to see her face in the mirror. The flicker of blue-black eyes stares back at her, little wisps of light from the center of the darkened pupils.

Motley stands outside the bathroom door. His legs are poised to run. He's unaccustomed to Scotty's hurried movement. The chink of glass bottles shifting on the tile floor. The spill and churn of the rushing liquor into the endless sound of water flushing down.

***

Talia slams her bedroom door and picks up her phone. Her thumbs are fire sweeping a dry plain in a texting frenzy. She makes herself stop before she sends it to Rachel. Her heart is racing so fast her blurred eyes only see the smudge of letters on the phone's screen.

"Dammit!" She forces her thumb to the "x-arrow" and erases the whole venting paragraph. She knows that if Rachel even gets the text, it won't take away the rock-hard cement ball in her chest.

She throws the phone on her pillow and drops with a defeated thud onto her bed.

It's been a long time since she and her parents had a fight this bad.

She throws herself backwards on the mattress, her eyes glued to the ceiling. She peels her hair away from her skull. If only she could squeeze the argument out of her brain and start over.

She thought she was clear. She tried to be calm. Focused. Mature.

They certainly made her feel like she was twelve! And not an adult that can make her own decisions.

What did you expect? That they'd shout hooray! And go back to their crossword puzzles?

The harsh reality of their reaction is still echoing. Snippets repeat. Cutting and sharp. Talia ticks off their top bullet points.

- Four Years of College Down the Drain
- All That Money Spent for Nothing
- What Else is There for You Except To Be an Architect?
- What the Hell is in Malta for You?
- Other Kids Your Age Are Already Working at their Careers

Then the most hurtful of all.

- When the Hell Are You Going to Get Real and Stop Your Whimsical Fantasies?

Talia feels like she's going to blow up. It's not just the way they acted. It's that she feels this Anya of Mahet is more real than ever before. And it's that she can't ever really explain it to them.

It's that they'll never understand what means the most to her.

She's glad the argument ended before she mentioned the dream woman. They'd lose their shit if they knew that's why they're all going to Malta.

Was she just hoping things would be different? She springs off the bed and starts digging through her bureau. Of course Scotty and Aunt Abby are supposed to be here in, what, forty minutes? The whole plan was to have them tell her parents about Malta. Leaving out the dream, Talia reminds herself. She should have just waited.

How stupid! She pulls on her socks.

She finds her running shoes on the closet floor and tugs them on with angry fingers, tying the laces like she's strangling them.

She opens her bedroom door. *Shit.* She didn't mean to slam it on the wall. *Now they'll hear me.*

She lifts her chin and marches past them in the kitchen. There's a perturbing silence thick enough to cut with a knife. Talia can tell they're boiling underneath. She makes it out the front door, where she starts running as soon as her feet are off the front steps.

She's breathing hard right away, but her thoughts won't quit.

Maybe Aunt Abby can talk to Dad alone first.

Talia has a moment of panic. *What if* Scotty *talks to Dad alone first?*

She almost laughs now.

Whatever!

There's too much here she can't control.

I'm a grown-ass woman.

Her slamming feet on pavement remind her of her body. The anger turns into power.

***

Talia's back in her bedroom. She hears the front door open and the low greeting voices. She almost gets up but her heart starts racing again. She's sure Dad's acting like a total fool meeting a famous person like Scotty. The tension in the house will be obvious. Talia should be there. But instead, she stays sitting on the bed. She still needs to cool off before she can go out there.

She's already showered and changed into jeans and a T-shirt. Her hair is still wet. She's rubbing it dry with a towel when she hears a soft knock and Aunt Abby's voice at her door. Scotty's right behind her. They sit in a row on her bed, knees touching.

"Sounds like things got a little heated today?" Aunt Abby says.

"Want me to hire a contract out on them?" Scotty offers.

"You friends with the Mafia?" Talia quips.

"I'm just sayin'." Scotty looks amused.

"I'm guessing they told you about our fight?"

"They didn't say what it was about. Want to tell us?" Talia's relieved Aunt Abby asks.

"I screwed up. I should have waited to tell them about Malta until you guys got here. But I wanted to break the news to them about not being an architect and also that I plan to move to New York after we get back. It all went so fast. The Malta part got away from me. The next thing I know we're screaming at each other. Like never before."

Talia looks at her Aunt. She sees her dad's face. The brown eyes, warm skin, the Renaissance lips and cheeks. That curly hair. She drops her head onto Aunt Abby's soft shoulder.

Scotty gets up to pace the room.

"You can't smoke in here. Mom'll have a fit."

"Copy that." Scotty pats the cigarette pack in her shirt pocket. She picks up a ceramic octopus from Talia's knick-knack shelf. Talia looks at her blandly.

"Art project?" Scotty inspects the underside.

"From when I was younger." Talia thinks maybe 3rd grade, but can't remember exactly.

Scotty holds the ceramic sea creature in her open palm.

"You know octopuses are, like, 300 million years old, right?" Scotty pretends to sniff one of the crooked arms. "I think he's from Malta."

Talia cracks up, amazed her mood is lifting. "Funny that you say that, Scotty. Because I made that guy in secret, before I started on the ships in bottles. I had a ritual with this one." She takes the rugged clay sculpture. "I remember I wanted all the stars of the milky way to collect on the body. See how I painted white dots on it?" She holds it up for Aunt Abby and Scotty to see more closely.

"I was obsessed with the dots. It took me days." She feels almost like she's swaying on a boat. "I said my own version of a prayer for each dot of white." She runs her fingers over the white specks over the black inky shaped creature. "Mom wanted to throw it away. She said it was ugly."

"My point exactly." Scotty takes it from Talia and puts it back on the shelf. "You have to remember why we're doing this, Nugget."

Talia makes a fist. "I haven't forgotten."

"Not a lot of parents would understand what we're up to." Scotty starts pacing again.

"So I have to be skillful." Talia sits back down with Aunt Abby.

"They just think that this is the way to look out for you." Scotty sits back down next to them.

"But it's not." Talia's suddenly exhausted.

"They think it is." Scotty's knee starts to jig. "So let's get in there and take the tiger by the tail. Doc and I will back you up."

Talia stands up.

Scotty looks at her from the bed. "Besides. We bought the fucking ticket for you already. So Mom and Dad don't have a choice."

"You did? Thank you!" Talia surprises Scotty with a bear hug.

"Doc approved." Scotty pats Talia's shoulder with an awkward swipe. "She's a smart one, your Aunt. She thought your folks might say no."

"So we're going? For sure?"

Aunt Abby gets up and opens the door like a maître d, inviting them to pass her. "We're going for sure." She keeps her hand on the door until Talia can walk through.

Before they head out, Talia grips Scotty's arm. "Don't mention the dreams."

Aunt Abby and Scotty bow their heads.

Talia starts to go then stops again. "And Scotty, don't curse. Mom's already on edge."

Scotty grins. "I promise, Nugget. I'll be a God-damn saint."
Talia walks out, feeling the two women behind her like two bolts of lightning skimming the surface of an agitated and vast sea.

***

The energy in the sun room is what Talia would call an awkward silence, but even worse.

It feels like something could explode. Talia's worried it might be her own short fuse that might blow. She leans into Scotty and Aunt Abby's knees, who flank her sides, their three butts squished on the small couch, helping Talia slow her pulse down. Mom and Dad are across from them in their antique chairs, making them both seem like regal visitors in their own home. Nona Gina's grandfather clock ticks in the dining room. Little rhythmic sparks of measured tension.

Talia's brought her octopus to this tricky little pow-wow. He sits on the coffee table in front of the couch. The sunlight plays on the little dots, helping focus Talia on their purpose.

Anya of Mahet is our purpose. Just look at everyone like they're players in the life of our Priestess, even if they'll never know it.

"Please have some espresso?" Kate holds the tray out to Scotty, whose long fingers reach for the handle in a deliberate pinch.

"Thanks." Scotty blows in the little cup.

"Abby? You good with your green tea?" Kate puts the tray down.

Aunt Abby lifts her mug as a yes.

"Biscotti?" Kate passes the porcelain plate to Scotty.

"Mmmm. Delicious." Scotty exaggerates.

Talia stifles a giggle and lowers her head so her Mother won't see. Scotty looks like a gerbil nibbling on a peanut. When she's done munching, Scotty leans back and crosses her ankle over her jigging knee.

"Can I smoke in here?"

"The patio is that way." Kate waves behind her.

Talia braces, expecting Scotty to twirl her cigarette and taunt her Mom into a whole new theme of conflict. But luckily Aunt Abby intervenes, her hand firm on Scotty's jigging knee.

"No problem, Kate. Scotty can wait." Talia watches her Aunt's private glare at Scotty. "Let's all take a deep breath. This isn't the easiest thing and we know you guys are all mad at each other right now."

That's all Kate seems to need for the floodgates to open.

"I just don't get it! Why Malta? Is this whole scheme the reason she wants to quit becoming an architect? What does *she* have to do with this crazy plan?"

Talia looks at Aunt Abby to answer, but it's Scotty's velvet voice that fills the room.

"Kate. Talia's a grown woman. You can trust her."

Talia sees her Dad look at his shoes. A muscle above his eye twitches.

"It's not that we don't trust her." Kate's voice is a thinning note.

"It's that you don't trust *me*." Scotty leans forward. "I know you Googled me. Everyone Googles me. You probably read things that concern you."

Scotty feels for her cigarettes in her shirt pocket, patting the bulge. But she looks more like she's thinking about the next thing to say.

"You have a job to do. I think you can do it."

"And what job is that, exactly?" Kate crosses her arms.

"Let your daughter be a grown woman."

Kate's back straightens. Her lips make a tight line.

Scotty slowly leans back into the cushions, her eyes flashing. "Look. I have a daughter, too. She won't speak to me. I have an addict son. I screwed up a lot with him. I'm an addict myself. I screwed up a lot. I'm in recovery. Now. For good." She looks at Aunt Abby, then goes on. "You're a better mother than I ever was. Talia's a strong woman. A strong twenty-two-year-old *grown* woman. She's that way because of how you raised her. She has natural gifts. Gifts she needs to discover on her own. She's plugged into something greater than all of us."

Talia looks down, trying to hide the tears threatening to spill.

Scotty goes on. "I think you know that. And I think that's why you care so much. You've done well to shield her from some of the worst shit this world has to offer. Scuze me. Worse *stuff* this world has to offer. She's lucky to have you. Both of you—a Mother and Father like you two. My own Mother died when I was seven. My Dad was a hardworking farmer who was too busy to care for me. He died, too. You're all lucky." Scotty's low voice is like a melodic rhythm, drawing Talia into the sound, seeming to fill the room with a gemstone gleam.

Scotty goes on. "None of us—not me, Doc or Talia—understand why we all have this fucking... Sorry. This *important* drive to go to Malta. But we do. I cancelled my tours! I promise you on my life, that I will take care of her. So will Doc, right?"

"Right. We have her back."

Talia's filled with relief when she sees Dad take Mom's hand.

"Your fucking job, Mrs. Talia's Mother," Scotty goes on, "is to know how fucking blessed you are and to fucking thank her for going on this fucking weird-ass journey with us."

Kate's eyes harden.

Scotty shrugs. "I have a potty mouth."

"She can't help it." Aunt Abby adds.

"I fucking can't. I even promised Talia I wouldn't curse. I'm fucking sorry."

Mom lets out a snort that turns into a long and airy laugh. She wipes her eyes. She looks at Dad.

Talia takes a deep breath. "Mom. I love these two women. Like Aunt Abby said, they have my back. Dad. You know your sister. We'll be okay. It's an adventure. And when we get back, I promise I will talk more with you both about my career. I know you both want the best for me. I'm just not sure what that is yet. Maybe after some time with these two wise women" *and our Priestess*, Talia can almost hear Aunt Abby and Scotty say out loud, "I'll know more."

Talia feels the tension in her body finally drain. "I'm sorry I screamed at you both."

"We're sorry, too." Mom gets out of her chair to pull Talia into a hug. "I worry is all."

"I know."

"Sis – you've been pretty quiet all this time." Dad looks at Aunt Abby.

"I'm just trusting that we can move on now. Also I'm glad no dishes were broken."

"Ha ha!" Dad gets up and hugs his twin, then his daughter, then his wife. He moves to Scotty, who gives him a fist bump.

Mom points a finger at Scotty. "Scotty, you're right. I Googled you. You're a mess!"

Scotty hoots a belly laugh. "I have never heard a more honest account of my sorry-ass self." She gets up and throws an arm around Kate. "I like you now, Mom."

Kate smirks. "Lucky us! Friends now."

"Does that mean you and Dad give me your blessing to go to Malta?"

"With one condition."

"Mom!" Talia buries her face in her hands.

"What might that be?" Scotty's green eyes are on fire.

Path to the Priestess Temple

"That you let us pay for the plane ticket."

"No chance."

"Then we treat you all to dinner tonight before you and Abigail go back to LA." Mom starts clearing the coffee table.

"That is a yes. As long as I can smoke." Scotty pulls out her pack from her shirt pocket. "And fucking curse."

"I'm okay with that," Mom says, "but outside in the garden please." She laughs. "For the smoking part." She stands up and hugs Talia again, who rocks into her Mother's body as if a setting sun on the end of a long day.

"You got it." Scotty says. "We leave from LAX in two weeks. Almasto, come watch me smoke. We can talk textiles. I have some expertise in wool rug burns."

Scotty heads out the patio sliding door. The room deflates in a willowy wash.

***

That night, Talia dreams she's standing on the shore of a brilliant, azure-blue ocean. The waves are softly brushing her ankles. The warm salt water flows in. Then ebbs out. In and out. In and out. The cadence is mesmerizing. She looks down to see her feet, the water washing over her tingling skin. She watches her feet leave the water, then walk through damp sand. Sand that turns into dry dunes. Then over rocks. Then onto a dry bed of brush. Now her feet cease walking. Still looking down, she sees that she stands on moist and fertile ground, deep browns and reds in a damp receiving spread.

Still not looking upwards, she feels the limestone statue in her palm. Without arms and legs, its smooth surface is shaped like a long tube. She easily wraps her fingers around it, the contours seeming to be made for her hand. Her thumb traces the shape, rubbing it like a totem of good luck. She kneels, eyes still low toward the ground. She places the little statue on the earth and begins to dig a hole with her hands, nails scraping the spongy soil. Another set of hands begins to carve out the earth with her. She sees a silver ring with black etched spirals on one of the fingers. She watches their hands move together.

She wakes before they bury the little figure. The sound of the waves lingers yet her eyes are still closed. A wash of peace flows over her when she hears the words come softly in her mind.

Child, you are coming home.

***

"Shit, Izzy's here."

Scotty's black SUV is idling with the passenger door open. It tilts at an angle on the curb in front of Izzy's single story ranch house. The neighborhood is quiet, with a lone dog walker on the opposite side of the street. He won't notice Scotty's quick maneuver.

"We have to be sly, Motley. So she won't see us."

Scotty almost drops the old ferret carrier. Motley lets out a woof-yelp. His little body is a rigid bundle inside as the cage tips sideways.

"Shush! I told you this is what we have to do. Shake it off."

Abigail, Talia and Scotty leave for Malta tomorrow. Talia already flew to LA to stay overnight with Abigail so they can all leave from LAX together. This is the last thing on Scotty's to-do list. Scotty knows she's on Izzy's shit-list, but she also knows even her estranged daughter will never turn her back on Motley.

Scotty proceeds toward Izzy's porch in a sneaky scudder. Her shoulders are so tense they almost hit her earlobes. She's attempting disguise in her green baseball cap and sunglasses. She's in orange sweatpants cut above the knee. Her black UGGs slap on the pavement. Her white T-shirt has sweat stains under the armpits.

She glances to see if anyone is looking from inside the window off the front porch. Izzy's Toyota is parked in front, but Scotty didn't tell her about this doggie drop-off. She hasn't seen Izzy for six months, maybe longer. She hopes Zeff isn't anywhere in sight. She hopes neither of them are anywhere in sight.

Motley's whimpering now. Scotty puts the carrier on the porch near the front door. She checks to see if the note she wrote is still taped to the top.

She turns quickly and jogs to her SUV. She grabs the box off the seat. It's wrapped in bad reviews she cut out about herself from the *LA Times*, *Rolling Stone*, *Vogue* and *Rock Bottom*. She's taken a red sharpie to circle her failures and made smiley faces around each quote. "Fuck yeah!" and "True that!" and "Right on!" are added in her penmanship to accent the scathing critiques. This editorial wrapping paper encloses the box holding the envelope of cash, her mother's diamond ring and earrings, Scotty's child-size mittens, the cassette of her mother singing with her and the tape recorder. Scotty's two drawings are neatly folded on top, with a written attempt at explaining the story behind them.

She intends to drive away unseen. Her plan is nearly complete as she carries the box back to the porch to leave it with Motley. Then the front door swings open.

"Mom, what the fuck are you doing here?" Izzy stands in the doorway with her arms across her chest.

She's a spitting image of her father Ryan. Tall, lanky. The darker tanned skin and thick waves of dirty-blonde hair like her dad. But instead of Ryan's sea blue eyes, Scotty sees her own fire-green eyes in her daughter's irritated face. It feels more like years than months since they've seen each other. Scotty's chest feels like it's been stabbed.

Izzy's hair is pulled back in a messy ponytail the way she used to wear it as a little girl, the feathery wisps askew along her face and neck. Like her Mom, she has tattoos, but unlike Scotty's they reflect a more playful sentiment. One arm artfully displays a row of rubber yellow ducks. The other arm contrasts with a harsh red hammer and saw, but intertwined with the tendrils of a winged sea creature climbing up to her shoulder.

Izzy's tank top strap is slipped off to the side, showing her blue bra peeking out along the top. Her black yoga pants show the profile of long, strong legs like Ryan's, her bare toes manicured with hot pink polish. Scotty notices anger splotches on her daughter's face.

"Mom? I asked what you're doing here?"

"Nothing." Scotty holds the box in both hands like a statue.

"Mom. That's a bunch of shit. 'Nothing' means you aren't standing here on my porch with a weird holiday gift and your dog in a suitcase." Izzy bites her bottom lip as if to create a dam to hold back the power of unspoken words.

"It's a different kind of nothing… dear." Scotty steps backwards off the stairs.

"No you don't, woman. You are not backing out of here like a burglar."

"Is Zeff here?" Scotty tries to change the subject.

"No." Izzy hasn't moved.

Scotty steps forward. She puts one hand up to say "truce" to her daughter. She takes another step toward her. "I'm just trying to get to Motley."

Scotty puts the box on the ground. She opens the ferret carrier. Motley bounds out and licks her face. Then runs to Izzy and jumps up to her knee.

Izzy lifts him up and kisses his head. "Hi baby. I've missed you."

He wiggles down, then runs past the open door into her house. Scotty hears his toenails clicking on the kitchen tiles.

"I asked you what you're doing here." Izzy still hasn't budged.

Scotty turns her back on her daughter, pulls a pack of cigarettes out of her sweatpants pocket, lights one and sits down on the top step of the porch stairs. She takes three long drags then throws it on the ground and puts it out with her UGG.

Izzy groans. "Fuck you, Mom." She sits down beside her. She puts her arm around her mother's shoulders. She leans her head into Scotty's baseball cap. "I hate you."

"I know," Scotty says quietly. Her arms are limp on her legs.

They stay like that for a moment. "Turn your damn car off and come inside." Izzy stands up and walks into her house.

***

"Do you want coffee?" Izzy asks from the kitchen through the back screen door. "You know I don't have liquor here." Carrying two cups, she pushes the door open with her shoulder. Motley's digging at her rose bush in the fenced backyard.

"I quit liquor." Scotty's sitting on the back porch steps now.

"Yeah, right. Motley! Leave my flowers alone." The dog runs to the back porch. He sets to sniffing shoes, an old bike tire, a dead fern in a pot. He sits down next to Izzy on the step.

"I did. I quit drinking."

"Mom, I've heard that so many times. I'll believe it when you mean it." She hands her mother the coffee mug.

"I do mean it." Scotty sips the coffee. Makes a face. Puts the cup down on the step.

Izzy rolls her eyes. "You don't like my coffee?"

"It's just really watery."

"Fine!" Izzy drinks her own. "Your loss."

Scotty shifts her weight on the stair. "I'm leaving for a while. I have a… thing… I have to do."

"That sounds dramatic. Are you going to off yourself, Mom?"

"That's not the plan right now." She rests her chin on her tucked-up knees. "I have some things I need to heal."

"Now you have my attention. I thought I'd heard all your bullshit stories. But this sounds different." Izzy's eyes search her mother's sideways profile. "You're serious, aren't you?"

"I stopped singing, too." Scotty picks at a foxtail growing around the edge of the back porch. She thinks about making a snarky comment about gardening. She holds her tongue.

"You what?" Izzy puts down her coffee mug.

"I'm not singing. I canceled my tours." Her tone closes Izzy's mouth, which is gaping open. "It's only temporary. Until I figure this healing shit out."

"You are serious. About all of this. I'm in shock."

"You'll be fine. Do me a favor, Izz? Keep Motley for me for a while? I wish I didn't have to ask. But he loves you. And I can't ask anyone else."

Izzy groans. "Mom, I work all day. How am I supposed to take care of him?"

"He fits in your big-ass purse. Just take him with you. You run your own company. You make the rules. Right?"

"Yes, but…." Izzy pauses. "I mean, it would be kinda fun. I have three employees now. We're all doing well with the sales. The herbalist has made a great addition to the staff, our body salves are a big hit. We don't have any pets in the office… yet." Izzy rubs the pup's head. "You'd keep me and Zeff company at night." She shoots a glance at her mother. "I mean. He's, he's…. Shit. I don't want to talk about Zeff right now."

Scotty sighs. "I don't either. So you'll take Motley?"

"I guess." Izzy drags him to her lap for a quick pet until Motley wiggles out.

"Thanks, Izz. Can you get that box I wrapped for you? Please." She sits back and watches her daughter rise and return with it in her hands.

"Why did you wrap it like this Mom? It seems demented."

"Define demented."

"Should I open it?" Izzy's hands are poised.

"Hold on. Let me tell you some shit first."

Scotty tucks her legs back up. Replaces her chin on her knees. Closes her eyes. Her fingers absentmindedly squeeze and release her leg flesh, then dig under the furry rims of her boots.

"I fucked up a lot with you. I fucked up a lot with Zeff. With Dad." She pops her hands free to punch her wet eyes.

"Mom, you're scaring me."

Scotty clasps her daughter's arm.

"I'm going away because there's something calling me. I don't want to pass along my shit to you anymore. You're a grown woman and I messed that up. There's something about being a woman with our lineage that I need to find out. If I fight hard enough for both of us," she looks at her daughter and sees herself in those eyes, "and if I can square away this sense of what's wrong with me, I'll be able to get closer to what I can do about it. And you will have a better chance in this world than I ever did. And this world still ain't right. For women. Even after all this time. So I have to go."

"Mom, I...."

"Let me finish. I have a, um, a teacher. A woman. Who is...." Scotty looks away, "like an old friend I haven't seen in a really long time. She's got some things to tell me about our lineage and how it might be more sacred than I could ever realize and I've got to learn a better way to listen."

She picks another foxtail and twirls it between her fingers. "I haven't been the best listener."

She looks at her daughter and starts to laugh.

"Who are you and what did you do with my Mother?" Izzy laughs with her. "I do not even know what to say to *any* of this, Mom."

"You don't have to." Scotty puts the box on Izzy's lap. "I want you to have this, but I only want you to open it if something bad happens to me."

"Mom!! You *are* going to off yourself! What the fuck?!" She tries to hand the box back to her mother. "No way. This is one of your mind-fucks."

Scotty gently pushes the box back into her daughter's lap. "It's not. I'm not going to kill myself. I swear to you."

"Then why?" Izzy pauses, "Why do I have to wait? Why would you say that to me? It makes me really creeped out."

"Because there's stuff in there that you might need to know about. But I'm not ready to talk about any of it. But if something happens, I mean I don't think it ever will, but if it does, then at least you have a way to try to understand me someday. I would like you to try. To understand me. Someday."

Izzy's hands lie still on top of the box. She brushes it like a silk pillow-case. "Promise me you're not fucking with my head?"

"Not on purpose, anyway." Scotty laughs. "I can do that on purpose if you want?"

"Mom. You gotta know I never want that. I never have. I never will." Scotty can tell Izzy wants to smile. It's a lifetime of regret to know that her daughter can't.

Motley's collar tags jingle as he scratches his ear with his back leg. The quiet between them cracks.

"Where is this old friend?" Izzy air quotes the last words.

"Malta."

"Will she cure your demented weirdness?"

Scotty snorts softly. "Not sure about that so much. But I do know I have to find out more about why I do the things I do. To myself. To Zeff. To you."

She looks at her daughter, who pulls the box closer into her chest, not taking her eyes off the solid ground, as if at any moment it might disappear right out from under them.

THEN

The Madre's chamber is drafty but at least has cover. I have been sleeping here since the temple walls fell. There is little shelter left in the temple proper, so those of us who live within what remains of these walls have had to share quarters. The Madre has not only provided for me, but for Na'akt and her wolf, Eon and Lael.

I have not given care to what happens to me since the death of my beloved. I do not care if I sleep, wake or walk. I have no hunger. I do not dream. I do not let in the minds of others or reach to them in theirs.

When the sun sets, I will lay down the body of my Priest. If I could follow him to the afterlife, I would. I cover my belly with my palm. Our daughter grows beneath my touch. I know I must go on for her.

Ceaseless whispers have been a constant sound only I hear. I do not understand the words. They are a hissing, constant plague since the earth shook.

I shift in my chair. Lael and Na'akt have wished for me to let them into my mind, yet I only wish to be left alone in my dark world of comfort and no light. After the burial ceremony, we will depart and make the long journey to Grandmother Oriana's. There, I can birth my daughter in the safety and peace of my childhood home, with my mother's mother beside me. I believe the Madre and the others think this will cure the depth of my despair. I do not think it can ever be cured. They say Grandmother's home still stands from the earth's shaking rage. From what we have heard from those who have traveled here from there, our own Temple of the Arch was destroyed, while other temples and homes remain secure. It is not lost on me that this temple was built to hold the Balance in the Bridge of Harmony between Goddess and God, and is now shattered. Perhaps the worst is indeed yet to come, as the Prophetess has always promised. I do not know how much worse it can be than now.

I feel Lael attempt to probe my mind once more. I have spoken but once since the fall, when I made it known that Eon would stand beside me in this ceremony to honor the dead. This place would usually be taken by a High Priest—By my Sondro. But my Sondro is gone.

This demand to have Eon stand with me was not met well. The Madre insisted that this is not the time to break the traditions. She was cross when she commanded that I have one of our other Priests stand in until I choose another High Priest.

I have never been cruel to the only mother I have known. Yet, I came close with this. I made it clear I will never take another High Priest. I refused to lead the ceremony of the dead unless Eon be made Priest by his brothers. Not High Priest, for that is a union of deeper intimacy than right for a young boy. Yet for this ceremony, I will have no other than the favored Initiate of my beloved to stand with me. The Madre had no choice but to succumb to my wishes.

Na'akt and Lael saw to Eon's robes, and they crafted a headdress of agate, wood and silk. I knew this would cause concern among the other Priests who have been practicing for many moons and feel Eon is not ready. His voice has not yet changed for the chanting tone that must be low to summon the blood of the Goddess that runs in our Priestess bodies. Yet none can deny that Sondro would approve. He trusted Eon, and in spite of his age, Sondro taught him well enough to be prepared to stand with me.

As I rise up from my chair, my body weaves to almost falling, and I feel Na'akt and Lael stop their preparations to turn toward my sudden movement. I wave at them to cease their worry.

"Call Eon to me." My voice cracks for lack of use.

"Sister." Na'akt comes to me, and sets me back down in the chair. "He is with the goats. Lael will send for him. Do you wish for tea? I can soothe you with the elderberry and chamomile tincture."

I shake my head in answer.

She takes my hand to her heart. "This will become easier, Priestess."

I am quiet, still behind my black curtain. Yet I find I am unexpectedly open to her kindness. "What is it you wish to say, sister?"

"You know we all grieve, yes?"

"I do."

"Your need for solitude is considered with the utmost care. Yet I must tell you this before the ceremony."

I feel my heart turn over in my chest. "I will hear you."

"The Prophetess Taniyeh." I hear Na'akt pause, perhaps to find courage to speak of her kin. "She was ill. Already dying. She had little time left. The fall quickened her end. But her time to walk among the dead was close."

"You chose not to say this to me before?"

"It was her wish. She was to announce it at council."

I feel a layer of loss upon the emptiness already within me. "This causes me to think of her way with me."

Na'akt's voice trembles. "You speak of why she pushed you so hard to realize your Prophecy?" Na'akt's tone brings a sour taste to my tongue.

"Yes. It is why!" Na'akt's voice becomes muffled. I sense she is holding her face within her hands. "She had less time than she wished to prepare you for your Prophecy."

"Less time for those she cared for."

"You must know she cared for you, Anya. Like her own kin."

I am quiet, yet the hissing whispers become louder within my mind.

Na'akt continues in spite of my bitterness. "I promised Taniyeh I would tell you that her dying words were that the earth's crack was a good omen. For it created a portal between the worlds."

"That was no good omen, sister." My tone is a whip to her kindness. I hold my hand up, for I hear her take in a breath to say more. I feel her withdraw.

"It is a burden you do not wish for now, but in time, I beg you to consider this." In spite of her words, I am impressed with Na'akt's will to convince me. "It did not surprise me that you had a circle of protection around you, where no rocks fell, Priestess."

The memory of this startles, yet I steady myself.

"I saw the three faces, Anya."

I return slowly to my chair, my legs trembling. "They saved me," I whisper.

"Because they are part of this." Na'akt kneels in front of me.

I know she speaks the truth, for it can have only meant such a thing that I still live. Na'akt's palms cover my fists in my lap. "The Prophetess knew not of the fall, yet even so, you were protected. Do you not see this as a sign that there is now a portal? And that those that are on the other side wish to travel to you and wish for you to know them?"

I have no words.

"My sister, Anya, I will speak of this no more. I see it upsets you. I beg you to think on it. Can you offer me that?"

I say nothing but give a terse lowering of my chin. I move to stand, my legs still willow branches under me. I gather courage as I hear Lael enter the Madre's chamber with Eon. He comes to me in a somber step to lay his forehead to my palms.

"Priestess."

"My Priest." I bow to him. "You have aged in this short time. I ask much of you to stand with me in ceremony."

"It is my honor, Priestess." His voice betrays no youth.

In a sudden loss of protocol, I pull him to my heart. His small arms reach around me. I smell the Priest's earthy resin on his hair, bringing memories that ache. I tap his Priest's knot, knowing how much it means to him. I step back that he may stand alone in his own reverence as fitting for his new role.

I wave to those in the room, my hand a sweeping gesture to clear them from my presence. "I must speak with young Eon."

I hear the rustling of robes, the scraping of chairs on stone, the worried whispers about me, as if I am as deaf as I am blind. When the room has emptied I sit, asking Eon to join me. I hear only the wood chair creak as he folds himself down to sit in silent grace.

I smile. "You have found the way of the quiet fox, young Priest."

"I try for the sake of my mentor."

"He would only be proud of you." I know better than to allow my voice to shake at the rising grief. I force words to come without emotion. "There is something I must ask of you."

"I am in service to you only."

"It is to serve my daughter."

Eon is quiet.

"If anything should happen to me, I wish you to care for her in honor of her father, your mentor. In honor of me."

"I will. Yet why not Lael? Or Na'akt? Or your Grandmother?"

I lay my hands open on my knees. "My Priest. There is something you must see."

I allow my darkened world to lift. As carefully as I can, I enter Eon's mind. A stream of light flows, making his body thrust backward at the power of it. The whispers cease as Eon regards the three floating faces of the three women of the future held in the light.

"These faces," Eon's voice cracks. "They are unlike any I have ever seen. So harsh, the first one, like burning flame. The other with light from her hands. The last with hair the color of wheat. How is it that I feel I know them?"

"You have heard talk of my Prophecy?"

"I have."

"That is how. The faces belong to Priestess's from a time to come."

"I do not understand."

"I believe you, too, have a part in my Prophecy."

I feel Eon battle his need for comfort for the sorrow I know moves through him.

"You would serve Sondro, to care for our daughter."

"I will serve your daughter as if she were you, Priestess."

I take his child's hand in mine. "Bless you, Eon, for this vow. Even knowing you cannot yet know what this may mean. You bring me courage." As I stand, I close my inner sight once more. My ears fill with the stinging sound of a bee hive. For when I raised myself back into darkness, the hissing whispers came at harsh speed.

"Please call the others. We must begin."

I motion to Eon to take his place before me. He leads me over the fallen stones, his hand a damp grip in mine. Lael, the Madre, Na'akt and her wolf-beast complete our procession. We pass where our great cherry wood temple doors once stood, the remnants in splintered pieces I feel underfoot as Eon guides my steps. We move to the meadow, through the gates and onto the path toward the burial where I hope these whispering voices will finally cease.

***

The wind is up, as if knowing the breadth of our task. I am uncertain if it threatens or if it desires to support this doing. When we get close to the stone circle and the entrance to the tomb of the dead, the whispers seem to take over my body. I choose to take my rightful place as leader of this ceremony and call to the darkness behind my eyes to disperse. I once again open to the light. At the great rush of brilliancy, the whispers dissolve.

I hear the Madre, Lael and Na'akt startle as I finally release what my inner sight offers to them. When I feel the palpable contact within my inner eye, their minds seem to expand with the intensity of the light. I realize in this moment that I will never again be without this light seeing through my blind eyes. The sacrifice for this is yet unknown to me. I sense it will be great.

I merge with the light and walk with it as my guide. The choice has been mine all along. As I step with my true purpose forward, I make enough room in my heart for whatever my Prophecy holds. I have lost everything already. I am empty now only to be filled with my destiny, whatever shape or form it takes. I feel a great relief at this surrender, yet no less weighted by the burden for all people that I know I must carry. I touch my hands to my belly, hoping my daughter has the strength of her father and of me, to know this journey in the very blood of her body and the mystery of her soul through all time to come.

With confident steps now, I lead the others past the low-ceilinged entrance of the burial chamber and descend down several stone steps into the depth of Mother Earth where the Priestess drummers and low toning Priests already gather. The heat from the fire-lights on the wall warms my skin as we pass through the narrow tunnels. We move past the table, laid with the customary feast of bread, wine, sweet meats as offerings and of the sacred statues and jewels for those that journey with the dead. My inner eye sees everything as moving lines of light and dancing shapes.

I motion to Eon to stand next to me. He seems to stagger as the light fills his mind and body. Yet my own legs have become anchors with such power, I am the Goddess herself. I open my body through the bottoms of my feet inviting the energy and vibration of the great depth of the earth to race through me. There is no hesitation as I say the invocation, take the sacred mudra stance and bow deeply.

For this moment, gone is my feeling of grief, of sorrow, of loss, of all that ties me to the worrying steps to now. I belong in body and soul only to the Great Mother of All Things as I invoke Her once more.

This time my bow is so low, I bend at my knees to Her. I lie flat on the earth, my hips resounding with Her heartbeat within my womb. My forehead lies upon the smooth rock underfoot. I tilt my headdress to allow the posture then place my palms on the stones. Even my shoulders and the bottoms of my arms that lay upon the cool rocks are pulsing in this earth-to-body harmony. Every part of me vibrates with power.

The women drummers echo this rhythm in my bones and flesh, then I rise to take my place next to Eon. He stands in the death mudra next to me, impressing on me that he is indeed the one to choose for this. I feel Sondro's strength and grace in him as Eon holds the world of the living and the world of the dead open for my prayer.

Sondro's shrouded body along with the Prophetess Taniyeh's are carried to me first. Next will be the Priests and Priestesses who are also awaiting my blessing. I feel grief threaten to rise in me and bid it to wait. I must be clear for this ceremony.

I open my arms to the skies above to come down to the depth of this earth chamber. I tone the deathing chant that will lift Sondro to his place in the afterlife. Then, I do so for Taniyeh and the others. Each are laid into the side walls of the burial chamber to rest, for it will take until the dark moon to ascend.

I see the lines of light move within Eon's body as he places the clay jar of red ochre next to Sondro's shrouded form. Eon is to lay the goat skin bag holding the nine limestone statues of the Goddess's guards next to him. They will protect this High Priest on his journey. My heart feels wrenched open.

I am to end the ceremony with an invocation to the ancestors to guide the dead as they transition. Here the hissing whispers begin again, making me feel suddenly so dizzy I think I may faint. My breath is in short gasps. I narrow the light within my mind outward to point it toward a shadow moving in the eastern corner of the chamber.

I shine the light from my inner eye forward in hopes it will be Sondro's spirit I see. Instead, the light-shape of the Golden Hair Woman in robes of white is illuminated. She holds one of the nine guard statues in the palm of her other hand, with its hollow eyes, no arms or legs. Behind her is the Fire Eye Woman and beside her, She of the Wise Hands. They speak into my mind.

We walk with you.

I raise the intensity of light, finally aware that my gift of blindness is the reason I have indeed been chosen. For I can see them only without sight.

My mind seems to disappear with the light. My body stays earthen, yet I leave it behind. Just as the dead might slip upward without weight. I know I still live. I hold my hands over my belly praying to my daughter to yield with me as we ascend. I feel carried and not surprised when my familiar world dissolves. Gone to me. Perhaps forever. I move away from all that is here, where I can travel freely.

As spirit, I step toward the Golden Hair Priestess and lay my forehead to hers, merging with her mind. I give her my hand to hold. She leads me into the whirl of light, a tunnel that consumes. The Fire Eye Woman and She of the Wise Hands walk beside us.

I know not where they take me. I only know I go.

NOW

Abigail checks her phone. It's only 8:00 a.m. That means she only slept for four hours and Talia is still asleep in the bed next to hers in their hotel room. Abigail's hungry and, if truth be told, too anxious to try to sleep any more. This trip seems insane now that they're doing it. She already misses Rufus. She was glad Nicole agreed to take him while they're gone.

She hates flying. And worse, they have to do a layover in Germany. At least they were smart enough to get a hotel for the night.

Her stomach growls. She can get breakfast in the café downstairs in the hotel lobby. She rolls out of bed quietly so she won't disturb Talia. They aren't supposed to leave for the airport for the final flight to Malta until this afternoon. She wonders if Scotty wants to join her for something to eat. She can knock on Scotty's door on the way to the elevator.

As she heads to the bathroom to get ready, she wonders if this whole thing is a mistake.

At the time they booked their flights, it made sense to get one-way tickets. She took her vacation time off work, but has no clue what to tell them if they end up staying longer. She can't think what could possibly keep them in Malta. Just how much time does it take a person to chase down an ancient dream Priestess?

Everything seems so unfamiliar and chaotic. She feels "tetas arriba," as Nicole used to tease her when she would become this exhausted and disoriented.

"I am tits-up, yes." Abigail mutters under her breath.

She jots a note on the hotel stationary to Talia in case she wakes up, then heads out the door, making sure the key card is tucked into her backpack's side pocket.

She's getting close to passing Scotty's room when she sees the door open. Abigail smiles and hurries her steps only to stop dead in her tracks.

A man comes out of Scotty's room. He turns in the hallway and faces the open door. Abigail sees Scotty's tattooed arm hand him his cell phone and his black leather jacket, which the man takes and folds in a wad under his arm.

He has thick black hair and a rugged look about him. Abigail sees that he's probably European from his M. Gemi shoes, the same brand that Almasto always buys when he travels for work to Rome. Abigail has sized the guy up in about half a second. Although she isn't sure why he had to take his coat from Scotty like that. Or why he's even at her door. Did he deliver something?

Then she sees him lean in for a kiss.

But Scotty's face appears and instead of kissing the guy, she pats his cheek, saying something to him that Abigail can't hear. She suddenly realizes she's standing like a frozen statue in the middle of the hallway. She hears the guy ask for an autograph, then Scotty's voice saying something, then the guy heads away from Abigail toward the elevator. He looks like the cat that ate the canary. He's waving as he's walking backwards, clutching his leather jacket like a football. "Non lo dimenticherò," he says to Scotty.

He's Italian. And apparently he 'won't forget that,'" Abigail translates under her breath in a sarcastic drone.

Scotty's head appears from behind the door frame to watch him step into the elevator and disappear, but then she turns and sees Abigail, who whips around and hurries toward her own room, digging for her key card in her backpack with clumsy fingers.

She's horrified when she hears Scotty's velvet voice. "Morning, Doc. Out for a stroll?"

Abigail sets her shoulders and turns back to Scotty, sauntering to her as if nothing was out of the ordinary.

"Just going to breakfast."

"Is that a fact?"

Scotty leans against the doorway, a white T-shirt almost touching the bottom of her green boy shorts. Her legs and feet are bare. Abigail sees a tattoo on her ankle of a cow with *RIP Rilke* underneath, the delicate coloring startling her, as if she's looking at some kind of hushed secret drawn on Scotty's skin.

"Yes, it's a fact." Abigail is still searching for her key card, head down, her curls falling into her eyes. She punches her hair back, glancing at Scotty. "So. You're up."

Scotty crosses her arms and leans deeper into the doorway. "Mmm. Hmm. I'm up."

Abigail tries not to let words out, but her fuzzy jet-lag and jumpy nerves get the better of her. "What the hell, Scotty? You're more in the vagina business than I am!"

Scotty grins. "Come in and sit down, Doc. You look like shit."

Abigail finally finds her key card, holds it up to Scotty as if it explains some great mystery, stares at it as if she doesn't know why she's holding it up, then puts it back in her backpack, shaking her head.

"I'm all tits up."

Scotty laughs. "I see. Well come in anyway. I'd love some breakfast. I just need a shower."

Abigail stands in the hallway, unsure of what she wants to do. She tries to hide her embarrassment, but Scotty grabs her hand. "Come on, Doc. It was just a little tryst for a sad and lonely rock star. I'm allowed."

"Of course you are. Sorry about the vagina comment."

Scotty leads her into the room but stops and turns to look down at Abigail, who's just short enough to feel like Scotty's hovering over her.

Scotty's eyes are daggers. "Doc. Promise me you will never say the words 'sorry' and 'vagina' in the same sentence again."

She brushes a rogue coil of hair away from Abigail's cheek. "Now have a seat and wait for me. And when I'm done showering, we can go downstairs and find some hog-nose tea or whatever the fuck they drink in this city."

Abigail can't help but laugh. "I must be worse off than I think. Hog-nose tea actually sounds okay to me right now." She flops onto Scotty's couch. "Don't hurry. I'm probably going to finally fall asleep. I've been way too jittery."

Scotty yawns and stretches her arms over her head and cracks her back. "You can be jittery. After all, we're about to find out how crazy we really are now that we're almost there."

"What if Talia's wrong about this Anya woman?"

"Then we have a great vacation in Malta. Stop worrying, Doc." Scotty pulls her shirt over her head on the way to the shower, and within seconds the water is going, bringing the sound through the open bathroom door. Abigail's body suddenly feels as heavy as a ten–ton car. The water sound soothes her so much she can't keep her eyes open another second. *Anya of Mahet, you better show up somehow. I need a sign that I haven't made the biggest mistake in my life by coming here.*

Over the sound of the cascading water, Scotty's voice carries in a low, deep tone.

The Queen she is falling. Falling. Falling.
The Queen she rises and moves through time.

Scotty's deep voice resonates in Abigail's bones, slowing her heart beat, leaving her feeling like she's being cradled to sleep. She burrows further down into the soft couch cushions. She finally lets herself doze.

***

Scotty's felt a pinching pain in her head on and off since they got to Malta. She wonders if this is the one and only Anya of Mahet knocking on her boney head, since they did what she seemed to ask of them. Come all the fucking way here. And now maybe she's talking to Scotty in some kind of ancient Morse code.

Scotty's been dreaming of the woman every night since they got here. Just her eyes. Shooting light into Scotty's pupils. Maybe that's why her head hurts. Maybe the beams of light are scorching her brain matter. All she sees are the eyes, then she's in that tunnel with Talia and Doc. Then Scotty always wakes up.

Now she just feels the sticky sweat on her skin where they sit in the heat of the sun outside the Ggantija Archeological Park on the Xaghra plateau on Malta's sister island, Gozo. Scotty winces at the raw stinging pain in her toe. She kicks off her black UGG and drops it on the ground.

She, Abigail and Talia just spent the last hour touring within the ruins in the heat of the afternoon and her feet hurt, with what must be another blister. The low limestone ledge Scotty's sitting on is rough under her butt. She's not sure if these rocks are from 3200 BC like the temple they just visited, but however old they are, the rough surface chafes her skin. She feels it even through the thick denim of her cut-off jean shorts.

She examines her foot and finds the skin rubbed raw on one of her toes. Of the three temples they've visited their first week here, these blisters on her feet are the only thing to show for all this toiling in the heat. They've hit only roadblocks when it comes to revelations about their visions of their dream Priestess.

"Do you have another fucking Band-Aid?" Scotty nudges Abigail who sits next to her with her backpack on the ground between her knees. Scotty holds out her hand to receive the Band-Aid Abigail pulls from the side pocket.

"Thanks, Doc."

"Why don't you ever carry anything other than your cigarettes and phone?"

"Because you have such a nice backpack." Scotty plucks at the wrapper opening. "I hate these finger nails." She waves them at Abigail. "See what no guitar playing does?"

"You can clip them." Abigail holds out her hand for the Band-Aid wrapper.

"I might need them for a bar brawl." Scotty pops the crumpled wrapper into Abigail's palm.

"We don't go to bars," Abigail mutters.

Scotty folds the Band-Aid around her second to last toe. She lifts her foot in the air and rotates her ankle. She admires her first-aid skills then examines the other wrapped toes. Three of the five on that foot are now wrapped. Another on her heel.

A tourist with a gold "Warriors" T-shirt stops walking and stares at Scotty. Abigail reaches over and pulls Scotty's green baseball cap more tightly over her eyes to cover Scotty's famous face from the passerby.

"You're going to be on Instagram in a minute, picking your feet in Malta," Abigail says to Scotty. They watch the guy take a photo from his phone with it against his hip as he walks past them. He pretends not to notice that Scotty and Abigail see what he does in plain sight.

"I've had worse things happen." Scotty watches him go, giving him an exaggerated farewell wave. She replaces her UGG, pulls out her pack of cigarettes from her short sleeve button down pocket. Lights one, inhales deeply and leans back into the rock's craggy surface. "Where's Talia?"

"In the Heritage Museum."

"Do you think she picked up any vibes about our Priestess in this temple?" Scotty hasn't mentioned the recurring dream yet. She planned to but Talia has been moody and Abigail has just been a total pessimist about being here. Scotty would prefer a more appreciative audience to bring up the dream. What she really would prefer is a fucking drink. But that's a done deal. She takes another drag of her cigarette.

"None of us have picked up any vibes in any temple yet, so probably not this one either. I swear Scotty! We aren't going to find anything today. Let's just go back to the villa."

"You're wrong, Doc." Scotty tries a different tact to convince Abigail. "We've gotten good intel today. The temple tour guide had a lot of cool shit to say about all that good mojo of the Goddesses and Priestesses of that time. I'm amazed I never realized our origins in Malta. How come nobody told me about this in kindergarten?" She rubs the sharp pain her temples. *Ironic that our heads have the same name as these ruins.* "I think we might be really close to something big."

Scotty pulls her baseball cap lower when another tourist slows down in front of her. Here in Malta, she's recognized less than in the states, but there is the occasional tourist who will ask for a selfie or autograph. She always agrees, but for the most part, Scotty's been getting used to becoming invisible. She's noticed she's beginning to like it.

"That's all true," Abigail says. "But why do you think we're close?"

"Just a hunch." Scotty flips the cigarette on the ground and stomps it with her boot. "Why wouldn't our Anya of Mahet come from a culture like this?"

"From what evidence?"

"Doc. You can't deny that she could have come from here. It was a true matriarchy. This was Priestesses-land. Didn't you hear the guide? They were respected in ways our civilization can't even imagine. People think the women of centuries ago just had babies and drew shit on the rock walls. But you heard it, right? It was the Priestesses who ran governments, education, agriculture and farming and did all kinds of science shit. Did you hear what that guide said about the Priestess astronomers? And what about all those rituals women led?"

"All of that's true. But how does that prove that our dream woman is from here and from that time?"

"All I'm saying is you should try thinking outside of the box."

"I want to. I really do. But I guess I'm stuck in that box until I have more proof."

Scotty slings her arm over Abigail's shoulder and pulls her into a wrestle hug. "Try. We've come all this way."

Abigail lets Scotty shake her side to side like a rag doll.

"It's easier than you think, Doc. These Priestesses were the ones who were really in the vagina business."

She watches Abigail's smile spread.

"You heard the guide today, right? About how sex was sacred back in those days. And how if a guy jumped some chick in the temple, they cut his balls off?"

"I don't recall those were the guide's actual words, Scotty."

"Okay—she didn't say balls. Or mention a knife. But you got it, right? It was the worst crime that could be committed. So it never happened. At least for a few centuries until things went all man-o-war in the world. Still goin' on, as we know."

"True. It was a woman's world without threat, or shame, for a long time," Abigail muses. "But I need to know if we're on the right path. I guess I'm scared if I find out our dream woman was truly here, that makes her real. And that feels like it's going to make me look at my life as a loss of some kind."

"How in the fuck do you get that from what I'm saying?"

Abigail sets her jaw. "We've made progress and now things are going backwards for women. I worry for my patients. My niece. What if she has a daughter? I'm even worried for you! And that's saying something," Abigail laughs. "It's not even that we should try to go *back* to something that was better for women. Even the word 'matriarchy' isn't relevant to what I'm trying to say. I love what I'm learning here about these women of the temple times that were so revered that there didn't even need to be a word like 'matriarchy.' Because the balance for all people just *was*. What does that mean for our future? You get that, right?"

"Think of it this way, Doc. There's been a veil over our minds, right? And it's lifting. You feel it. I know you do. You wouldn't be here if you didn't. How else could you and Talia and I all have seen the same thing? You can't explain it, right? So don't try. Can't you let that be enough for now and then see what happens?"

"I don't know. I'd just like some kind of proof that we're on the right track."

Scotty scans the adjacent view. The mosaic of color is transmitting a tangible story she feels just out of reach. The sharpness of the blue sky is nothing like the sometimes hazy blue at home. Who in the past has looked up at the horizon the way she is right on this very rock? So many lived even before this time. The huge overgrown cactus, clumped in groups, looking like some kind of prehistoric council discussing ancient vegetation. The grey and mustardy-pink ancient stones are randomly set, impossibly heavy, but like some giant dropped them from the sky above like stone dice on a little game board. The allure of this place is real.

There's a small breeze coming from the ocean not far from here. Scotty's glad it's cooling her down. The back of her neck is bristly from her conversation with Abigail. The air smells fresh with salt and the heat off the rocks. She seizes the cleansing moment to disperse with their discussion when she sees Talia trotting toward them.

"Hey, Nugget. You look happy. Did you just have sex in the museum bathroom?"

"I should ask the same of you, Scotty." Talia clutches a white plastic bag.

"No. But there's still time," Scotty winks. "What's in the sack?" Scotty reaches for it.

Talia's smile seems too big for her freckled face.

She slowly pulls out an object from the plastic bag.

Scotty's knee starts to jig. She hears Abigail gasp.

The little stone statue fits snugly in Talia's palm. The hollow eyes stare out of the body with no arms. No legs.

"Replicas of our mystery statue! They were for sale in the museum gift shop! Look." Talia pulls out a leather pouch with a drawstring. She tugs the leather ties open. One by one, she takes out the other eight statues, laying them across Scotty and Abigail's laps.

With the sensation of the statues on her, Scotty's body begins to tremble. She sees Abigail's knees shaking so much the little statues vibrate in her lap.

"Well, well, well." Scotty looks at Talia. Then at Abigail, whose face is suddenly rapt.

"Just like he gave to me in my dream." Talia's breath catches.

"Talia! This is amazing." Abigail's almost whispering. "It's a set of nine. Just like we learned. They look just like you drew from your dream!"

"See, Doc? I told you. We're close." Scotty pinches Abigail's arm.

Abigail picks up one of the little statues and smooths her hands over it, her smile inward and serene. Scotty hasn't seen that look on her face since they got here.

Before Scotty gives the statue back to Talia, her head blasts with another sharp twinge of pain, so intense her eyes hurt. It's like she looked right at the sun, even though she hasn't. It's suddenly so bright she sees dots of intense white light moving like strobe lights in her vision. The pain in her head sharpens. She drops the statues into Talia's leather pouch. Abigail pulls Scotty by her wrists to stand up.

"You okay?"

"All good, Doc. Let's take these weird little people home to the villa and lay them out. Talia, did you bring your Ouija board?"

Scotty hopes her joke will stop the others from noticing her knees going out from under her. She links arms with them feigning a jovial mood, hoping she can hide that she lost her balance. The last time her knees gave out like this was when she first saw that face in the mirror. The light blasts again. She loses her balance once more, making her grab Abigail and Talia in an awkward jerk. She feels them wordlessly lift their arms to steady her. They walk down the path together, their feet in time with each other. As Scotty lets them help her, she's suddenly panicked. It takes a minute for her to realize why. She is, at least for these few steps, totally blind.

THEN

Na'akt is sluggish with the heat of the day's relentless sun. Sweat drips into her eyes from under her Priestess head wrap as she moves along the dirt road, deep in thought. The others keep in step under a silent blanket of heavy grief. They toil along beside her, their footsteps on the dry earth a rhythmic chore. They should arrive at Oriana's homestead by the next sunrise, their fourth on this journey. Ba-leh pants next to her. She remembers from previous travel that there is a small pass along the edge of a carob tree grove that runs along a stream at the next set of large rocks. The night will fall soon, so they can stop there. The large trees will provide a way to hang their provisions and offer shelter should there be a strong wind come dark. Bah-leh can drink his fill from the stream and they will bathe and leave an offering to bless the water and replenish their goatskins with its bounty.

Na'akt's bow and arrows lay over her back, leaving a stained sweat line across her robe on her chest where the leather holds it. Between her skills with the arrow and her wolf's wise ways, they will make sure no harm comes to the others as they sleep under the stars. Lael will make the fire bright. Once the rabbits that Na'akt secured for their meal and the strong-toothed sea fish Ba-leh hunted are seared by the flames, the day's hunger will subside well after the setting sun.

Na'akt watches the Priestess Lael's heavy step in front of her, leading one of the donkeys from the temple that pulls the cart. Na'akt has not been able to keep Anya steady on her feet, so the cart has been useful to carry her along with their supplies. Since the burial, the High Priestess has not been the same. She does not speak, not even to eat or drink. Na'akt has seen only emptiness in Anya's eyes. She has not shared an image with Na'akt or the others since then. Nor has she seemed to want to be shown images of the life around them. She seems to be fading into herself. Eon walks beside the cart, often taking the High Priestess's hand that lays listless over the side edge. His face is a scheme of worry and shadow. His young brow wrinkles, bringing creases to his eyes. Even the small dark crescent mark of birth that touches the side of his chin seems to carry a burden he claims as his own. Na'akt aches for the hastening loss of youth this grief has brought him.

She hears the Madre's labored breath behind her. The older woman uses a walking stick with her one good arm, the injured other wrapped close to her chest.

"We will find a place to stop soon, Madre. Do you wish to lie beside Anya in the cart again?"

"I will rest when we stop. How does Anya seem?"

Na'akt looks ahead at Anya's limp body. "She appears to be resting, but it seems she is still not with us. I think she travels in trance. I have seen this many times with the Prophetess when I have assisted her in her Oracle Visions. That is when I have seen Taniyeh so taken with her journey she seems lifeless, when in truth her spirit travels as the Goddess with vitality in worlds beyond. We can only hope this is true for Anya."

"Yet we gave her no tea. No medicine to travel."

"No Madre, we have not."

Na'akt holds her tongue, wishing not to worry the Madre. Yet Na'akt cannot help but worry herself. She does not know if the child Anya bears will be enough to make her wish to bring her own spirit home. Or if her loss of Sondro will keep her seeking him. She wonders if that is where she walks now. With him. Or if she instead travels with the three faces in a world that frightened even Taniyeh.

The thought of her kin and the memory of the falling temple makes Na'akt close her eyes tightly. The sound of the rocks crashing down in the council room still haunts her. Ba-leh looks sharply at her, as if following her thoughts. She flicks her wrist at him to gather the goats who have scattered. They move along with the travelers, stopping to forage. They eat quickly, nosing the brush, then trot to catch up. The bronze bells on their necks ring along with their bleating mews. Ba-leh gives chase, making Eon laugh. For a moment all seems normal. Yet Na'akt's thoughts soon turn to spinning as quickly as the wind on a dandelion seedling.

It will be the time-between soon. They must stop to rest. Once the fire is lit, Na'akt will stay awake and take her place by the flames to pray to the Great Mother for guidance and protection. She knows that Anya's Prophecy must live through Na'akt's own actions now, a task she feels as a weighted shroud.

She hears the stream now, and watches Ba-leh's long legs carry him in haste to the path along the carob trees. She waves to Lael to turn the cart toward the water.

Na'akt looks again at Anya, her arms by her sides, her head rolled back. They cannot get to Oriana's soon enough.

∗∗∗

As the rocks crash with the sound of thunder in the council room, Sondro remains on his knees. He keeps the tone for as long as his breath can empty, then resets to tone again. He is aware his head has been hit and he should feel intolerable pain, yet he feels nothing. His eyes, as a promise to his prayer, remain closed. He only feels the wet blood by its spill on his cheeks. His tone increases, searching for his brothers' voices through the sounds of shouts, of rocks crashing, of the thunder of the sky as it seems to fall down in cascades of rough edges, cutting and flattening around him.

Then his voice is unfit. No sound comes forth, even though he shapes the vowels precisely. His knees no longer feel the pillow under him, for his body is at once too light to move his limbs. When he finds himself secured high above the fallen rocks below, held by air alone, his eyes now open. He tries to descend. He cannot command his limbs to do his bidding. From here he looks down and he sees himself lying on the ground, not knowing why he is both here and there. He sees Lael move to his body below and wonders what makes her fold over his chest. He thinks she is injured as Na'akt comes to carry her to Anya. He floats in frustration, disturbed by the unreasonable way he cannot move his body. He grows weary with the effort.

He drifts to sleep.

When he wakes, he is alone in the council room. This time when he wills his body to move, it floats forward a little. He swivels it. This way. That way. He gains momentum and begins to wiggle and wave in an awkward manner until he can choose where to move it. He strains to hear the Priests' tones. Surely they call to him.

A faint note draws him to their sound. He knows not how he is transported to them. They are few in number, on their knees praying in the 8th syllable of the Goddesses' Secret name. He is not sure why they sing this as it is the death chant. He wonders who has died.

They are in a dark cavernous place, which he slowly realizes is the burial chamber near the Temple of the Arch. When he sees Anya performing the deathing ceremony, he tries to lower himself to her side. As High Priest, he is to serve the dead along with the High Priestess, for this ceremony cannot be done properly without him. He sees it is his young student Eon who holds the death mudra next to Anya. Sondro floats his body to them. He tries to put his hand on Eon's shoulder, for it is Sondro who should be standing there. His hand moves through the young boy's flesh and bones.

The shock of this creates more confusion. More frustration. It is then he sees his own body, this time shrouded and ready to rest in an open grave in the wall of the cave.

Floating to the corner of the burial chamber, he watches, finally understanding he is in the afterlife. His emotions wash away, the truth bringing clarity.

He hears a hush of whispers then sees the leather pouch holding the nine Goddess Guardian statues next to his body, left there to protect him on his journey to the world of the dead. He finds himself moving away from the burial. Away from his body. Away from Anya. From Eon. He does not know why he travels, or where he is to go. There is nothing he can do but allow himself to be carried.

His body, no longer moving, hovers now above the Golden Hair Woman asleep in a bed of linens. He understands now.

With swift but gentle deliberation, he moves into the Golden Hair Woman's mind. He sends an image of giving her one of the limestone statues. He tells her to bring it to Anya of Mahet to the Temple of the Arch and bury it. This will give Anya what she needs.

To open the doors between worlds.

He floats in seamless peace now, knowing his vow has led him here. His vow to serve. To anchor Anya's Prophecy. He needs nothing else.

He sleeps again.

This time when he wakes, Sondro finds he is now within a small room he does not recognize. Rather than stone, the walls are of wood. He chooses a high corner to view what lies below. He senses a motion then sees a young man, sleeping on a raised mat, thick and off the ground. It is a shape he is unaccustomed to seeing, as it appears to be on wooden legs. The man's hair covers the pillow under his head, strewn around his face in thick black waves. His long honey-toned limbs are spread wide, the linens in a heap rolled around his waist and one leg. Sondro waits, for he senses he will know more when the young man awakens.

When the light outside begins to fill the room through the wooden window, Sondro lets his awareness take in the unfamiliar objects. He sees a wall of shelves filled with thick parchments stacked sideways. He notices a chair of brown hide in the middle of the room with thick cushioned seat, arms and back.

A squawk sounds abruptly. He watches the young man pick up a black tablet the size of his hand from a small table next to the raised mat. He touches the tablet, which seems to stop the sound. The man seems to be close to Sondro's age of twenty-three summers. He wears a tight wrapping around his hips with openings for his legs and a tunic with short sleeves. There is an etching on one arm of a sacred labyrinth that Sondro has seen in the temple's meadow. The circles within circles spiral into a maze with no end.

The young man runs his fingers through his thick hair, twisting it with quick fingers into a knot, then wrapping it with a band he pulls off his wrist. The tablet makes another chirping noise. The man plays his thumbs on it but no sound comes forth. He taps it for some time, the tablet now chirping again. He drops it on the mat, then walks to a pot that sits on a table by the wall. The young man presses a finger on it. The pot soon emits the sound of water heating into a bubbling gurgle yet, quite perplexing to Sondro, there is no fire to cause this.

The young man looks up toward Sondro. Except for the absence of a beard, and the presence of two sets of bronze rings in each earlobe, the man's face is somehow familiar. The dark eyes and brows grace his shapely cheeks, nose and lips. Sondro floats closer to gain more view. There, on the side of his chin lies the dark mark from birth. The waning crescent moon. The touch of the Goddess, just as he has seen on his young Initiate Eon's face.

The man suddenly tips his head in silent question at Sondro. Sondro moves back, his instinct to lessen any fear for the man, knowing how he must seem in his floating form. Yet, the man bows his head in quiet greeting to Sondro.

The man turns and moves through a small doorway near the mat, pulling off his garments on his way, revealing effortless, sinewy muscles. Soon Sondro hears water rushing. When he emerges, the man wears a wrap of thick linen around his waist. He dries water off his body, takes a garment from the table's drawers and pulls his legs through, securing the leggings with a string. He unfurrows a roll of sticky fabric on the floor, then lowers his body onto it. He moves into a series of Sacred Mudras, his breath sinking in the rhythms of his body. He holds postures much like the Priests' body prayers Sondro practiced all his life in the temple. When seeming to be complete, the man bows then pulls a circular pillow from under the brown chair and lowers to rest on it, his legs crossed, his back leaning against the chair. Sondro drifts closer, intrigued.

The man closes his eyes, places his palms together and bows his head as he tones a short salutation that Sondro recognizes to be to Kali-Ma Om. Sondro moves closer to the sound of the chant to the Great Mother, then rests in stillness over the man's left shoulder.

That is when Sondro sends him the vision.

NOW

When they get off the bus at the bottom of the hill in town, Talia takes one of Scotty's arms, Aunt Abby the other.

"I'm sure you'll be okay," Aunt Abby tries to reassure Scotty.

Scotty's weight pulls on Talia's shoulder as they trudge up the hill to the villa.

"Let's just get you home." Aunt Abby gives Talia a look of concern over Scotty's head.

"It's probably a migraine," Talia offers, lifting her eyebrows to her Aunt. "Could that be it?"

"It's not a fucking migraine." Scotty almost shoves them both away, but then leans on them again. "I can see now. The pain is what's so fucked up."

"Okay. At least you can see." Aunt Abby stops them. "Drink." She holds up her water bottle to Scotty.

"Vodka, right?"

"Mmm hmm. Straight up."

Scotty drinks the water. "Thanks, Doc."

"Better?"

"Getting there. I'm like a crotchety old woman you found in the alley, leaning on you both like this." Scotty snorts.

"We're almost there," Talia encourages them further up the hill. She's totally spent and needs to take off her tennis shoes and hopefully take a swim at the beach just across the road. While it was kind of terrifying for Scotty to lose her sight like that, she seems to only have a bad headache now.

It's only a bit further, even though it's straight uphill.

The rented three-bedroom house is on Gozo, Malta's sister Island. Gozo is only a thirty-five-minute ferry ride from the northern tip of

Malta. Talia's glad they were on Gozo today and didn't have to take the ferry here. It was just a short bus ride from the temple they were visiting when this eye thing happened to Scotty. The bus let them off in the center of the town, down the hill from the villa, so they're almost there.

When she studied Ancient Malta in college, Talia read about the theory that during the Ice Age, these two sister islands Malta and Gozo, might have been connected but became two after the ice melted and raised the sea level. There are even cart tracks on Malta that end on the edges of cliffs and flat rocks, some that seem to go right into the sea, making the theory plausible. It was even thought that before the Ice Age, Sicily was also once attached to Malta, making it about a four days' walk from Gozo. Talia loves that idea, being that her grandparents are from Sicily. Whenever they've taken the ferry from Malta, Talia lets her imagination go wild, pretending she's going "home" to "her" temple.

Once they go past the garden and into the villa's stone interior, they all blow out a breath of relief. They're all sticky with sweat and the cooling stones act as a natural air-conditioner. The home is a four-hundred-year-old farmhouse, remodeled but timeless in how it feels inside. It's cozy and elegant, with its thick stone walls, high ceilings, echoing hallways and terra cotta pavers. Everything is oversized, even the leather furniture and massive window dressings. But the best is how cool it is when it's hot out and how balmy and inviting it's been when it's rained.

The views in the surrounding landscape stretch in gorgeous display. Gozo's terrain is hilly, and the villa shares a vast meadow with a scattering of tree groves. The breeze is never harsh as it swoops over the flatter meadow and then slows to scoop through the huddles of trees in random bunches on the horizon. The ocean is just a short walk across a pot-holed road and down a winding dirt path. There's a gentle inlet where the waves roll in languid crests on the sandy beach, which can be viewed from every window of the front of the old farmhouse.

"I'll make us a snack. Does your head hurt too much to eat, Scotty?" Aunt Abby's already opening the fridge.

"I can eat." Scotty lifts her sunglasses off with tentative fingers.

"Were you really blind?" Talia asks.

"All I can say, Nugget, is that there was so much intense bright light all of a sudden, it was like I went blind. But I'm okay." She pats Talia's arm.

"Good."

"Thanks for being my crutch up the hill."

"Anytime."

Relieved that she's got some time alone now, Talia goes down the hall to her bedroom, kicks off her tennis shoes and peels off her shorts and T-shirt. She slides her hair scrunchy off and wraps it around her wrist. She runs her fingers through the strands, shaking her head so her golden mane falls evenly onto her shoulders. She slips on a cotton white sundress, enjoying the soft fabric on her skin. But when she looks in the mirror, her reflection shows her how wired she still feels. She's been buzzing ever since she purchased the nine little statues.

How weird it was to find all nine of them displayed on their individual, tiny podium blocks inside a glass case next to other artifacts of ancient times. Talia looked at them through the glass unable to move until her toes went numb from standing still so long. When she wandered aimlessly into the gift shop next to the exhibit, she almost fell over when she saw the leather pouch of the replica statues for sale. They were casually sitting on display next to cards, magnets and key chains for sale.

Now, she pulls the leather pouch out from her backpack, opens her dresser drawer then pauses. Her nimble fingers pull the drawstring. She takes out the statue that most resembles the one the Priest gave her in her dream. It's not the tallest of the nine. Or one of the two animal figures. This one is mid-sized, fitting into her palm easily. It seems to stare at her with those hollow eyes. The sides and bottom are smooth, no hard edges with any arms or legs. She holds it to her chest. "I'll be back soon." She tells it, then she restores it with its mates, closing the pouch and burying it under her socks.

By the time Talia's back in the dining room, Scotty looks a lot better.

"So about those weird little statues," Scotty says as she takes a piece of apple from a plate of hummus, fruit and bread on the table.

"Eat more. You probably have low blood sugar, too." Aunt Abby slides the plate closer to Scotty.

Scotty takes a piece of bread then opens her hand out to Talia. "Let's have a look at them again."

Talia shakes her head. "Let's wait. I'm all jacked up. I'm going on a bike ride. We can look at them tonight."

She tucks her arms through her backpack and sits on the chair by the door to put her sandals on. "I'll take one of the villa bikes." She kisses Aunt Abby's cheek and hugs Scotty's head, who still sits at the table.

Scotty winces at the squeeze on her forehead. "Have a good ride, Nugget."

The bikes are leaning on the side of the garden wall. Talia pulls one out and throws a leg over the seat. She pedals toward the beach across the road, the bike wheels making dust on the dry dirt. She feels like her body is a coiled wire and wants to bounce loose with such furious speed that she begins to peddle without any idea of where she's going to go. She pants with the effort, enjoying the sting in her lungs, the bitter saliva rising in her mouth.

The colors and view from up here are breathtaking but her restlessness presses her on. She glides down the hill, making an arch around the corner of the street at the bottom.

She stops her bike at the neighborhood local Pastizzeria at the bottom of the hill. Talia discovered the first week they were here that she loves Maltese street food. Especially the diamond-shaped Pastizzi even more than the popular squared pizza, sausage rolls, and unique pies found in shops like this one. She loves the light, flaky crust of the phyllo pastry and the warm stuffing inside. Her mouth is watering at the heavenly aroma coming from the shop.

She leans her bike on the wall outside and heads in. She orders two pies, one with ricotta stuffing and the other with peas, which she brings out to the sidewalk in search of a table. There are often long lines at this shop, so she's lucky to find a seat. She can't resist biting into one of the pies before it cools. As the steam wafts out, she takes her time, tasting each bite. When she finishes, she can't help but lick her fingers clean, then wipes her mouth with a paper napkin, sips her last bit of her iced tea and carries her dirty plate inside.

She's just about to get on her bike and go back to the villa and take a nap when she notices that the little bookstore next door to the café is open.

It-Tempju Tal-Ktieb, has been closed since they arrived. When she first saw it, she looked up the name to mean The Book Temple in Maltese. She leans her bike on the side of the building and moves to the bookstore entrance.

A ratty dog lies across the open doorway, her white fur streaked with sand and dirt. She rolls on her back when Talia steps over her. Talia grins and leans down to rub its warm tummy. The dog's tail slaps the cool floor tiles. "Hey pup! Nice place for a nap."

When she looks up, a woman is smiling at her. "Rami."

Talia tilts her head to the side, raising one shoulder in question.

"Rami. My dog's name," The woman says. "She's Rami. I'm Cathleen. I see you're not from around here." Her accent is only slightly hinted with the Maltese inflection with a possible British tone. "America?"

"Yes. I'm Talia." She thinks the woman's eyes might be twinkling.

"Rami loves the American food. Pop Tarts and McDonalds." Cathleen enjoys a low chuckle. "I can see she likes you."

"I like her too! I'm from California."

"We went to San Francisco last year. Very nice."

"I'm from only a short distance to the Golden Gate Bridge. Did you see the bridge when you were there?"

"Yes. Very beautiful." Cathleen smiles and moves back behind a small desk. "Please take your time with the books." She sits down and resumes shuffling through some papers.

Talia moves to the shelves. Most of the books are in Maltese, while some are in Italian, Arabic and Greek. Fewer are in German and French. Talia searches and finds books in English scattered throughout the shelves. There seems no logic to the order.

Talia turns to Cathleen. "Can you please show me any books you have on the boats of Malta?"

Cathleen looks surprised. She moves behind a large bookcase toward the back. These shelves seem to be in some semblance of order. Most are on temples and the history of Malta.

"Anything along here." Cathleen points to a section of a long shelf that goes from one side to the other.

"Oh! So many on boats!" Talia can't hide her excitement.

"You like boats?" Cathleen's wavy dark hair slips off her shoulder in surprise.

Talia turns to face her, realizing she's almost a foot taller than the woman, but she feels smaller. Cathleen wipes her hands on her skirt, a full wrap of flowing orange and blue fabric. As she starts to pull books from the shelves, her many bracelets jingle.

"What kind of boat would you like to read about?"

"I'm looking for anything on the old ships from centuries ago."

"I see." Talia smells incense on Cathleen's blouse she is so close. Talia steps backwards.

"Mum?" A resonant voice pitches right into the center of Talia's body. She swivels around to see a young man about her age has quietly appeared. Talia looks behind him and sees he's emerged from a back room behind

Cathleen's desk. The door is open enough to see an oversized brown leather chair in the middle of the room with a green yoga mat rolled next to a purple meditation pillow sitting on the floor in front of it. Talia can smell coffee from the pot she sees on an old dresser leaning in front of a wall of books.

As he walks toward them, Talia lets a quick breath in. Her knees feel weak. She's never had this kind of reaction to seeing a guy. The man steps closer to where she and Cathleen are tightly squeezed in the aisle between shelves.

The man puts his hand on his mother's shoulder, but his eyes are locked on Talia's, which she meets with deep curiosity. She has no desire to look away. Her body downshifts with a palpable drop, her jacked up energy from before, now melted. She takes him in like a warm drink on a cold night, quenching a craving thirst she only this moment realizes she feels.

His eyes are amber brown. Dark eyebrows accenting. His light brown skin seems to invite her touch. He's somehow familiar, like she intuitively knows how that skin would feel to touch. Smooth, erotic. Sweaty-sweet. She smells a peppery cologne, which flutters the tendrils in her nose, even making her mouth go moist. She senses how he would feel wrapped around all the freckled surfaces of her own body, bringing a burn to the surface. She notices a birthmark on the side of his chin, like a sideways crescent moon. The sight of it brings a wave of edgy, sensuous hope. She steadies herself, thinking her knees might buckle again, but not minding this time. Heated nectar could spill to her thighs if he even so much as seemed to move any closer to her.

"Mum. Are you harassing the tourists?"

Talia can't help but smile. The British accent darts right into her body, like an erupting chortle. She notices his light blue T-shirt and the pair of soft cotton sweat pants. She lowers her head, catching a glimpse of the tattoo on his forearm. Circles in circles with no beginning or end, giving her goosebumps. His feet are lazy in a pair of red flip-flops. As she lifts her head, her eyes pause at the shape of his soft lips, then at the two sets of gold hoops in each ear.

Slow to break the trance, Talia notices Cathleen who holds a book to her chest trying not to seem amused. "My son." She pats his arm. "Niko, this is Talia from the Golden Gate Bridge."

Talia's elbow catches a loose book on the shelf and knocks it to the ground. She bends to reach for it but Niko beats her to it. When she takes it from him, her hands are trembling.

"Mum," Niko's eyes remain locked with Talia's. "Maybe we should give Talia from the Golden Gate Bridge a little space?" His smile spreads into his eyes. "We seem to have backed her into a mighty corner."

Cathleen moves off to return to her desk. "Take your time Talia. My son can help." Her voice fades.

Talia waves the book at him. "I don't know where it goes?"

"Bit of a muddle here at the Book Temple."

"It is a sort of book temple isn't it?" Talia says.

"Because it's in ruins, yes," Niko laughs. He takes the book from Talia and slides it next to a random book. "Mum'll dig it out someday and then rejoice at finding buried treasure." He lowers his voice out of Cathleen's earshot. "She has absolutely no idea where anything is."

"She led me here. These boat books seem in order." She runs her hand across each spine with her fingertips.

Niko follows with his own. "Not a lot of people come back here."

"I'm looking for a book on boats from Malta from long ago. Hopefully written in English." Talia tilts her head to read the sideway spines.

"You're interested in boats of Malta?" Niko pulls one out and puts it back. "That one's in Pharsi."

"I've been making miniature Maltese boats in glass bottles since I was a girl." She stops herself, surprised that she exposed herself so suddenly without thinking.

She sees a flicker in the corner of Niko's eyes.

"Everything okay?" Niko asks.

Talia forces herself to return her gaze to the bookshelf. "I'm fine. I just don't ever tell that to anyone." She keeps her eyes on the books, glad Niko doesn't ask more.

They move in a rhythm down the line of shelves.

"Here." Niko pulls one out. "It's in English. Boats of Malta." He hands it to her quickly. But not so fast that Talia doesn't see his hand tremble like hers. She smiles at him.

Noticing, Niko draws his hands into fists, rubbing them together. "Guess I'll skip that second cup of coffee."

"Of course." Talia smiles again.

Niko leads her out of the bookshelf aisle.

"I'll take this one." She holds the book out to Cathleen.

"Mum. Paghero per questo," Niko says to Cathleen.

"That's okay. I'll pay for it myself." Talia pulls off her backpack.

"You speak Italian?" Niko asks.

"Better than Maltese for sure." Talia confesses. "I'm glad everyone here seems to speak at least three languages. But Italian's easy for me since my grandparents are from Sicily. My father and his twin sister, my Aunt, are fluent. I was raised hearing Italian in my family to know enough to get by."

"Then you know he's buying this book for you." Cathleen winks at her.

"Mother, behave."

Talia feels her cheeks turn red. "Thanks. But I'll get this." She opens her wallet. "Quanto?"

"Sette euro, grazie," Cathleen says, as Talia counts seven bills.

As he leads Talia over Rami in the doorway, Niko takes her elbow.

"I hope you'll let me buy you a book another time?"

They walk to her leaning bike. Talia puts the book into the basket then grabs the two handlebars with her long fingers.

"Or a cup of coffee, sometime?"

"I'd like that." Her tone seems to pitch from a rising well.

"Where are you staying?" Niko stands on the low curb of the street.

"We're in a villa on Vjal Mezzodi."

"South Avenue isn't far." Niko doesn't move.

"No, not so far."

"Can I walk with you?" Niko's eyes shine.

Talia's smile is a slow simmer. "I'd like that more."

"I'll just get my phone from the flat." He looks at her as if she might disappear.

Talia tilts her chin upwards to him. Her golden hair spills over her cheek. "I'll wait."

***

Abigail's eyes wander over the open page of a well-thumbed paperback novel. It must be from previous renters as she got it from a row of random, tired-looking books on a shelf in the living room. She read the same sentence moments ago. She glances over the top of the book at Scotty, who lays prone with a washcloth over her face on the couch next to her, her legs across Abigail's lap.

Abigail wonders if the washcloth is still cold on Scotty's eyes and forehead. Maybe it got warm from resting there, taking in body heat. Abigail starts to reach over to check, then changes her mind. She draws her fingers tighter around the book.

A page drifts open past her grip, poised in a slice of mid-turn, losing Abigail's place. The current of energy from Scotty's legs into Abigail's thighs feel like her own blood pumping. She should get up and stomp her feet on the woven throw rug over the living room ceramic pavers. But she doesn't.

With Scotty's face covered with the washcloth, Abigail takes a hushed second to steal another glance at her friend, feeling drawn to reach over, this time to slip the washcloth off and feel Scotty's cheek with the back of her hand. She imagines her fingers moving through Scotty's black hair stopping at the bleached tips to play them along her knuckles.

Instead, Abigail spreads her palms across the book's wordy page. She closes it loudly.

"You mad at your book?" Scotty says muffled under the washcloth. She lifts up an edge and squints at Abigail.

Abigail lets a list of topics she'd rather not mention fly through her mind at high speed. She settles on an easy chat. "I'm restless. Today was weird. With the statues and all. And then Talia just bolts out of here like a runaway train."

"Don't worry, Doc. She's just being a kid."

"Says the expert parent."

"Touché." Scotty folds the washcloth corner back down.

"Sorry. I'm grumpy." Abigail opens her book again.

Scotty folds her arms across her chest. "I noticed."

Abigail thwacks the book closed again.

"What the fuck is going on with you? I'm the one who's infirm here." Scotty's mouth is moving the washcloth up and down.

"I know. Sorry. You up for dinner out tonight? Or Talia and I can get something to go? I'm not up for cooking."

"Sure. When Talia gets back."

"I think she's back now."

Scotty's feet slip off Abigail's lap onto the cushions as she gets to catch a peek at her niece.

"I hear her talking." Abigail shuffles to the window.

Scotty hauls herself up to join her. "Who's she talking to?"

Abigail sees the white cotton sun dress contouring Talia's body in a light breeze as she walks her bike on the flat part of the road after the rise up the hill. But she's not alone. "A person!"

"She's fucking a Malta boy!"

Abigail slaps Scotty's arm. "Shhh. They're coming in!"
They both swerve around to face the front door, frozen in place.
"Scotty? Aunt Abby? What's wrong?"
Abigail moves toward her niece, "Sorry honey! Scotty and I were...."
"Spying." Scotty finishes.
Abigail winces as she sees Talia's face go bright red. The young man next to her gives Abigail a wry smile.
"Niko, here's my... unique family." Talia seems to be trying to hold it together. Her tone is almost formal. She leads him into the room. "My Aunt Abby."
"Piacere di conoscerti," Niko presses his palm to hers. It's warm in Abigail's hand.
"Pleased to meet you, too. It's nice to hear Italian!"
"And this is Scotty." Talia presents her. Abigail's relieved to see that Niko doesn't notice Talia's warning stare aimed at Scotty.
Scotty offers the hand without the wet washcloth.
"Whoa!" Niko sputters in recognition. He takes Scotty's hand with one then both of his. "I'm a fan." He turns to Talia, his accent a jovial jab. "How have you kept this secret from me in all the time I've known you?"
Talia laughs. "As you can see, we need more time than a walk up the hill to explain Scotty. Or any of this, actually." She waves her hand, an easy white flag of surrender.
Talia reaches past Niko and gives Scotty a peck on her cheek. "I'm glad you're feeling more yourself. Thank you for embarrassing me only once in the last two minutes."
"No problem, Nugget." Scotty snuggles Talia into her ribs with one arm.
"Niko, do you want something to drink?" Talia starts toward the kitchen.
"Hold on a minute." Scotty reaches her arm out to Niko. "Do you know anyone with a guitar?"
"My Uncle Marcello has an acoustic."
"That can work." Scotty releases Niko's arm and sits down again, her fingertips tight on her forehead. "Can I borrow it?"
Niko pulls out his phone from his back pocket. After a few chirps, he looks up. "I'll get it tomorrow."
"Great. Come at dinner time." Scotty throws a look at Abigail. "Doc's cooking. Aren't you?"

"Apparently." Abigail beams. It will feel good to have company.

"Niko, let's see if there's something I can give you to drink." Talia starts toward the kitchen again. She aims a warning glance at them over her shoulder.

"I'll only stay a bit." Niko bows to Abigail and Scotty. "I have to close up shop for mum." He follows Talia into the kitchen.

Abigail follows them. Scotty follows her.

"Hello? Privacy?" Talia whips her head around to them as she and Niko keep walking.

"I'll make us some tea!" Abigail starts toward the cabinet.

"It's okay, Aunt Abby."

"Of course." She sees her niece's red cheeks again. "Scotty, don't we have something we have to do? Outside?"

Scotty gives her a blank look.

"On the patio?"

"Have you become a smoker?" Scotty crosses her arms.

Abigail pushes Scotty in front of her in a quick exit.

***

As the sun begins to set, Niko leaves the villa to start walking back down the hill to the bookstore, but changes his mind. He stops and kicks off his flip-flops, chucking them upwards into his thumbs. He crosses the road down the little path to the water's edge. The Black Wing Stilts stab their long beaks on the water's edge, in stuttering picks into the deep sand. They share their evening hunt with the sheen of the brilliant green and orange Kingfishers along the water. A flock of Pelicans sweep past, low on the waves. Their prehistoric wisdom seems as old as the rocks beyond them. Niko often wonders if his Maltese ancestors used to gaze at Pelicans the way he is now.

He sees a boat anchored a short distance off shore. Its unhurried shape is easy on the water, seeming to stop time. This western ridge of the island stretches in an easing yawn of eternal spread above this part of the calm, inviting sea.

He and his two older sisters used to love leaving the humid summer heat of London to be on this island with his grandparents. Before Nannu and Nanna died of course. He shifts his weight in the sand as memories come. Like when Nannu used to let him drive the family boat, fondly named *The Trusted One* in Maltese. When Niko was young he thought *Il Wiehed Fdat* was a huge ship, rather than the small, compact vessel it was. He loved when Nannu let Niko stand on his tiptoes to grip the knobby tiller to steer. Those long, end-of-the-day rides after swimming and floating on the rafts they strung off the boat rails were days of heaven. He loved being on the water, lingering out on the sea as the sun set in a fury of orange and pink. Bringing fresh Amberjack, Snapper or Dorado home for Nanna to cook on the coals in the fire pit in their garden, sharing the outdoors with an army of mosquitoes. Niko can smell the same heat of the day turning to the cool, blue Malta evening now as he remembers. The nighttime boat rides were the most cherished of all memories. Nannu would drink his grappa with one hand on the wheel and float through the moonlit waters. They even anchored right here, across the very road he just walked across from the villa. It was always hard to leave them to go back to London at the end of the summers.

His eyes mist into half seeing, half sensing. The sea seems to come up to him, spreading around his feet like a wandering song. But his mind snaps back to the last two hours. How it all seemed to start with seeing the new spirit in his flat, different from other visitors he and Mum have noticed over the years. If he tells her, she'll do her thing, burning herbs and spraying her essential oils. But as he remembers how he felt with this one, so at ease, he realizes he won't tell Mum this time.

He thinks about how random it was that he woke up to seeing the shimmering body high in the corner. The headdress threw him, but once he got past that it was like he was looking at someone he knew. He felt unusually comfortable just continuing his yoga. As if the fellow was an old friend.

But everything tilted sideways after that when he came out of the flat and saw Talia. Like it was all supposed to happen. It shouldn't have surprised him, given what came to him in his meditation.

Niko shakes his head.

Nothing about this is normal. Now he's standing at the water on an island where he's spent most of his childhood, yet feeling like he's somewhere he's never been before.

His mind goes warp speed back to the bookstore and the moment he laid eyes on Talia. She was the only one in the store. When he heard Mum talking, he went out, feeling like he had to. Her voice. The cadence. It seemed to pull him out of his flat. When he saw her, he almost fell over.

It was a weird flood of some kind of deja-vu.

His heart was pounding. It was everything he could manage to keep his face blank.

He conjures her image now, remembering how he scanned her body, her face—all of her—as if dialing into a memory rather than a first impression.

Her shiny golden hair, spilling past her face, her freckled cheeks he wanted to brush with his lips. Her deep brown eyes with those long lashes, not even a stitch of makeup needed to accent. Her strong body, tall, with long legs like his. Her curving shape just right in the places where he knows his hands want to go. Her speckled skin. That look of secrecy on her face. Like she thinks she's hiding something, but clearly isn't. How she blushed. How her hands shook. Just like his. But the thing that surprised him the most was how she seemed to belong with him. His heart's been fluttering since that moment.

He pulls his phone from his pocket, turning it over and over in his hands. No. Not yet. Too soon.

He slips the phone back in his pocket and turns back up the hill to the dirt road. He drops his flip-flops on the pavement, rubs the undersides of his feet on his sweatpants, pops his toes around the thick rubber coil, then starts the walk down the hill to the store.

As he invokes Talia's image again, the hair stands up on the back of his neck.

He's almost certain the specter in the headdress is accompanying him down the hill.

***

Even though it's after hours when Niko gets to the bookstore, Mum's still inside. She's sweeping the floor, which, given the ever-present layers of sand and dust, Niko suspects she never does. He's wondering why she's lingering.

"Going home soon?" Niko sits and rolls the squeaky desk chair backwards to make room for his long legs.

"Pretty soon. I was waiting for you." Cathleen pulls on her cardigan.

"All good, Mum." His smile is meant to keep her from a line of questioning he knows is coming.

"How's Talia from the Golden Gate Bridge?"

"Now, now Mum. You know better."

"Very well then." She zips her lips with easy fingers, bracelets jangling.

A quiet moment settles between them. She slides her hip on the desk. Niko leans back and stretches his arms behind his head. Cathleen reaches over to her desk and hands Niko a book. Its heavy weight feels good.

"Boats from Ancient Malta." He notes the title.

"For Talia. I found it after you both left."

"Thanks, Mum."

She opens her arms for a hug. "You can come for dinner? Dad made Timpana."

"Hard to resist my favorite." The chair protests under him as Niko gets up to hug her. "Even if the chef is a Brit."

She shoves his knee with a playful swat. "You tease, but he's a good cook."

"Hard to botch up macaroni pie, Mum."

"He's taught himself well."

"Only because you're Maltese and can't tolerate tasteless food."

"You'll come?"

"I'm knackered. Better to stay here then go and come back round after."

"Of course." Cathleen collects her keys off the desk. "Rami stays?"

"She's good company."

Cathleen kisses Niko's forehead. "Holm ħelu, ibni."

"Sweet dreams to you too, Mum."

He closes the door behind her and locks it. He flips through the boat book as he stands over his Mum's pile of books and papers, until his eyes wander to another messy pile on her desk. His eyes catch the corner of a book cover he's never seen. Maybe Mum just ordered it. He slowly moves the papers that are partially hiding the photo on the cover, when his heart suddenly pitches to high speed.

His legs move him to the desk chair, where he drops with a thud. He holds the book in his lap, his hands resting on the glossy cover. He doesn't move. Not even when he thinks he feels a hand on his shoulder. Not even when the last of the sun sets, blinking to a dimming light on the scraped and dented bookstore floor.

✳✳✳

Talia's stomach is a rumbling gurgle. She only had two pieces of toast and a bite of apple since this morning. Aunt Abby went to the market this afternoon and picked up fresh rockfish for the Aljotta she's making for dinner. She said the favorite Maltese fish soup is a lot like Nona Gina's Bouillabaisse recipe but without the shellfish. The mint and lemon will complete it with the right Mediterranean flare. The kitchen smells like a four-star restaurant.

Talia lifts the pot's lid. Her skin moistens in the whisk of fragrant steam. The artful display of colors brings on another belly growl. When she turns toward the sink window, her eye catches Niko coming up the hill on his white motor scooter.

She watches him park next to her bike, his leg sliding off the padded seat in easy balance. A soft, black guitar case is slung over his shoulder. His dark hair is still pulled back, accenting the shape of his face, his steady eyes and full lips. His body moves like liquid mercury to the front door. His tight jeans show off his long legs, his yellow T-shirt a bright fill above his waist. He slips his feet out of the flip-flops and leaves them in a carefully arranged pair on the steps.

Talia slows her jog to a methodical stroll to the door. Pausing her grasp of the doorknob, she waits for his knock before she opens it.

She steps aside to let him pass. She smells soap and that peppery cologne.

Niko lowers his head as he steps into the foyer, even though his height clears the high ceiling by several meters. He stands, regarding her without hurry, making every nerve stand on delicious edge.

His slow smile is a mischievous stretch. He holds up the guitar.

"I'll get Scotty," Talia says.

Scotty appears from the hallway. "I'm right here."

Talia can't help a secret smile at Scotty's face. She looks like she's reaching for a lover.

"Man, Niko." Scotty folds her fingers around the strap of the neoprene guitar case, her other hand cupping the curve of the bottom as if the guitar inside could break. "You really pulled through for me."

As Scotty turns to go, Talia sees a worried look cross Niko's face.

"Everything okay?" Talia asks.

"Brilliant."

He seems distracted. His eyes follow Scotty down the hall. Then he seems to shake it off. Talia feels his eyes back on her.

"Are you hungry?"

Niko still stands in the foyer. He takes her hand, bringing her fingertips to his lips.

"Ravenous."

***

The sun is just beginning to set on the sweep of the sea across the street. A flicker of dimming sunlight makes a lacy curtain over the patio in the villa's front garden. Talia lights a match to the candle on the round table as Aunt Abby brings the Aljotta out. She sets the steaming pot in the middle, then sets a bowl of rice beside it. Talia pulls out her chair next to Niko and sits, her knee brushing his. They flash a smile at each other. The coo of the doves settling in for the night blends with the sound of the distant waves. Talia can't remember the last time she felt this peaceful.

Aunt Abby's just about to sit down. "I forgot the Ftira bread. It's warming in the oven. Talia, can you please fill everyone's bowls with the rice and soup? I'll be right back."

"Are your eyes better now, Scotty?" Talia asks, passing her a bowl.

"Still just the headache now, Nugget." Scotty takes the bowl, giving Talia a look to say no more in front of Niko about her recent affliction.

Aunt Abby returns with an overflowing plate of the sliced warmed Maltese bread, enough for a family of ten. "Can't even think of having soup without bread to soak it up."

"This looks so good, Aunt Abby!" Talia takes a piece of bread from the plate Aunt Abby passes.

"Bon appetite!" Aunt Abby barely gets the words out before Talia digs in. The succulent broth and the fresh herbs burst with the first taste.

"Niko, did you grow up in Malta?" Aunt Abby asks.

Niko shakes his head. "I grew up in London with my family. But my grandparents are from here. They owned the bookstore down the hill that Mum inherited. I spent most summers here with my two sisters, though. My Pop's British, but Mum's Maltese and grew up here."

"Do you and your parents live here full time now?" Aunt Abby passes the plate of bread around to eager hands.

"I'm only here since I graduated Uni in London last spring. Mum and Pop moved here but Pop still goes back to London some. Mum is quite content to be back in her homeland."

"Do you live in the bookstore?" Talia's voice has gone low, remembering the moment she peeked into the room he came out from.

"For now." He smiles at her. "Mum likes someone there at night."

Scotty raises her water glass. "To Uncle Marcello."

Niko raises his glass back to Scotty. "He was well chuffed when he heard the guitar was for the likes of you."

Scotty looks down. "I stopped playing. So."

Niko holds a piece of soaked bread mid-air. "Come again?"

Talia watches Scotty's jiggy knee.

"What I mean is. I didn't want to play. Until now. So." Her hands are fast anchors pushing her up. "Mind if I play a tune?" Before she can respond to the hoots of excitement around the table, Scotty vanishes.

"She took a break from playing for a while," Talia explains to Niko.

"Maybe that's over now," Aunt Abby's adds, "thanks to your uncle." She raises her water glass to Niko.

Talia reaches over for another helping of soup, when she sees Scotty come out from the villa with the neck of the guitar in one hand and a book in the other. Talia slowly puts her plate down, seeing the look on Scotty's face.

"What the fuck is this?" Scotty waves the book at them. "Why was this in the guitar case?"

She chucks the book on the table. It slides down in a crooked slam, the cover revealed.

Talia feels like her heart stops.

Aunt Abby jumps up, shoving her chair backwards almost tipping it over. "Niko! Did you put that book in your uncle's guitar case?"

"Wait!" Talia puts her hand on Niko's shoulder. "He can't have known."

"Known what?" Niko's confusion is clear.

"About those statues!" Scotty points at the book's cover.

The nine limestone statues are set in a symmetrical arrangement, looking like a group of armless, legless troubadours. Their odd shapes are accentuated by a lacquered black background. They feel alive, emerging from a dark hole. The title "The Xagħra Stone Circle Statues" is in white lettering on the top of the cover. Even that seems to vibrate.

Niko slowly picks up the book. He stares at it for a long time.

Scotty lets her body drop into her chair. "I'm not mad. None of us are mad."

"What'd you do when you're really pissed off?"

Scotty seems to reset herself. "We're just shocked."

"There's an explanation." Niko lifts the book up as if about to do a lecture. He sighs.

"It was meant to be a gift to Talia." He slides the book cautiously in front of her. "I didn't get a chance. The book went off with the guitar case when I handed it to Scotty. I had hopes of nicking it back later." Niko swallows. "I didn't mean the book to cause such a row. Though I can't say why it is. But I swear I didn't mean it to."

"There's more." Scotty's knee is back to jigging.

Talia feels a wave of nausea. "Don't. Please, Scotty?"

"The man needs to know." Her knee's a drill now.

"Know what?" Niko looks around at each of them, clearly alarmed.

Abigail puts her hand on Scotty's arm. "Give it a second, okay?"

"If you say so, Doc." Scotty flips the guitar onto her knee. She starts to tune it. The notes reaching to find harmony seem to reflect the same dissonant vibe around the table.

"Niko. We're here, in Malta, for a kind of expedition." Aunt Abby uses her Doctor-voice over the sound.

"I'll wager it has to do with these statues." Niko throws his chin at the book.

"It's a long story." Scotty finally lands on tuned notes and begins to strum in a soothing background lull.

Talia feels a subtle energy around her like she's in a warm spot in an otherwise cool stream of water. It seems to guide her to her bedroom. She knows what she's going to do, even though it seems like a crazy choice. She watches her hands open her dresser drawer, like they don't belong to her. She reaches for the leather pouch. She glides back to the patio. Once there, she sees sorrow in Niko's eyes. She knows the risk she's taking. She wonders if he knows what's at stake, too.

"Niko, I'm going to tell you something. It may be that you'll run out of the villa. I want you to stay. More than you could really know. But you might not."

To her disbelief, Niko seems to relax. "I need to tell you something."

Talia holds up her hand. "Not yet. Listen to me first, okay?"

"I really need to tell you this."

"It has to wait." Talia isn't surprised at her conviction. The leather pouch seems to throb in her hands. Scotty's calm now. Her hands are feathers on the strings, the sound a sedative.

"I've got your back, Nugget." She casts her eyes downward, still strumming.

"Aunt Abby?" Talia waits for her Aunt's response before she goes on.

"Tell him." She's been standing up until now and seems grateful to finally sit down next to Scotty.

Talia opens the pouch and takes out each statue, one by one. They sit in a row on the table, illuminated by the candle flickering in the lantern. The effect is haunting. They look alive.

In spite of that, Talia feels clear. The energy she felt moving her to her bedroom is a current through her now. The force of it is palpable. Familiar. *My child, you are coming home.*

She turns to Niko. "I've been dreaming of a Priestess and a Priest from long ago. These dreams have been coming since I was younger. The Priestess is called Anya of Mahet. We believe she was alive here in Malta in ancient times." She glances at Scotty, who's stopped her strumming.

"Scotty and my Aunt Abby have had visions and dreams of her, too. Sometimes they're even the same dreams. It's why we came here."

"Blimey, Talia! You have to listen to me." Niko's urgency causes Talia to pause.

She sits down.

He reaches to one of the statues on the table. He lifts it up and cups it in his two hands, rolling it gently. He closes his eyes. Talia's skin goes cold. The statue he holds is the one the Priest gave to her in her dream. The one she was guided to bury. Niko opens his eyes.

"Did your Priest have a headdress on?" He seems to know what her answer will be.

Talia nods slowly, speechless.

"Did he tell you to bury this statue?"

Her skin goes from ice to fire, the blood rushing to the surface.

Niko holds it out to her. "He told me to bury it too. With you."

The candle in the lantern suddenly blows out.

***

Until now, Sondro has been aware of only floating close by the young man with the Mark of Birth on his chin. At times, Sondro has simply allowed himself to sleep near him. Yet, when he moved his weightless body quickly past the little flame on the table to extinguish it, he knew the time had come that he must stay alert.

He was already able to reach both the minds of the young man and the Golden Hair Woman. He was already able to bid them to bury the statue at the site of his shrouded body.

Yet whether they follow his guidance is uncertain. He senses fear in them.

This makes his vow to Anya uncertain.

He moves closer to the others at the circular table in the garden below. The Fire Eye Woman. She of the Wise Hands. They stand in alarm in the dark night. Their chairs are askew behind them, pushed to fall when Sondro stopped the flame's light.

None here see him.

Sondro senses a warning.

Even with his efforts this far, they still do not know their part in Anya's Prophecy. They still do not know why they must heed to his call to bury the statue. If he is not thorough now, all could be lost.

He must stay close.

The Golden Hair Woman suddenly flees. She runs from the garden, across the road toward the vast sea.

Child, wait. He tries to send the command to her mind. She is in too much haste to know his call. He floats swiftly above her, following.

The young man runs behind her, down the path toward the sea. Sondro hears him call her name. *Talia.*

When the young man catches up to her, Sondro sees him take her elbow.

She pleads with him. *Niko.* Tells him she does not understand.

He who is called Niko speaks softly to her.

Sondro watches him lead her to a flat stone, close to the water's edge. The one called Talia sits.

Sondro moves closer, observing.

Niko stands flustered. He speaks in quick tongue. He paces. He pulls his hair out of the knot in frustration, casting the band that ties it aside. His long hair spills in a cascade around his shoulders. He scratches his head in brisk and flustered flicks.

Talia beckons him to sit beside her. She reaches to him, bringing her fingers through his hair.

Niko leans into her, their foreheads touching. Sondro sees this calms them both.

She wraps her arms around Niko's neck.

Sondro watches their lips meet in a yearning kiss.

Sondro sees a boat moored not far from the shore. He moves to it.

From there he can see the one called Talia. The one called Niko. They are in an embrace on the flat rock.

When they look to the boat at sea, they point at him.

When they see Sondro floating above the sails, he is glad.

His heart longs to have the voice he once did. To bring a low note to bless their sacred union.

To gift them with his toning prayer. To praise them for understanding his message.

He watches them glimmer in the light of the half-born moon.

When this moon is full-born, Sondro knows they will bury the statue. Then his time here will be done.

∗∗∗

Thinking about the statues that still lay on the table half lit by the moon, Abigail's aware that she feels like stone too. After what just happened, she sat back down. She feels so dense she can't even get up from the patio chair. The wooden slats make creases in her thighs. She barely feels it. Now she's alone.

Talia ran off. Niko followed her. Scotty disappeared with the guitar.

Abigail scans the remnants of the meal she spent all day preparing. The Aljotti is cold. The bread still in a tipping pile. The bowls need clearing. The unlit candle seems to stare at her.

The statues are still lined up like a row of mini-soldiers. They look so alive they could get up and march in a drill if they had legs.

She shudders.

She'll leave them right where they are for Talia.

She longs to run across the street to her favorite spot on the beach. But if she goes now, she risks running into Talia and Niko having their little chat. Or fight. Or whatever.

That spot on the beach has been a good reset for her while here. She usually goes in the early mornings alone to watch the sunrise. Or in the afternoons to sketch portraits of the rocks, the beach critters and boats in the distance.

Right now she'd like to feel the soothing contouring stones that fit her spine and comfortably support her lower back. Like a pair of warm hands on her. She likes to sit on the sand leaning into the power of the thousand-year-old rocks and gaze with half-closed eyes over the majesty of the sea. That's the place she learned to allow her thoughts to settle while here in Malta. For her breath to ease. For her scattered, anxious mind to relax. At least attempt at the practice to let go of her need for logic, where apparently there isn't any!

Like Niko knowing to get that book for Talia.

She feels the niggling anxiety again. She wonders what emotion is really buried under it. Tension. For sure. And under that? Her jaw is clenched. She's afraid.

They were all scared when Scotty found that book in the guitar case. Scared of the wild confusion. Of Niko's confession. Scared at that damn candle going out like someone snuffed it.

Her mind sees Scotty's face throwing the book on the table. Those flashing eyes, how they always look so....

Let's not think of Scotty now!

Abigail forces one of her deep breaths into her lungs as she pushes away the image of Scotty's eyes. So intense. Such a pull. Then there's her lips around a cigarette. Her hands on the guitar. The memory of that voice, making Abigail's skin always feel like it's melting. If Scotty's aware of how Abigail feels, she hasn't shown it one bit. At least that's reassuring. That's the last thing Abigail wants. All of this is adding to a crowded twist of emotions she doesn't like feeling.

She stands up in a forced push off the chair.

She's dizzy from getting up so fast. A breath starts as a tickle in her nose. It opens into her throat, forcing air through her lungs in a shuddering upward wobble. The tight skin around her ribs protests the pushing, yet yields anyway. The breath whooshes through her mouth. It's more like an act of courage than a freeing release! Bravery to let it flow. *Trust* the breath seems to say. *The opposite of fear.* She's grateful her legs are now unglued from the chair.

She thrusts herself into action. She stacks the dirty bowls in a pile, silverware clanking to the top in a messy collection. She stops, hands paused. Why is she always looking for crap to get busy with and always distracting herself from this relaxed self who she's beginning to actually like?

She conjures up the memory of that candle going out.

This shit is real, Doc. She can almost hear Scotty's voice in her head.

Back to Scotty again. Abigail groans.

She takes the precarious stack of bowls and silverware into the kitchen.

***

Abigail's finished cleaning up from dinner and about to turn in for the night when she hears Talia and Niko's low voices in front of the villa. She looks out the kitchen window and sees Niko getting ready to start his scooter. She hurries to the front door to find Niko straddling the baseboard and Talia's already on the seat, her hands on Niko's waist.

"You guys leaving?" Abigail tries to pitch her mother-hen voice low. She hears Scotty come out the front door and step up behind her.

"You guys make up?" Scotty lights a cigarette, blowing the smoke away from Abigail.

"We weren't fighting, Scotty," Talia says with a little vinegar. "We were just scared I think."

"I know I was." Abigail crosses her arms. "That was intense."

"No more than normal these days." Scotty stubs out the rest of her cigarette.

"Talia, the statues are still on the patio table. Can you collect them?" Abigail asks.

Talia shrugs. "Sure. I'll leave them here in my room. Niko and I are going to his flat, so I'll be quick." She shoots Niko an apologetic look.

"A sleepover." Scotty rubs her hands together. "Momma and Poppa are so proud. Do you have condoms?"

"Jesus, Scotty!" Talia stops dead to glare at her, then runs into the house to get the statues, her voice a fading promise. "I'll hurry, so she won't say anything else, Niko!"

"I can handle it." Niko leans on the scooter seat, legs easy and crossed at the ankles, hands folded like he's waiting for a bus. "It's a fair question."

"That you do *not* have to answer." Abigail bumps Scotty with her hip. "Behave, please."

"Okay fine. But how in the fuck did you know to bring that book to Talia?"

"It's a bit of a long story." His face lights up when Talia comes back. She sits back down on the scooter's cushion. "I was meditating." Niko looks like he wants to say more.

"He sees spirits," Talia explains.

"And the one I saw when I meditated said that I should give the statue to Talia and that we should bury it. Actually," Niko rubs his chin, "it was more of a visual thing than words."

"But he hadn't met me yet," Talia adds, grinning.

Abigail feels like she's got cotton in her mouth. "How?! I mean, does any of this make sense?"

"I'd say normally no," Niko sighs. "But when I came out of my flat, Talia was standing right there with my Mum in the bookstore."

"And the 'he' that told you what to do was the Priest?" Abigail's beginning to shake.

"Definitely Talia's bloke with the headdress," Niko answers.

A crisp energy passes through them, and Abigail raises her arm to show them the hairs standing on end. "It's a strong presence, isn't it?"

Niko clears his throat. "It is. I've gotten some intel. I've been doing some research. The statues are replicas of the ones that were originally found in a burial site on Gozo. This site is mostly known as the Xagħra Hypogeum. Or the Brochtorff Circle. It's a Neolithic funerary complex, from about 3000-2400 BC. The caves collapsed sometime after then, maybe even as early as 2000. I have a sense there were earthquakes here a long while ago. Anyway, it's not clear what the statues were for. But I believe they could be considered some kind of protection for the dead."

"That's where we'll bury the statue," Talia announces. "Niko and I decided."

"I have a mate that works as a watchman there. We can go at night."

Abigail's about to protest but Scotty speaks up. "Good plan, Nugget. It's why we came here."

"But what about the temple from Talia's dream?" Abigail asks. "The Temple of the Arch? Is there such a place, Niko?"

Niko shakes his head.

"It's inside us," Talia says in a matter-of-fact tone.

"How?" Abigail is ready to explode with frustration. "How do you know that?"

Scotty lights up another cigarette. "Doc. Listen to your niece." She blows smoke. "There's no building called the Temple of the Arch. It's us. We are the temples of the arch. So when we bury that little guy, Anya of Mahet will open the doors between the worlds. Through us." Scotty takes a deep puff then throws the lit butt on the ground. Sweeps sand over it with her bare toes.

Niko turns and straddles the scooter, his eyes pouring such kindness that Abigail finds herself fighting back tears.

Scotty notices and touches Abigail's arm. "Let's let these two go, okay Doc?"

"Okay." Abigail's glad for Scotty's direction. "I'll make us brunch tomorrow when you come back."

"Deal." Talia's hands find Niko's waist once more.

"Buona notte, kiddos," Abigail's voice has calmed to a soft wish.

"Il-lejl it-tajjeb," Niko answers.

"Good night." Talia taps Niko's back before he starts the scooter. She gets off and hugs Abigail. "Get some rest, Aunt Abby. You seem fried. It will all be okay. I promise you. Swear on my life."

Abigail smells the sea air in Talia's hair. "Okay. Okay." She shivers as she watches them glide down the hill.

"Cold?" Scotty asks.

"No. I'm scared."

"Yup."

"I noticed you're not wincing in pain anymore." Abigail restrains herself from feeling Scotty's forehead for a temperature. "Is your head better?"

"It is." Scotty squeezes Abigail's shoulder, her hand lingering a moment longer than usual. For a moment, Abigail's breath catches.

"See you in the morning, Doc."

Abigail can't quite make out the look in those green fire eyes. She swears they're shining two beams of light right into her heart.

***

When Abigail wakes up suddenly she sees no clock reading 3:45 a.m. No curtains, bed covers, walls or familiar sights in her villa bedroom. The moment is so vivid she thinks she can't be dreaming. From a faraway place in her mind she knows this is real.

Her body lifts from the bed and glides toward a throbbing beat of drums. She hears a low humming, its yearning shared note intermittently joined by a toning bell.

As she attunes her ears, she realizes the drums accompany a huffing-out sound of women breathing together. The methodical swoosh of it pulls her closer. She sees that the sound comes from within an old stone kitchen, dated from very long ago. There's a fire going in the fireplace, the hearth made of flat, large stones. There's a low bed on the ground next to a window, with a cypress tree just outside. A table is pushed to the wall, next to a door that opens out. She can see the sea's easy lapping on the shore not far away. She hears the bleating sound of goats meandering outside, their bells tingling.

A woman comes into view in the middle of the kitchen. She's squatting low to the ground, her knees bent to her sides. Abigail's not surprised to see the blue-black eyes of Anya of Mahet. Her long black hair is pulled in a knot, with loose strands sticking to her sweaty brow and neck. She clutches the back of a wooden chair to allow her lowered body to anchor. It takes only a short moment for Abigail to realize Anya is surrounded by a circle of women who are the source of the swooshing breath she hears. They kneel with their arms linked, woven together in a semi-circle around Anya. As they inhale, their bodies tilt one way. As they exhale, their bodies move as a unit in the other direction. The exhale is with powerful purpose and intent. Anya's pregnant belly bulges and glistens by the light of the fire from the hearth. Her engorged breasts seem ready to burst. Her golden skin is slathered with oils. No robe covers her that would encumber her birthing body.

Abigail feels a fluttering in her skull, then an image appears as if she's being shown a movie of Abigail walking to Anya and placing her hands on the crown of her head.

Abigail moves to Anya without hesitation, looking right into the emptiness of the blue-black eyes. Yet within the center arcs lie lines of light aiming into Abigail's own pupils. She places her hands on top of Anya's head, surprised to feel such life force dive into her palms. As the cadence of Anya's voice fills Abigail's mind, tears can't help but well up. The voice is the long draw of a low cello.

She of the Wise Hands. I call you here.

With your sacred hands you Bless this birth as the Priestess you are.

Feel the temple that is you. Awaken to me within it.

Abigail wakes up in her bedroom. The open window curtains frame the quarter moon high in the night sky. The Milky Way holds it as a cup of brilliant possibility.

***

4:30 a.m. has always been a favorite hour of the night for Abigail. There's always an enchantment to the energy that is not yet early morning and no longer the middle of the night. When she's on the night shift at work, the whole hospital seems to fill up with mystery at this hour.

Now she stands next to the counter in the villa kitchen. The blanket she pulled from the bed is draped over her shoulders and arms. Her nighttime camisole and underwear peek out from under the sides.

The dream lingers. The sound of the cello voice.

The feel of Anya's life force in her hands.

Her own hands. They feel the same now as they did in the dream.

She sweeps the marble top of the counter amazed at the vibrational pulse she can feel in her palms. She sees the black surface, the sinewy white veins. Their quickened vibration is a bubble of energy, tickling her palms, like dew drops of essence. She runs her fingers over the curling lines. Feeling along the way. She's amazed at herself to intuitively ask the creases and lines to tell her how she can feel this kind of thing in a stone. But it's the same kind of thing that she feels when she's touching the belly of one of her expectant patients. Life within. She'd laugh out loud with glee if she didn't think it would echo in the stone villa and wake Scotty.

She slides her hands to the other side of the counter and opens the fridge, feeling her way. It, too, has vibration. She pulls out an apple. Her hands crackle with the energy of the fruit's surface. She puts it back. Her taste buds race as if she's already bitten into it. The bitter, sweet, succulent juice could be dripping from her tongue. She moves to the front door, leaving it open, and wanders across the quiet road to the beach. Her toes feel as if they're magnets. The soft grainy ground seems to pulse up into her feet as easily as the marble countertop found the heat in her palms. As she makes her way to her spot on the beach, her whole body erupts into electric, sensual crests of energy. They rise through her feet, as if they're open wands of sensation. Her spine ripples in ecstasy. The intense pleasure of it swallows between her legs. She drops to her knees. She rolls off her hips. The sand is cool. A skin-to-skin caress. This quickens and opens her as if to a lover underneath. Her nose and mouth fill with the salty texture of the sea air.

The water laps at the shore nearby. She has no desire to rise from the grooves she's shaped with her body into the sand. She gazes over the water's surface.

She touches her forehead. *What is happening inside here?*

After the dream her head feels as if it has no bounds within it. Her brain, once rigid and thumping into boxes of ideas and words, has no way to formulate such things. She tries, then can't. She sees she's functioning and moving around like she always does. But nothing is the same.

Her skull feels like it's full of warm water. No restrictions there. Like her brain is malleable and made of some kind of taffy. She knows she isn't made of taffy! She studied neuro-science in med school! But the inside of her head feels almost chewy.

This makes Abigail's forehead wrinkle as if just thinking about such things is not, in this moment, all that easy.

She isn't sure of anything right now. But she does know that nothing she ever studied talked about this kind of distinct awareness she's currently experiencing. She sees and knows things that have great purpose. Yet she can't seem to piece it all together. Yet there is bliss with this notion rather than intellectual hunger.

She feels her body again, watery and pulsing. The sand opens her once more to a rush of heat in her loins, her body becomes fire again. She can't contain the cresting.

What is going on here?

She hears the cello-voice of the dream. *You are remembering.*

Now as she leans back on the rocks of her special spot on the beach, she gazes up at the moon, pulling her blanket tightly around her.

This is the first time since they've been here that she's come to her spot on the beach at this magical hour. She's amazed how her back feels warmth in the stone at this time of night, when the air is crisp with damp wind. The ocean has a film of fog on it, shifting in random directions as the tide pushes and pulls at the vaporous substance. The sight gives the impression of a breathing sea.

Abigail closes her eyes, taking in the fresh salt air to fill her lungs.

She wishes she could have seen the face of that child. To hold the child of this Priestess. To bring the child to her mother's breast. To feel the women around her. The power among them. One mind. One soul. Helping the birth. She didn't want to leave any of them.

Even so, the short dream felt like more than a lifetime of purity. It fills her even now with more tender peace than she's ever allowed herself to feel.

With your sacred hands you Bless this birth as the Priestess you are. Feel the temple that is you.

She thinks back now to when she was younger. That first time she saw that face. That she even forgot about until recently. Those blue-black eyes. That hair—that Priestess—in the church confessional. She was nursing a baby then.

Abigail knows with certainty that the baby she saw in her vision then is the same baby in the dream she just had.

She startles. The sound of a footfall on a cracking branch comes like a bark through the cavernous night.

She pulls the blankets with fists and stands up, her heart racing.

"Hi, Doc."

"For Christ's sake, Scotty! You scared the living shit out of me." Abigail drops to her knees.

"I tried to be un-scary."

"It's 4:30 a.m. I mean, really? How would this not scare me?"

"Relax, Doc. It's over now. Here." Scotty hands her a hot cup of green tea. "Truce?"

"You are full of surprises, my friend." Abigail takes the tea, her hands feeling the cup sing into her palms.

She looks up at Scotty standing with the dark night behind her. "You must be cold in just your shorts and T-shirt." Abigail offers to share the blanket with a raised arm holding one corner. "Get in here."

Scotty slides down next to Abigail, who tucks the other corner of the blanket under her arm to seal them in. Scotty's leg is ice against Abigail's thigh.

"You're shivering."

"You're warming me up, Doc,"

Abigail sips the tea, feeling the warm liquid roll nicely down her throat. "Thanks for this." She passes the cup to Scotty.

"Don't mind if I do." Scotty blows on it, then sips. "Tastes like hot toilet water." She passes it back, smiling. "So, what brings you out at this hour? Couldn't sleep?"

"I should ask the same of you." She nudges Scotty's shoulder with hers.

"I was awake. I heard you come out."

Abigail's body begins to sway. "I dreamt of her."

Scotty is quiet, listening.

"It was," Abigail turns to Scotty, searching those green eyes for the words. "Beautiful."

Scotty still says nothing.

"I think I understand this more."

"I think I do, too. Look at me, Doc."

Abigail returns her gaze to those eyes.

"I see light." Scotty keeps them on Abigail's face. "When I look at you, I see lines of light. Colors shooting off of you. You're surrounded by pink and gold and," she squints, "shine."

Abigail isn't surprised. "What happened to your headache?"

"Gone."

"Your momentary blindness?"

"Gone. Just this now."

Abigail thinks before this dream tonight she'd want a slit lamp to inspect Scotty's pupils. Yet there's nothing but trust in her heart. She sees light shining from the greenest moment inside the deep fire-lit centers. Abigail feels almost lifted into them.

"I see you." Scotty says simply. She leans over, setting their lips together. An electric pulse spreads through Abigail as the kiss lingers, overriding her surprise. She lets her lips answer, softening, easing into the supple shape of Scotty's skin on hers. When she finally can pull away, she can only speak a notch above a prayer.

"You are a terrible tease."

"I'm not teasing."

Abigail looks at her friend. "Why now? You must know I have been pushing these feelings aside since we got here."

"I do."

Abigail's voice drops to a sotto voce, muted and almost inaudible. "I thought you only liked guys. Like that Italian dude in the hotel in Germany."

"This is not that."

"What is it then, Scotty?"

"Don't think, Doc." Scotty kisses her again. Abigail lowers her tea to the sand, lips still meeting in wonder. She pulls Scotty into her, tongue to tongue, reaching, softly finding.

Abigail's heart is thumping. Scotty slowly stops the kiss.

"Something happened for you tonight. With the statues. And your dream I assume." Scotty slips a lock of hair behind Abigail's ear, brushing her cheekbones. Her chin. "Light is still flickering off your skin."

"Clearly something happened for you, too."

"When the candle blew out at the table, all I saw was light. Everywhere.

My headache was gone. I went to my room. I sat there on the bed for like an hour after that, just looking at everything. Fuck. There was no way I could sleep."

She puts her chin on her knees, her arms hugging her legs under the blanket. "Now this."

"But you haven't…. well, I mean… you say you know I've had feelings for you. I didn't know you had feelings for me."

Scotty laughs. "Sister, I haven't had a real feeling in about three decades. But I know what this feels like." Scotty takes her arms slowly out from under the blanket and reaches for Abigail. She pulls her forward, sliding her hands up and down Abigail's back.

"I want you, Doc. I want to taste you. Sing into your skin. Watch the light explode. Take us both home. Priestess to Priestess."

Abigail feels the velvet of Scotty's voice spill into the suspended night, lifting the heavy weight off shoulders that she didn't know carried the world. She takes Scotty's face gently into her hands. Her palms and fingers seem to become a part of Scotty's skin. She lifts her fingers off the surface and still feels the living force of blood, of essence of a movement even deeper below the skin. Scotty's body shudders, feeling Abigail's hands, even though she is inches away from Scotty's skin.

"Your hands are kissing, without even touching me." Scotty turns her head sideways to lay her cheek into one of Abigail's hands.

Abigail stands, up letting the blanket drop to the sand. "There's more where that came from."

She pulls Scotty up to her, now touching Scotty's lips with her fingertips, feeling the life force respond.

Scotty teases her hand between Abigail's thighs raising her fingers in an upward, slow glide.

Abigail smiles, putting her hand on Scotty's, keeping it there. "And more there too."

Scotty picks up the blanket laying it around them, bringing Abigail into the weave of their bodies. They lean their heads back to look at each other, their eyes laughing. Abigail thinks she sees, for just one moment, a blue-black hue accented in those pools of sparkling light.

***

Niko sits on the edge of the bed in his flat, naked and awake. The clock says 7:00 a.m. Talia's asleep next to him on the narrow mattress, the blanket swept under her and halfway covering her stomach. She's on her back, arms splayed sideways, her head tilted on the edge of the one pillow he owns. A drizzle of drool spills out of the side of her ever-so-slightly-snoring mouth. He's amazed at his response, ready again. For a third time.

After they first made love and dozed off, a tangle of legs and arms in a glossy stupor, they woke up reaching for each other again at around 3:00 a.m. Then they drifted, sweaty and sated, back to sleep until now. He wants to wake her again with his mouth on her breast, his tongue flickering her electric skin, his ache to move inside her once more building, but he stops himself. She looks so peaceful sleeping so deeply. He reaches over to the nightstand to drain the last sip of the Merlot from the bottle they opened that he found stored on the bookshelf in his flat.

He considers letting Rami out. She's been a good dog. When they got here last night, she didn't jump on the bed, once she realized there was too much motion to contend with. She spent the night in the brown chair, oblivious. She paid no attention to their moans, their animal growls, their sharp cries. Their laughter, their tears.

The dog probably wants to go out, but Niko slides under what covers he can snag out from under Talia. She rolled on top of them while he got up to go to the bathroom, and now she's taking up the entire bed.

He manages to lie down and shift himself to stretch out without waking her. This bed is definitely too small. He's tipping over the edge, his head on the bedside table instead of the lone pillow. But here at the flat at least, they could make all the noise they wanted to. If they had stayed at the villa, they'd have a bigger bed, but he can only imagine breakfast with Scotty the next morning. Those stone walls carry an echo for sure.

He crosses his arms behind his head, looking at the corner of the ceiling, wondering if the Priest will make another appearance, when he suddenly feels a probe in his mind, like a trickle of crawling bugs. An image appears, just the way it did when he meditated. But this time he sees himself standing next to what is clearly the Priestess Anya.

His breath catches, stunned at the sight of her. He stays dead still, worried that if he moves her image will vanish. As he looks at her in awe, energy trundles through his body like a series of shock waves. Her presence feels so magnetic, it's like he's watching an exotic, extinct animal he'd never want to disturb. He watches her raise her arms upwards, blue-black eyes cast above. She wears a blue robe tied at the waist, her long black hair is underneath a blue stone headdress with gold folds over her ears. The image probes once more and shifts. He startles even more when he sees himself standing next to her. Like he's watching his own body in a movie. But he's young. He looks the way he used to when he was maybe ten or eleven years old. He's surprised to see he's wearing a headdress, too. He hears the Priestess speak into his mind, the voice a somber plea.

Promise me you will care for my daughter.

Then the vision is gone.

Niko sits up in a spastic thrust upward. "Bloody hell!"

He's used to visions of spirits but now he's shaking like a rattled pack of nerves. This felt too real. Even personal. Like an out-of-body experience.

He throws his legs over the edge of the bed, fully alert, feet planted, hands on thighs. He's about to get up, not even sure what he wants to do.

What would I know about your daughter?

Talia stirs. She reaches for him in a drowsy arch. Her hands find his hips, the back of his butt where his spine ends. She teases her mouth there, arousing him again. She inches her lips around to the front of him, slipping her arms and head over his lap, joining her tongue with her fingers around his growing hardness. Her mouth and touch sweep away his fear as if it was never there.

He folds his torso over the side of her, laying over her like a playful otter, his loose hair skimming her back. He scoops her body easily and slings the rest of her torso around with one chuck of his arms. She laughs, letting him move her to sit on his lap, upright now, facing him. Her legs slink and lock around his hips, ankles folded on the sheets. Their hungry mouths bite, lick, kiss, taste skin. Necks, shoulders, lips, cheeks, nipples. He slides into her as he leans his arms back on the bed. She grips his shoulders, moving her hips on him. He burrows deeper into her, cupping her butt, their bodies a slippery mosaic of limbs, wet skin, sticky hair, the scent of their heat. His eye catches the sensuous curve of the underside of her chin as she moans and arches back.

Niko pulls her to his chest, squeezing her as if she might disappear like the vision of the Priestess.

"I feel like I've known you forever," he whispers.

Talia's fingers make dents in his back in answer.

"I-unika qalb tieghi," Niko murmurs into her hair.

"What does that mean?" Talia purrs in his ear.

"My only love."
Talia brings her fingers gently to the crescent birth mark on the edge of Niko's chin, her eyes a curious wonder.
"I-unika qalb tieghi, Niko. I-unika qalb tieghi."

***

Scotty hears syncopated drums beat in a hypnotic trill, only to realize with a slow blink that she's in Abigail's bedroom, not on stage singing as she thought. The more alert she becomes the more the drums fade to silence. Her surroundings come more into Scotty's alert focus.

She's lying at the bottom of Abigail's bed where she fell asleep. Abigail's naked leg lays under Scotty's tingling arm, numb from not moving. She wiggles her fingers to get the circulation going. She's cold even though the morning sun is heating up the day already. She sees specks of light dusting the topside of the bed, where Abigail is lying on her back, the blue cotton sheet halfway slipping off. Abigail's breath lifts her chest upwards then downwards in even meter. Scotty sees light rays arch and spark with each breath. Violets, golds. Crystal clear sparks interwoven with a dust of white. She reaches to the floor to grab the cotton blanket they shared on the beach that still lies where it fell next to their clothes in a heap. As she lifts it, tiny particles of light shift like liquid sand off the fabric. She lays the blanket over Abigail, tugging gently to smooth a wrinkle from one corner.

Scotty's tempted to lie back down. But she gets up and picks up her clothes on the floor. She carries them in a muddled wad, swinging in an easy walk down the stone hallway to her bedroom. She smells her arm pits. Considers a shower. Inhales the skin on her elbow, her wrist, detecting Abigail. She pulls on Zeff's sweatshirt.

She tosses the hood over her bed-head hair, and digs through the hamper in her closet for the warm socks she knows are there from yesterday. She shakes out the sand, watching the light specks spill, then pulls the socks on, rubs her thighs to warm her hands, then heads out to the patio.

She lights up a cigarette and blows out a stream of smoke.

Her mind plays images of last night. Slick skin. Mouths. Fingers. Movement in sweaty meter. Still thundering.

She lets a wistful smile spread, then takes another drag.

***

It's 10:00 a.m. Abigail has showered and is starting to get brunch ready in the kitchen when Scotty comes in.

"You're up." Scotty leans against the fridge, her hands in her hoody pockets.

"When did you get up?"

Scotty shrugs. "Before you. I didn't look at the clock."

"How're you doing?" Abigail hands her a cup of black coffee.

"Thanks." Scotty seems genuinely touched. "You don't like coffee."

"True. But I like you." Abigail smiles and pours hot water over her green teabag. "I notice you didn't answer me. Let's go sit."

She takes Scotty by the hand and leads her out to the patio.

Scotty puts her coffee cup down on the patio table and pulls two of the lounge chairs side by side. She motions for Abigail to recline.

"You're turning into a sweet person," Abigail teases, sitting back, letting her legs stretch out in front of her.

Scotty shoves her hands back into her sweatshirt pockets. "I'm trying it on."

Abigail knows Scotty means to sound flippant but it comes out breezy.

"I like it." Abigail puts her tea mug on the table, then pats her lounge chair. "Come sit with me." She wiggles her butt over to make room.

"About last night." Scotty slowly sits.

"Mmmm hmmm?"

Scotty pulls her hands out of her pockets, winding them together in her lap. "It's the first time I can remember that I was sober."

"For sex?"

Scotty dips her chin in an almost imperceptible waver.

"I wondered." Abigail opens her arms and invites Scotty to lean into her. Scotty looks like she'll protest, but then she slips easily down and lies next to Abigail.

"Do you want to say more?" Abigail asks.

Scotty picks up Abigail's hand and traces her palm. "I'd rather take you to my room and put my mouth on you."

Abigail feels a vibrating heat pitch between them. She shifts her body lower to wrap her arms around Scotty, sliding down so their legs weave together on the length of the lounge chair.

"I'd like nothing more, but…," Abigail pauses. "Please don't be mad at me for saying this."

She feels Scotty tense. "Okay."

"You're an addict."

Scotty offers no answer.

"Do you think it's possible that you're thinking sex with me fills some kind of empty hole that drinking did? Maybe what you crave isn't really me."

Scotty shrugs a shoulder. "It doesn't feel that way to me."

"Or maybe what's happening between us is because of how altered we both feel with the way Anya's world is impacting us?"

Abigail's surprised that Scotty's eyes well up with tears. "Is this too hard to hear?"

Scotty rubs her eyes with the back of her sleeve. "It's true for you. So no, not hard to hear."

"It's not true for you?"

"I feel different. It might be from what you say. But last night was," Scotty stops speaking.

"Last night was off the charts amazing." Abigail chooses her next words carefully. "But something big is going on for me. The dream I had last night was life changing. I'm finally okay that Anya's a real thing. That my life has been a part of hers for a long time. I know, deep down inside, that I have a purpose and she's part of it. But I don't know what it is yet. And I need time to figure it out."

"I get it." Scotty sighs, then tucks her chin over Abigail's head, squeezing her in.

"Besides," Abigail's voice is muffled by Scotty's sweatshirt arm. "When this is all over, you'll probably end up going back to being a rocker with a hot man on each arm and I'll have to watch you with them on the red carpet on TV while I pine for you at home, knitting a scarf I'll never give you."

"Doc. Look at me." She turns Abigail's chin toward her. "I told you. This is not that."

"People fall in love with you all the time, I bet."

"People fall in love with their *idea* of me," Scotty says. "Not you. Not now. Not with all this." She sweeps her arm at the garden, the beach, the sky.

"So you agree we need to see where Anya's taking us?" Abigail hopes her answer will give them what they both need.

"We do."

An electric current shoots through Abigail's body.

Scotty notices. "Seems like your body knows better where it wants to take us."

Abigail sits up, unfurling her arms and legs. "Let me be clear, Scotty D. Jones."

"Clear about what, Doctor DiGiorno?"

"If there weren't an ancient Priestess from the past knocking on our doors, or you just sober for not even a month, I would be leading you back to my bedroom right this second, and your cute boy shorts would be on the floor in a New York minute."

"Now you're the tease," Scotty smirks. She shifts to sit up. "Let's go make some brunch for the kiddos."

Scotty's almost standing when Abigail grabs her arm.

"I'm serious, Scotty. If you still feel this way in… say, six months, then we can talk."

Scotty takes Abigail's hand and kisses the palm, folds her fingers through. "Only six months? Keep your motor running, sister."

"It turns out I'm not in control of my motor. Or of any of this," Abigail laughs.

"Now that is one thing I do agree with."

For a moment, Abigail can see through Scotty eyes. As if she's inside Scotty's cranium, yet orienting her own sight from within. If she closes her eyes, she sees it even better. Her forehead seems to serve as a telescope for the vision. Now it's like a window through which they merge their shared inner sight. Amazed, she not only sees light burst into the space between them, but her own face as Scotty gazes at her. Then she's seeing from her own location where Scotty's face once again is across from her. Abigail stares in wonder at this sudden dazzling display as light literally rains over them. The tendrils of pure iridescence spread until there's no difference between its shine and Scotty's hand that she still holds in hers

THEN

I have not forgotten that when I buried my Priest, the grief pulled my body to the earth. I followed the women of the future. The Golden Hair Woman. The Fire Eye Woman. She of the Wise Hands. I have not forgotten how I rose and lifted through the veil of time.

Where I still remain, even as I am also here, in the home of my grandmother by the sea.

Such is my fate. My task has been to embrace being in two worlds all along. I refused to accept it, for I feared loss.

Yet the women led me through the tunnel. When I am with them, the light sees all that is through them. Through me.

I was meant to return here from their world to give birth to my daughter Solisheh. To find solace within the kind embrace of my Grandmother Oriana's gentle homestead. To grow strong for the task of my Prophecy's path. To ready for what is to come.

Na'akt tends to me. She understands well that I live in two worlds. What is now and what will be. The Madre has gone back with our birthing and drumming sister Priestesses. Grandmother worries, Lael fusses. Eon seems overcome at the loss of his teacher, bereft at my weakened state.

Na'akt is the one who does not rush me through my healing. She has been giving me a tincture made of the bark of the Oak to root my spirit to the earth. It does not help as much as she hopes, for my heart is moving away from here. Yet I have come to be more alert since being brought here and I agree her healings have seemed to make me stronger.

My daughter birthed in this room where I sit at the same hearth. Next to the same the fire pit. I used this same chair I sit in now, to hold me steady as I labored. My Priestess sisters linked arms in the breathing force right here. I remember their power waking in my body.

I was not surprised to see She of the Wise Hands when I gave birth. I reached into her mind for her Blessing. She did not hesitate to look right into the darkness of my eyes. When she did, I saw my own face in the light that came from her. She touched her palms to the crown of my head to Bless me with her pure hands. I know this sealed us in a bond that will never be broken.

I rest as Solisheh suckles. It is good to hold her. To smell her skin. Her hair. To brush my hands along her back. To let her squeeze my finger in her tiny fist. I bring her closer, my heart swelling.

I hear her sweet rutting hunger, the gulping and whimpering in little hiccups of filling. When she has had enough, she drifts to sleep. I slip my finger into her mouth and slowly let her leave my breast with a popping sound. I use the sleeve of my robe to wipe the drip of milk from my breast, then from her mouth. She makes a hollow *huhhh* sound with each sleeping breath out. Her dreams are quiet.

Eon comes to the table where I hold Solisheh in the high-backed chair. He kneels at my feet, for I feel his sleeve brush my leg. He lays his head in my lap, then brings his hand gently to my daughter's feathery hair.

"Such a little bird," he whispers.

"You are kind to her." I am grateful to the young Priest.

"It is my vow to you, Priestess. Yet were it not, I could not help but open my heart to her."

His words bring comfort to me, for I know he will keep her safe.

I begin to fall to sleep, traveling as I do, to the trance world.

I see the women.

They are ready.

NOW

Sondro hovers outside the chamber where his body was laid, shrouded and blessed for his journey here in the afterlife.

His task is not to track time gone by, or to linger over his bones. He feels no need to pay homage to what was once his body.

His endeavor is to wait.

He hovers and sleeps.

He comes alert when he sees a guard with a flame-less light leading the one called Talia, the one called Niko, the one with Fire Eyes and She of the Wise Hands. The night is lit by the full moon.

The guard lays out his hand for an offering then leaves them alone.

Sondro floats behind them, waiting at the entrance to his grave.

***

I feel no grief at Sondro's burial site. Here in the future, I know I am complete. There is no longer a need to mourn the loss of my beloved High Priest.

I see Sondro floating before me, in the doorway of his tomb. He calls to me.

Anya my love.

There is no measuring for the soaring ecstasy I feel at the sight of him that I see with the light as it knows itself through me.

I know we will never again be apart.

He brings his forehead to my palms.

We descend into the tomb that holds his grave.

He floats to my side taking his place as High Priest.

We reach our minds to the future women to stand before us.

The Fire Eye Woman bows her forehead to my palms.

She of the Wise Hands bows her forehead to my palms.

The Golden Hair Woman runs to me to bow her forehead to my palms, then turns and walks her consort to me, who bows his forehead to my palms.

Sondro moves to him, whose mark of the birth is revealed.

I am elated to see him. I thank him for his vows. He inclines his head in wise understanding of his birth reborn.

We are all now of one mind in the light and stand in circle. I speak into the women's minds.

First we make you Priestesses.

They stand strong, arms at their sides. Palms to me. I move to the Golden Hair Woman and kneel before her, my hands blessing her feet.

These are the feet of the Goddess.

I bless her knees.

This one bends with her wisdom.

I bless her womb.

This is the Temple of the Goddess.

Then her breasts.

For purity and nourishment for those in need.

Then her heart.

To open only to the truth.

Then her mouth.

To speak with power.

Then her eyes.

To see the unseen.

Then her forehead.

With a mind without bounds.

Then the crown of her head.

This one is blessed as Priestess, on the Path to the Temple for this life and all lives to come.

I do the same for the Fire Eye Woman. For She of the Wise Hands.

Now they understand their tasks. They are Initiated. They are Priestesses. Now and Then.

I send an image.

The Golden Hair Woman and He of the Mark of Birth carry the guardian statue forward.

They kneel and dig together until the guardian statue rests under the earth.

We feel thunder under our feet.

I raise my arms.

This one calls to the ancient ones.

Taniyeh floats toward us. She leads a line of ancient Priestesses. Some in headdresses. Some in sweeping robes. Skins of many colors. Eyes alert with conviction. Some Warrior Women with sword in hand. Some holding the snake of power and truth. Some holding the drum. Some holding the knife and the wheat. Some the moon in all her phases. Some the key to birth, to music, to song, to dance, to sex, to grain, to the sea creatures, to the forest dwellers, to the mountain rocks, to the stars, to all life and all death. Some are veiled. Some are larger than the mountains. Some are of seamless ether; some are of translucent light.

They join our circle making us strong.

I invoke the change.

This one Opens the Bridge Between Worlds.

My arms crash downward, bringing the arch of the bridge to its place between time.

I know now why our temple fell. It was indeed to create this portal.

I see Taniyeh glimmer as she floats above the bridge, bowing low before dissolving to a point far in the distance that blinks out.

Her work is done.

Sondro moves to He of the Mark of Birth. He places his hand upon the young man's head, Blessing him.

This one is now Priest.

He of the Mark of Birth bows his head to my palms once more, then moves with Sondro to the bridge's other end, their Priest's stance a steady anchor. They begin to tone the low chant. Centuries of good men who know the Way appear in form, in memory, in what is to come. They join the note knowing their vows are to uphold our Sacred Woman Ways through time.

They wait at the ready.

The Golden Hair Priestess, The Fire Eye Priestess, She of the Wise Hands Priestess flank my sides.

With the ancient ones behind us, we wait.

Then we see it.

A sea of women begins to move over the bridge toward us.

There are as many walking as stars in the vast sky.

They come in a never-ending stream, bowing to us as they pass. Some sing. Some walk in silence. Some carry sacred objects in front of them in graceful power. Some are scorched from bodies burning for nothing more than being women. Some seem dazed and unsure. Some run. Some crawl in sobbing relief. Some are soaked from forced drowning in water. Some clothed with only blood and tears. Some carry dead children. Some have had their eyes gauged, their limbs severed, their sacred genitals cut away. I feel them. I feel their pain. I feel their loss.

I see what has become of our revered place as women in life.

My sorrow is not able to be measured.

I feel the power of the Future Priestesses behind me, determined and clear.

We will not forget. The Golden Hair Woman, The Fire Eye Woman, She of the Wise Hands vow as the Priestesses they have become. *We will carry on what you began.*

We hold this doing as the moon sets.

We hold this doing as the sun rises.

Our bodies do not tremble, for we have become more than our flesh.

More come over the bridge. Now among them are not just women but men. Not just daughters but sons. Not just sisters, but brothers. Not just mothers, but fathers. Women in men's bodies. Men in women's bodies. Sexual beings in all shapes and sizes. Children someday born. Leaders in the making. They seem dazed, then clear to understand.

They come from Then. From Now. They come from Yet to Be.

When the last traveler is over the bridge through time, Sondro and He of the Mark of Birth return to our side to stand with us as we watch the bridge dissolve. The Priest tone ends. The elders, the ancient ones, those that came to help, fade.

I stand with Sondro and take his hand in mine.

We float toward the stars.

Looking back, I see the Priestesses of the Future below us.

They raise their faces to me. They do not look away.

NOW

The Maltese sunlight is especially vibrant this morning. The pure azure waters marry the indigo and white clouded horizon in ecstatic union. The regal rocks on the cliffs embrace their wonder with quiet majesty. The sense is that they hum together, commenting among themselves that the earth's axis has perhaps found a new gravity.

Niko shifts the gears as he drives Uncle Marcello's old canary yellow Citroen up the hill over the potholed road. Talia grips the handle above the passenger door, but she leans out her open window, her hair in a wild scatter. Abigail holds two overstuffed beach bags on her lap in the back-seat. Her hand plays the waves of air out her window, rising and falling in even pace, in spite of the jagged thrusts of the car's groaning effort. Scotty's face is a marble Pieta, the fire in her eyes reflective embers. Her tattooed arm hangs easy over the rim of her open window. She bangs a rhythm on the side of the car, encouraging it to not give up just yet.

Niko lets out a hoot when they make it to the top, then leans back in the driver's seat as he down shifts to coast the descent toward the docks. He pulls over into a well-worn rut on the side of the road. The little car's exhaust blows one last puff before everyone piles out.

Abigail and Scotty pull two more oversized beach bags from the tiny trunk, handing one each to Niko and Talia. Niko spins like a dancing cat, walking backwards with a grin, when they arrive at his family's fishing boat. *Il Wiehed Fdat* looks like she's seen better days on the water. A gash of rust is visible on the bottom, just above the line of silt marking the waterline. The canopy above the hull is dented.

With one foot on the deck and the other on the dock, Niko offers his hand to the others one at a time. The boat tips out of balance with every move.

Talia climbs the short ladder to the hull, running her palms along the mahogany wheel.

Scotty and Abigail tuck-in onto the cushioned bench in the narrow stern.

Niko unties the docking rope. He climbs the ladder above the hull to join Talia in the shaded console. He starts the engine.

"We rock and we roll!" Scotty sings out in a long, enthused note.

The vessel backs out, putts along in a tugboat sputter, until Talia takes the wheel. They start to speed up as they near the open sea. The wings of the gulls flying alongside the boat sound like applause. They seem to know this day is worth celebrating.

***

Il Wiehed Fdat is anchored far enough away from the shore, but close enough that the rugged and layered textures of the thousand-year-old stones in the distance can be seen from all sides of the boat. The sea caves within the ancient cliff's spread are visited by a slew of tourists, far enough away that the sturdy vessel floats in quiet respite.

They have been anchored here all day, taking in the sun. Swimming and resting on floating rafts they secure to the rails. The fishing lines have been left alone for the most part, to catch just enough Gilt-head bream and Amberjack to take home for their last dinner together. Abigail had spread lunch on the small folding table on the boat, which is now empty of the plates and delicate crumbs. The gulls expedited the meal's completion, in their thwarted attempt to scavenge the remains of the bread, olives, tuna and tomatoes.

Niko rests with his legs stretched on the ice chest that holds the day's catch. Abigail and Scotty sit on the bench with their arms slung over the rails. The sun will soon blink out before they pull up anchor to head home.

Talia stands at the rail, taking in the varied range of blues in the water below. The accenting teal. The regal cerulean. The mix of cobalt and robin's egg adding a transparent sheen on the surface. A translucent, phosphorous gleam shifts in liquid motion. Underneath it all, the blue-black deep of the ocean bottom holds all that fills to the surface in mysterious solidity.

A primal stillness pervades the moment, as the others move to stand with Talia. Her long fingers unloop the leather pouch she holds. She takes out two of the limestone statues, then passes the pouch to Niko. He reaches in without looking to pick out two more of the statues. He passes the pouch to Abigail. She finds her two statues with slow, deliberate collection. Scotty turns the pouch sideways to shake out the remaining two, leaving the empty leather pouch on the cushion of the stern's small bench.

Talia raises her two stone figures to the setting sun, her eyes closed. The others follow her gesture, a silent current of reverence passing between them. Without speaking out loud, they bring the statues to their lips, breathing into the stones their private vows to the High Priestess, Anya of Mahet.

They bring their hands over the rail.

They open their palms, dropping the eight limestone statues into the iridescent sea.

They watch the ocean water envelop them, forever joined with the grounded past.

They stand in hushed silence, the boat rocking softly on the water.

THEN

Na'akt wakes with a jolt. Ba-leh is up on his feet next to her on her mat, his ears pricked in taut attention. His fur is up, his tail a straight arrow of alarm. The fire is out, the night cold. Na'akt hears the cry again, throws the rug she's used as a blanket around her shoulders and lurches to the front door, Ba-leh following close behind. Lael, who has been sleeping with Anya on her mat, wakes as they move past. Alone under the linens, Lael throws them off and rushes behind Na'akt out the door toward the cry.

It comes from the shore, not far from the homestead. They run to the edge of the water, Ba-leh racing ahead, his growling whine building. Na'akt grips the rug around her, her blood racing.

They see Anya's wolf fur lying on the sand, wrapped in a bundle, next to her quiet body. She lies flat on her back on the shore, her arms spread wide. The baby's exposed leg and foot stick out from the bundled fur. Ba-leh licks the infant's soft skin, between distressed yips and whimpers. Na'akt moves to the wolf's head, laying her hand on him. He quiets, yet his eyes do not move off the child. Na'akt picks Solisheh up, still wrapped in the fur, as her cries dissolve into a gurgling whimper. Na'akt hushes her, bringing her close to her breast, the rug now dropped in the sand.

Lael's tears spill in silent sobs, her chest and arms flung over Anya's lifeless body. Na'akt folds the rug over them, hoping to bring comfort and warmth to Lael's back. The blood rushes from Na'akt's limbs. She lets her weight drop to the sand, Anya's daughter now cooing in her arms. She clasps the child's cold foot, warming it and tucking it under the fur. She hears someone behind them. Eon stands under the full moon, face empty, hands hanging by his sides.

Na'akt looks up to the stars, hoping for strength. She reaches her palm to close the lids of skin over the open blue-black eyes. She leaves her hand there, rocking Solisheh in the other arm. Slow. Slow. Slow.

NOW

Scotty pulls off her black UGGs, flipping them onto the floor of her dressing room backstage. Chicago is colder than it was the last time she was here. *Feels like a couple of centuries ago.* She turns to the mirror, remembering that the last time she looked at her reflection in this dressing room, she jumped out of her chair. Now she turns her chin side to side, watching the light radiate in her reflection back at her. A dusting of gold and white pinpricks illuminate the edges of her skin.

She reaches for her mascara, but stops when she hears voices behind her closed dressing room door. She swivels in her chair to see the door open.

She jumps up, her arms open wide for a hug.

"Hey, Nugget! Glad you made it!" Scotty pulls Talia into her arms, squeezing extra tight, feeling Talia's backstage band pass wedge between them. Niko's tall frame rolls in to join Scotty's bear hug.

"Glad your flight didn't hit delays from San Francisco." She leans back to look at them, still holding their hands. She's about to ask how it went with Niko meeting Talia's parents, when her fingers graze the metallic outline of their rings.

"Let me see them!"

They hold up their right hands. Scotty inspects the etched spiral patterns with no beginning or end. The black onyx circular design is overlaid on silver bands.

"Didn't we see this pattern at one of the temples?" she asks, impressed.

"They're from a Neolithic design," says Niko, as he twirls the ring on his right ring finger.

"We designed them and found a jeweler in Malta to make them for us." When she zigzags her fingers through Niko's, the rings looking like they're one continued set of spirals.

"What's the right-hand thing about?" Scotty asks.

Talia holds up her right hand inspecting the ring. "When we were researching rings, we found out that when a wedding ring is on the right hand, it signifies renewed vows." Talia grins.

Scotty squeezes them once more. "Eternal love. Perfect." Scotty laughs. "Also perfect that you got the rings before the wedding."

Talia and Niko exchange private smiles. "We did our own ceremony already." Scotty sees sparks of light burst between them. Pretending to ignore the quick blush that heats her cheeks, Talia goes on. "We'll do a formal one for our families. Maybe even in Malta."

"Got a date?" Scotty asks.

"Not yet, but you're singing for us. That much we know!" Niko announces.

"Wouldn't miss that for the world." Scotty shakes a finger at them.

"Neither would we." Talia laughs.

"Where's your aunt? Didn't she meet you in the airport?" Scotty straddles her dressing room chair backwards, arms crossed on the back.

"She's resting in the hotel. She should be here soon. She's been pretty busy with setting up the curriculum to bring women's wisdom practices into the education system. Niko and I are moving to Los Angeles to help her. We'll start with the West Coast. We hope to bring it across the U. S., and then reach out abroad. I'm designing a building for us that will be home base. It'll be our temple where people can also come to study." Talia gives Scotty a wistful blink. "Did you know?"

Scotty's voice goes quiet. "I heard. Yes." Her knee starts to jig. Then stops.

Talia's face shifts. "Scotty. You seem good."

Scotty's palms make a prayer mudra. "Sober for seven months, three weeks, two days and forty minutes." She watches a pink-gold ray of light flicker across Talia's cheekbones. "Still seeing light, y'know."

"We hoped so." Talia looks to Niko, who gives an ardent shake of his head.

Scotty feels no need to say more. The refined flecks of light are now more violet and blue, spreading to Niko's face. She watches the display slow then diminish.

The dressing room door flings open suddenly.

"Izzy! I want you to meet two people who were in … uh… rehab with me." Scotty shrugs at Talia and Niko's surprised looks.

Izzy waves. "Hey." They smile back.

"Talia," Scotty pulls Motley from Izzy's grasp, "You remember my Candy-Dog?"

"Sure do." Scotty plops Motley in Talia's lap, who kisses the top of his furry head.

"Where's your brother?" Scotty asks Izzy.

"I'm here." Zeff's tall frame ducks under the doorframe. "Hey." He smiles at Talia and Niko, then shoves his hands in his long coat's pockets, eyes cast down. Scotty throws an arm around him, his cheek leaning on the top of her hair.

She watches Izzy absentmindedly twiddle her backstage pass, then reach to her back pocket. "Been meaning to give these to you, Mom. I've had 'em for a while." Izzy hands her two red child-sized mittens.

Scotty takes them slowly into her hands, searching her daughter's green cat-eyes. She pulls Izzy into a hard squeeze.

"God, Mom! You're hurting me!" She play-shoves Scotty away.

"Sorry." Scotty lets her go. She wiggles the mittens at her, then turns away, slipping her fingers over the droplets of tears threatening to show.

"Now all of you get the fuck out of here. I have to get ready."

Scotty shoos them out the door, closing it softly behind her. She weaves the mittens between her fingers. Puts them on the dressing room table. Pats them.

The light from her mirrored reflection plays on the angles and contours of her face in dancing specks. She sees the dressing room door open behind her through the mirror's view. She swings around to face the door.

Abigail's standing there with her hand on the doorknob.

Scotty goes to her. She inhales the skin on Abigail's neck, feeling the curls of black hair tickling her cheek. Scotty leads her in, closes the door, sits her down on the couch next to her. She takes Abigail's hands. They're cold. She rubs them.

"So?"

Abigail laughs. "What?"

"I haven't seen you in six months. How's that motor?"

Abigail tilts her head, her eyes in half-closed mischief. "It's never stopped."

***

194

Scotty walks on stage, the sound of the even steps of her platform boots drowned out with cheers the moment the audience sees her enter. Her acoustic guitar is slung in front of her waist, held by the strap over her shoulder. She waves to the erupting audience as she moves to a stool that's lit under a single spotlight. She sits, resting one foot on the lower rung of the stool, taking in the whistles and hoots, the sound a salve to her bones. The guitar rests on her knee, its shape seeming to rise from her ligaments and flesh. She feels the band behind her, a silent but ticking buzz of energy ready to explode. They are dimly lit so the audience sees only her under the bright scope of the light, spilling a cocoon of shining glory over her. She sits quietly still, gazing out at them. A microphone is set at the level of her face and another one lower down set on her guitar. She glances backstage at Talia and Niko, Abigail, Izzy and Zeff. Their bodies make shadowed silhouettes of different angles and sizes in the darkened wings, not visible to the audience, who clap and chant. *Scotty D. Scotty D. Scotty D.*

She smiles inwardly to herself, then raises her hand up at the stomps and shouts and the hovering anticipation. The energy in the audience runs through her like a wild fire. She keeps her arm up until they settle down.

"Hi everyone." They start up again, hooting and hollering. She waves the mittens at them. "My Mom gave me these a long time ago. Like them?" The audience roars. "I'll just tie them here." She attaches them to the guitar strap. "You can all remember her with me." She glances backstage at Izzy in the shadows.

Scotty plays a few soft chords, adjusting the microphone's angle to her mouth. "It's been a while." Scotty's buttery voice fills the hall over the sea of people. "I want to start this tour with a little present for you. How 'bout I sing you a little song by myself to start?"

The applause and hoots burst again. Scotty chuckles as she waits for them to settle one more time. "The guys can get all hot and bothered while they wait." She tosses a thumb at the band behind her. "I just want a moment alone with you all."

She strums a chord. "It's a new song I wrote just for you. It's called *The Path to the Priestess Temple.*"

She sets her fingers on the frets, breathes deep as the notes rise from the earth into her. She watches the light filaments like nerve ends, cast outward, collecting every soul sitting there into her song.

I want to see with the light in your blind eyes
I want to know the Queen returns
I want to live what lies beyond my eyes
I want to help the time to turn

Anya we see you
Anya we know
Anya we see you
The bridge rose from below

I want to be the one you hoped for
I want to turn the world around
I want to change the way we hold it
I want to fight for what went wrong

Anya we see you
Anya we know
Anya we see you
The Priestess path was closed

I want to be the home I wasn't
I want to tear the lies apart
I want to rage until the night falls
I want to set what we need right

Anya we see you
Anya we can
Anya you're here now
The path is open again
The path is open again
The path is open again

THEN

At seventeen summers, Eon's body is full and at ease. His long legs, neck and wrists seem to have stretched the past two seasons. His hair is loose this night, a swerving arch of black silk. He hands Solisheh her shawl as they pass the chairs in the cook room. At seven summers, she is a beauty just like her mother. Just like her father.

Solisheh takes Eon's hand in hers as they tiptoe past the goats under the table. The little one bleats. Eon pats the goat's knobby head to quiet her.

The deep of the night is on them. Eon moves past Na'akt's sleeping body on the mat next to Ba-leh. The wolf lifts his head at the sight of them, then yawns back to slumber. Eon puts his fingers to Solisheh's lips to signal her to stay as quiet as a mouse past Lael's bed. Solisheh's smile peeks at him in the dark. This is their secret ritual every full moon. Even Great-Grandmother Oriana does not know.

They move outside, Eon's hand tight around Solisheh's. They chase the night down to the water's edge. He stands beside her, gazing at the sea stretching out before them. The moon casts its illuminated fullness onto the shining liquid surface. Eon tucks Solisheh's shawl tighter around her, making sure she is warm.

He kneels on the sand, his legs effortless under him. He pats the ground next to him. Solisheh drops down beside him. She pulls her long hair from under the shawl and holds it out to him.

"Can you braid it the way you wore it before you became a Priest?"

She turns her back to him. Eon wraps the strands through his nimble fingers, separating her hair into three sections. The golden color glow of her hair seems part of the moonlight. The wheat toned strands are so different than his own black hair yet with the same graceful sweep.

"Can you sing mama's braiding song?" Solisheh whispers.

He clears his throat watching his fingers appear and disappear through her shining locks of hair.

I want to see the light in your blind eyes

I want to know the Queen returns

The song blends to a soft lull from Eon's low tone, through the weaving hair, and back.

The night seems to stop and listen.

The Path is open again

Eon stops his fingers with the last word of the song. He binds the braid with his own hair tie that he slips off his wrist. Solisheh turns to him, smiles her thanks and fondly pats the Mark of Birth on his chin.

Eon smiles back at her. "Let us practice now. Are you ready?"

"I am ready!"

He closes his eyes and joins her inner sight, sharing the image of a Priestess with long black hair, a light blue robe, with a headdress of Lapis Lazuli and a bronze orb the shape of a moon.

"It's mama! I see her black hair. She wears a big bowl on her head."

Eon opens his eyes, watching the spirit of his beloved High Priestess hover next to her daughter. He is sure he sees the blue-black eyes flicker.

ACKNOWLEDGMENTS

Gratitude to my writing sister Crissi McDonald, this story's midwife and cheerleader. I honor and appreciate our shared laughter, tears and ache for the voice of truth. To Linda Shreve for proofreading my final draft, and for her inspirational teachings on Goddesses, sacred herbs, Priestess Temples, and for the more than four decades of friendship and sisterhood. To Suzanne Hardy, for her wise compass through the flames of transformation and healing. To Sara Neto-Brown whose empty cottage gave me many hours of writing solitude under the Redwood trees to listen to my characters tell this story. To Rachel Burke for her enthusiasm, bright laughter, and help with tips on British slang. To editor Elisabeth Kauffman, who helped me shape my story with firm kindness and direction. To copy editor Kara L. Stewart's enormous heart and refined final touches. To Jane Dixon-Smith for her fabulous skills at the final digital design and formatting. To talented cover artist Melissa Stratton-Pandina of Deshria Design. Co-creating with her has been a highlight of this journey. To Dr. Laurie Marston for her belief in the magic of this story and for her medical consultation on Abigail's surgery scene. To John Lawrence for his expert advice on Scotty's rare and coveted 1985 Hamer Phantom A7 guitar, as only she would use. To Tobi Lessem, for her help with tips on rowing. To Candra Severson for her illuminating author's photo. To Lilith House Press for their good work and committed role in publishing support for women authors. To my parents Marna and Tony Howarth for their belief in me. I count myself as lucky to be raised in an atmosphere of passion for creativity. To Tina Diaz for her intuitive feedback on choosing my final title. To my son Carson Fox Harvey, for support with the final title and his inspiring and stunning heart that sparked courage for me to listen to the wisdom of Niko's youthful voice. To my beloved husband Frank Preston Adel. You are my Sondro and will forever be the love of my life.

Printed in the USA
CPSIA information can be obtained
at www.ICGtesting.com
LVHW041726241023
761957LV00002BA/146